ON THE SLAB PIE

ON THE SLAB PIE

AUNTIE CLEM'S BAKERY
BOOK EIGHTEEN

P.D. WORKMAN

ISBN: 9781774682333 (KDP Hardcover)

ISBN: 9781774682296 (KDP Paperback)

ISBN: 9781774682340 (Large Print)

ISBN: 9781774682302 (Kindle)

ISBN: 9781774682319 (ePub)

ISBN: 9781774683446 (Lulu Paperback)

pdworkman

ALSO BY P.D. WORKMAN

MYSTERY/SUSPENSE:

Reg Rawlins, Psychic Detective
What the Cat Knew
A Psychic with Catitude
A Catastrophic Theft
Night of Nine Tails
Telepathy of Gardens
Delusions of the Past
Fairy Blade Unmade
Web of Nightmares
A Whisker's Breadth
Skunk Man Swamp (Coming Soon)
Magic Ain't A Game (Coming Soon)
Without Foresight (Coming Soon)

Auntie Clem's Bakery
Gluten-Free Murder
Dairy-Free Death
Allergen-Free Assignation
Witch-Free Halloween (Halloween Short)
Dog-Free Dinner (Christmas Short)
Stirring Up Murder
Brewing Death
Coup de Glace

Sour Cherry Turnover

Apple-achian Treasure

Vegan Baked Alaska

Muffins Masks Murder

Tai Chi and Chai Tea

Santa Shortbread

Cold as Ice Cream

Changing Fortune Cookies

Hot on the Trail Mix

Recipes from Auntie Clem's Bakery

Zachary Goldman Mysteries

She Wore Mourning

His Hands Were Quiet

She Was Dying Anyway

He Was Walking Alone

They Thought He was Safe

He Was Not There

Her Work Was Everything

She Told a Lie

He Never Forgot

She Was At Risk

Kenzie Kirsch Medical Thrillers

Unlawful Harvest

Doctored Death (Coming soon)

Dosed to Death (Coming soon)

Gentle Angel (Coming soon)

AND MORE AT PDWORKMAN.COM

For those with secrets
And the secret keepers

CHAPTER 1

I've never even heard of a slab pie before." Erin studied the materials that her best friend and assistant Vic had assembled for her. "It must be a Southern thing, is it?"

"Suppose so." Vic shrugged. "I've never lived anywhere else, so I couldn't tell you. I guess if you never heard of it in Maine…"

Erin shook her head again. "In the North, the only pies I ever saw were round pies made in pie tins."

"Well, if you have a whole crew to feed, it's a lot less trouble to roll your pastry out onto a cookie sheet, add the filling and a top crust if you're doing one, and pop it in the oven. Then you just cut it into squares to serve. A lot less fuss and bother than cutting and filling half a dozen round pies."

"And people do double-crusted too?"

"Most of the ones you see now are dessert, and they just do a single crust. But you can make meat and potato pies, and then you do a double crust, so you can pick it up and eat it for lunch."

"Like an individual-size meat pie."

Vic nodded. "But a lot less bother. It would be pretty fussy to make individual meat pies for your whole field crew or mining shift. Or for a mom with a dozen kids, putting them in everyone's lunchbox."

"I never even thought of such a thing. But it's very practical."

"And good for a picnic or fair." Vic grinned widely. "You can get really fancy, laying out your fruit in a pattern or picture. Looks good, tastes even better, and it's quick and easy to serve."

"Okay," Erin agreed with a nod. "I'm convinced. That's what we'll do for the Statehood Day picnic."

"Great. We can do a run-through now, and I'll look up some recipe ideas tonight so you have something to start with. Then we can come up with something traditional but unique."

Erin wasn't sure she would be able to repeat the success they'd had with the mile-high stack cake at the Fall Fair, but she and Vic would come up with something good. She had perfected several gluten-free pastry recipes since she had first opened Auntie Clem's Bakery, so that part would not be difficult. She was sure that it would cook up just as well in the large cookie sheet as in a pie pan. Though it might need to be a little stronger to make sure that the pieces in the middle were substantial enough to remove from the pan without crumbling, even if they would be eating them with a plate and fork rather than out of hand. They would come up with something that would work with a tweak or two.

After they had closed shop and gone home, Erin had a light dinner by herself—Terry was on an evening shift with the police department, and Vic was having dinner with her boyfriend, Willie—and debated going out for a walk.

It was a beautiful day, and she knew that she should take advantage of the cooling evening. She and Vic had vowed to spend more time watching the sunrises and sunsets and enjoying the natural beauty around them. What was the point in working all day indoors and never getting out to enjoy the beauty around them? Not only was Bald Eagle Falls a paradise in the midst of some of the most gorgeous scenery Erin had seen, but she literally had the woods in her back-yard. Or separated from her backyard by a fence. And the woods were hers, inherited from her aunt Clementine along with the house and the storefront that had been the original Auntie Clem's Bakery, the only gluten-free and allergy-friendly bakery in driving distance.

She could take a short walk through the woods, enjoying the lowering light shining through the dappled leaves of the brilliantly green trees, return to the yard for her tai chi practice, and then head to bed for a few minutes of reading and, hopefully, quickly drop off to sleep.

It was always harder falling sleep without Terry there. Unless, of course, Terry were also having trouble sleeping, and then they just kept each other awake tossing and turning and kicking each other. But Orange Blossom, the cat rubbing against her legs and complaining that his kibble bowl was already empty, would snuggle with her in bed, and he was never too restless. He didn't seem to have any kitty worries or trauma that kept *him* awake at night.

"You don't need any more to eat," Erin chided him. "You're getting too fat. You want Doc Edmunds to put you on a diet?"

Blossom yowled more loudly. He had the loudest voice of any cat Erin had ever heard. The windows were open and she didn't want any of the neighbors complaining that he was disrupting their evening.

"Shh. You don't need anything else. You need to be quiet now."

But he wasn't quieting, and Erin eventually broke down and added a little more dry kibble to his bowl, hoping that would satisfy him. Marshmallow, the brown and white rabbit, had quietly eaten his dinner and lolloped off to the living room to sleep it off without any complaints. But then, he never complained. Orange Blossom more than compensated for Marshmallow's silence.

She decided to make her escape while he was occupied with his second course. Then at least if he started howling for more, she wouldn't be close enough to hear him and he would eventually get the message and have a nap.

After stepping out the back door onto the porch, Erin took a deep breath of the warm, sweet air. Even though she had grown up in the northeast, moving to Tennessee had been like coming home. She had only vague memories of the times she had visited Clementine before her parents' deaths, "helped" her aunt in what had then been her tearoom, and dug around in the garden or thrown rocks into the river. But the smell of the plants and flowers growing around her and the wind blowing over the lakes was unique. It took her right back to her childhood, confirming that Bald Eagle Falls, Tennessee would always be her home no matter where she lived.

She wandered into the woods beyond her fence, following the animal trails that had become familiar to her since she had returned home. She didn't know the woods nearly as well as Adele, the woman she employed as a groundskeeper in exchange for her use of the summer cottage and a small salary. And she wouldn't be comfortable walking around it late at night by herself like Adele did. But there was plenty of daylight left before she started worrying about that.

She could feel the tensions of the day and any stress over upcoming events or promotions or worries about employee scheduling or short supplies of flours that she needed falling away. Her muscles relaxed and she breathed more deeply. It was a good idea to take more time to enjoy the nature around her.

Erin could hear a crow cawing loudly nearby and wondered whether it was Skye, Adele's crow. He wasn't exactly Adele's pet, but he came to her for food and companionship, and sometimes when Erin was out in her yard, she would feed him a few peanuts or some other treat.

The crow's voice mixed with another loud bird. A magpie, Erin decided, listening to it. Both were scavengers and were probably fighting over some tasty morsel dropped by a passerby or the remains of a fox kill. The path she was taking would bring her closer to them. For a moment, she hesitated and considered taking a branch off in another direction to avoid disrupting them. But she was curious about what they were fighting over. If it were Skye, then he wouldn't leave just because Erin showed up. He knew her and would just ignore her unless she had a treat for him.

In a moment, she could see them both. The crow on the ground, his wings flapping, making himself big, and the magpie dive-bombing from above. Erin got closer. She probably didn't want to see exactly what they were fighting over. Scavenging birds weren't exactly known for eating fresh fruit or flowers.

She crept a little closer, her eyes on the ground, trying to discern any objects in the shadows of the trees. Late in the day, the shadows were long and it was hard to make out the shapes in the foliage. Tree stumps, litter, whatever it was the birds were squawking over so excitedly.

Erin let out a soft cry when she got close enough to make out the shape of an animal in the undergrowth. And not something dead; it was still alive. She hurried closer, shooing the birds away.

"Get out of here! Go on! Get out!"

She leaned down to peer under the bush and found herself looking into the round green eyes of a kitten.

CHAPTER 2

The kitten was not as young as Orange Blossom had been when she had found him, barely old enough to have left his mother. This cat was probably half-grown, but terribly thin, his coat patchy and bloody in places where the birds had attacked him.

"Oh, look at you." She knew that he would be too skittish for her to just reach down and pick him up. Even if he was hurt, he would still try to leap away, avoiding her. "There, little one. Are you okay? Where did you come from?"

There were feral cats around town, of course, though with both traffic and predators to deal with, they did not have long lifespans. And there were barn cats from nearby farms, and many people in Bald Eagle Falls didn't believe in keeping their cats indoors where they were safe, but insisted that a cat needed to roam outside. Erin looked around for something that would help her catch the cat so that Doc Edmunds could see to its injuries.

Terry had caught Marshmallow—when he had been feral—by throwing his coat over him. Erin had layered a loose blouse over a sleeveless t-shirt. Not being able to think of any other solution, she unbuttoned the blouse and took it off, moving very slowly and, she hoped, in a non-threatening way. The cat continued to watch her with big, round eyes, perhaps unsure whether she had actually seen him or not. Or maybe just hoping that she would walk away and leave him alone to lick his wounds.

Erin threw her blouse over the cat and, miraculously, it actually covered him. Erin had never been the best at sports. But she had never played any sport that involved throwing clothing, either. She shuffled a bit closer and bent over to pick up the cat inside the shirt, wrapping it tightly around him so that he would be still and she could transport him, as she had seen others do.

As soon as her hands closed around him, he slithered out from under the shirt, darting away and hiding behind a tree to watch whether she would pursue him or not. She could see his sides heaving and quivering.

"Poor thing. Just let me catch you, and I'll take you somewhere they'll make you feel much better."

He didn't look disposed to do as she said. Erin could hear Skye— if it was Skye— cawing high overhead. Disappointed that she had chased him away from the potentially tasty morsel?

Erin picked up her blouse and looked around for help. If Adele were nearby, or another neighbor, maybe the two of them together would be able to trap the cat.

A few feet away, she saw a boot. And was it a pile of clothes? Or the shape of someone sleeping on the ground?

Adele had previously mentioned that someone had been sleeping in the woods, as she had found areas where the grass and vegetation were still crushed down from someone being there for an extended length of time. After all that had transpired, Erin had assumed that the person in the woods had been Theresa, watching Vic and those she interacted with from a distance before making her move. Theresa and Vic had been a couple before Vic's gender transition and Theresa had decided she wanted to renew their relationship. But Vic was not interested in Theresa and, as was often the case with crazy Theresa, things went quickly from bad to worse.

But that was in the past. Vic was fine. All of Erin's friends associated with Vic were safe and well, and Theresa had failed in her aims, foiled by someone who had been watching her as she watched Vic.

Erin shifted her stance and shuffled sideways a bit, not towards the cat, but in the direction of the dark shape with the boots to get a better look.

She would not confront someone who was sleeping in the woods by herself. She would get Terry or Adele with her shotgun to back her up. She had no desire to face an angry vagrant on her own.

It was starting to get darker, the sun setting over the horizon. That made it harder to make everything out. But she knew something was wrong. Something was very, very wrong with what she saw.

Erin fumbled for her phone. It took several attempts to get it out of the small purse she had brought with her, slung diagonally across her body. For some reason, her fingers felt numb and fat and weren't working the way they were supposed to.

When she was baking, her hands flew; she was so familiar with the processes of stirring, rolling, shaping, and all of the other things she did automatically while she was preparing the goods for sale at Auntie Clem's Bakery that sometimes she just watched her fingers, surprised that they knew what they were supposed to do and moved so automatically and gracefully. But that wasn't the case as she clumsily separated her phone from the purse and tapped at the screen, trying to unlock it multiple times and then unsure what to press when she finally got past the lock screen.

Her sluggish brain fed her the instructions. Tap the phone icon. Find Terry's face in her favorites list. Tap on it a couple of times until the phone figured out she wanted to call him and tried to make the connection. She stared at the phone, waiting for something to happen. It was a few moments before she realized that he had answered but that she hadn't put the phone up to her ear to answer or pressed the speaker button. She lifted the phone to her face.

"Terry?"

"Erin? Is everything okay?" His tone was light, but with just a hint of concern. He knew only too well that as idyllic as everything might appear to be in Bald Eagle Falls, things didn't always go as expected and there were dangerous people or circumstances to contend with. Or maybe he was just worried that Erin might have chopped the tip of a finger off while getting a bedtime snack or had forgotten that he was on shift and was expecting him home.

"Umm… no. I guess not. There's something in the woods."

"In the woods?" his concern raised his tone another notch higher. "What is in the woods? Where are you?"

"I just went for a walk. And I stopped because I saw Skye and a magpie fighting over something, and then I saw that it was a little cat."

"A cat." He blew his breath out in relief. "You had me scared for a minute there. Don't tell me that you're adopting another stray."

"No… I didn't see… there is something else here. I saw the boots, and then I smelled something, and…"

"Boots?" he echoed, trying to make sense of her babbling. "What did you smell? Is there a fire? Some homeless person camping out back there?"

"No… it's… well, maybe he was camping here. But he wasn't. And there's no fire. It's okay."

"He? Who is there? Do you need me to send someone on his way?"

"I need you. And… I don't know who else. Everyone, I guess." They didn't have a very large police department. Something like this would require all hands on deck. "You see… it's a body."

CHAPTER 3

*T*erry's response to her announcement was not repeatable. He was usually so mild mannered and calm that Erin was shocked by his response.

"Where exactly are you?" he asked urgently, once he got the expletives out of the way. "What are you close to?"

"The stream with the little waterfalls in it. Uh… south of the summer house, I guess?"

"Stay there. Are you okay? Is there anyone else around? Have you seen anyone in the woods while you were walking there?"

"No. I didn't see anyone. I've just been by myself. I saw the birds, and then the cat… and then the body."

"But you haven't seen anyone else nearby?"

"No."

"Good. I'm going to hang up to put a call in to the dispatcher and get everyone moving. And then I'm going to call you back, and I'll stay on the phone with you until I get there."

"Okay."

Erin's voice sounded far away from her own ears. As the call ended, she tried to work it through in her own mind. Terry's instructions had not been complicated, yet she found herself having difficulty processing them. He was getting help. He was going to be there. If she could just hold on, he would be there soon.

Bald Eagle Falls was not a big place. If Terry were driving from the farthest point away from Erin, it would still take no more than ten minutes to reach her. And he had lights and a siren if he was in his car rather than on foot. And the others in the police department might be closer than he was. They wouldn't all be on the other side of the town.

Bearing out this line of logic, a siren sounded somewhere close, getting louder as it drew near. Erin heard the sound of a car door slamming after it pulled onto the nearest street, but it was a few minutes before she could hear footsteps getting closer.

"Erin?"

"Over here."

Officer Terry Piper, who Vic teasingly called Officer Handsome, stepped through the trees toward her. He was currently looking rather grim, his mouth a straight line, eyes hard, and no sign of the dimple she found so charming in his cheek.

K9 marched at his side in perfect formation, not running ahead like an untrained dog might. If he could smell the body, as Erin had no doubt that he could, he had the self-restraint not to react, but he obeyed his schooling and did what Terry expected him to.

Erin pointed to the body so that Terry couldn't miss it. It would be rather embarrassing for him to trip over it because he was looking at her.

"I just…" Erin tried to figure out what to say to him by way of explanation. "I just looked, and there it was."

"You didn't see or hear anyone else out here?"

"No. No one."

"Earlier in the day? Did you look out the window at suppertime?"

"No. I didn't see anyone."

Ever since Theresa's last reappearance, Erin had been very cognizant of any activity in the backyard or any of the woods she could see beyond it. She couldn't control everything in Bald Eagle Falls, but she did her best to be aware of anything going on within her own sphere. In her house and yard, Auntie Clem's Bakery, news about things happening in her friends' lives… She couldn't change anyone else, but she felt safer if she knew what was going on around her.

"Stay," Terry told K9, leaving him a few yards from the body. "Where are Vic and Willie tonight?" Terry bent over the body to take a careful look. He didn't touch anything or even pull on his gloves.

"They were eating in. At Vic's."

Vic lived in the loft apartment over Erin's garage. Erin would have known if either of them had been out wandering in the woods. But of course, they hadn't been and neither one could be accused of having anything to do with this death. She was sure of that.

"Did you touch anything?"

Erin shook her head, but he wasn't looking at her. Of course, by "anything," he meant had she touched the body. Because what else would she have touched? They weren't going to be fingerprinting the trees. Erin hadn't seen a weapon but was sure that there was probably one close by.

"No. I didn't touch anything."

Skye cawed overhead; a loud, long call repeated several times. Erin heard footsteps approaching from the other direction. Not the closest street, but in the direction of the summer cottage.

"Who's that?" Terry called in an authoritative voice.

"Just me, Officer Piper." Adele's melodious voice reached them before she pushed her way through the brush to get close enough for them to see her. She cradled a shotgun in one arm. "I heard the siren. What's going on?"

Then her eyes fell on the body Terry stood over.

"Oh. I see. Who left that there?"

Terry chuckled. "Not you, I assume."

"Erin pays me to keep the woods clean. I wouldn't clutter it up with bodies."

Adele looked around, her eyes sharp. Skye swooped down from above, calling loudly again and landing in a tree close by.

"I chased him away," Erin explained. "That's probably what he's complaining to you about. He and a magpie were attacking a cat."

She looked around for the black cat, having forgotten it the moment she saw the man's body in the undergrowth. "Where did he go?"

Adele looked around. She shook her head. "Ran away, I expect. The birds guard this as their own territory. A number of them have nests close by. The cat probably got too close to one."

"I don't think they were afraid of him. I think maybe he was sick and they were trying to… well, they had pecked him. He had bloody spots on him."

Terry looked up from his examination of the body. "You're sure it was the cat's blood? He didn't get it from…" He drew a little circle around the body with one finger. "Over here?"

"He might have been attracted by the smell of the body. He was really skinny. But he was hurt. I saw the wounds."

Adele nodded. "I'll look for him. See if there is anything we can do for him."

"Would you? Thank you." Erin shook her head, looking around. "I don't know which way he went or where he came from. Poor thing."

Their eyes were all drawn back to the dead man.

"At least it's obvious where *he* came from," Terry observed.

CHAPTER 4

It wasn't long before all of the Bald Eagle Falls police department law enforcement officers, full-time or part-time, were on the scene. The department was so small that they needed everyone out in force to deal with the investigation for a crime like this. And probably law enforcement officers from one of the nearby towns, the staties, or the FBI, depending on what kind of crime it was. They would need all the help they could get.

In this case, Erin didn't think it would be very long before they saw someone from security at the penitentiary and the FBI.

The orange coveralls the man was wearing were a *dead* giveaway as to where he had come from. Erin rolled her eyes at her own lame humor as the thought passed through her mind.

"Could you tell how he was killed?" Erin asked Sheriff Wilmot as she sat in his car and again gave her story. She would, she knew, probably tell it another half dozen times before they let her go back home and get ready for bed. And would she sleep? It didn't seem very likely. It would take a long time for her to unwind enough to go to sleep, and then she had to be up very early to start the baking at Auntie Clem's before they filled the display case and started their day.

"You didn't see?" he asked in a kind but neutral tone, careful to give nothing away. She'd heard what hadn't been intended for her ears too many times in the past. He knew that he had to watch everything he said around her or she would figure out information that they hadn't intended to release to the public.

"No. I didn't actually look very closely. I saw his boots, and then the clothes, and realized that it wasn't just a pile of clothes and that he wasn't sleeping."

"How did you know he wasn't sleeping?"

Erin was trying not to picture the dead man's body or his face. The less she focused on it, the less of a chance there would be that she would see him in her nightmares or be constantly drawn to think about him and what had happened to him. It had been a quick look. She had caught only a glimpse of him. Just enough to realize that something was wrong.

"He... wasn't lying like he was sleeping. You know, people rest their heads on their arms, try to find a comfortable position. But he was just sprawled there like he had fallen down or been dropped out of a plane." She paused. "He wasn't dropped out of a plane, was he?"

That would be weird. But weirder things had happened in Bald Eagle Falls.

"No, he wasn't dropped out of an airplane," Wilmot agreed. "It was apparent that he had... sustained a serious injury."

Terry had mentioned blood. Erin was glad that she had not looked closely enough. She really didn't like blood.

"And his face. He was so pale... gray... Was there a prison break?"

Wilmot nodded. "There was."

Of course. Did Erin think that people just wandered around Bald Eagle Falls dressed like prisoners for something to do? It wasn't Halloween. The prison was only a couple of hours away. During Charley's short incarceration for her boyfriend's murder, Erin had visited her half-sister there, in the section of the penitentiary reserved for those who were awaiting trial. They didn't wear uniforms in that section. The orange jumpsuits were reserved for those who had been convicted and sentenced.

"How did he get out? And why did he come here?"

"We will be looking into all of those questions. Someone from the prison is on their way over, and the feds are going to be involved. Just leave it to us."

Erin nodded. Of course she would. She had no intention of getting mixed up in a murder investigation.

Not again.

"So the first sign of any trouble was the birds squabbling?" Wilmot asked, taking her back to the beginning of her story once more. "That's what attracted your attention?"

Erin sighed and repeated it all one more time.

She returned home on her own. She had hoped that Terry would be off and would be able to go home with her, but he still had work to do and probably would not be home until late. Erin's queasiness and confusion upon finding the dead body had dissipated. She was feeling well enough to handle things and declined a police escort to her back door.

Erin made herself a cup of tea and sat down on the couch with the animals, pretending to read. But she wasn't actually seeing anything she put in front of her face. She was glad for the company of Orange Blossom and Marshmallow, who were happy to snuggle and for her to pet them and talk to them about her experience. Seeing the skinny cat had reminded Erin of when she had found Orange Blossom as a tiny kitten and later, the brown and white rabbit they would dub Marshmallow. It was hard to believe that each had once been a stranger to her. They were so much an integral part of her life in Bald Eagle Falls.

Orange Blossom had been such a dirty, skinny little puffball.

Eventually, Terry's truck pulled up to the curb in front of the house and she watched him walk up the sidewalk to the door. She didn't bother to get up to open the door for him, which would mean disturbing the slumbering animals. He let himself in, punched in the code for the security alarm, and locked the door behind him. He smiled at Erin and the animals cuddled up on the couch.

"Any room left for me?"

"Lots."

He gave K9 a hand signal to release him from duty, and K9 lay down on Erin's feet with a thump and a sigh. She laughed. Terry loosened his duty belt and sat down beside her, tugging her over slightly so that she was leaning against his shoulder.

"Aaah," he sighed.

Erin closed her eyes.

"I don't suppose you have any thoughts of going to sleep any time soon," Terry said.

"No. Starting to get tired, but… my head is still whirling with questions."

"I'm sure it is." He leaned over and kissed her forehead gently.

"Sheriff Wilmot said that he was seriously injured."

"Well, yes. People don't generally just drop dead. I mean, it does happen. People have heart attacks. Other illnesses. But when you're talking about an escaped prisoner… it's more likely to be violent causes." He looked searchingly into her eyes. As well as needing to keep certain information confidential, he would want to shield her from anything violent or gory. Erin appreciated that.

"I don't need a lot of details. And it will be in the news. I just want to know the basics about how he died."

He stroked her hair and leaned against her. Erin leaned into him, enjoying the closeness. She felt warm and protected.

"He was stabbed. It would have been very quick."

Erin closed her eyes and nodded, trying not to picture it. "Do you know who he was?"

"The man's name is Christian Bruel."

"Do you know him? Is he from here?"

"No. He's never lived in Bald Eagle Falls, as far as I know."

"Why would he come here, then? Wouldn't it make more sense for him to head in the other direction, toward a big city instead of a little town like this where he would be bound to be noticed?"

"We have some theories about that."

Erin raised her brows. "Yes?"

"You know I can't share inside information with you."

"You'll have to release something to the press."

17

Terry was silent, thinking about it. He must have had a conversation with Sheriff Wilmot already about what they could release and what they would hold back. It was a conversation they always had.

"*Two* prisoners escaped."

"Oh." Erin supposed that explained how Bruel had been killed. His partner had double-crossed him. "Who was the other prisoner?"

Terry licked his lips. He rested his chin on top of Erin's head momentarily, holding her close to him.

"The other prisoner was Davis Plaint."

CHAPTER 5

DAVIS PLAINT.

*E*rin's heart sank. But at the same time, she didn't know exactly how she should feel about this news. She had been instrumental in putting Davis in prison. But she'd felt bad about doing it, knowing that part of what he was had been the result of his traumatic childhood and the murder of his father, which he had witnessed. How was a kid who had grown up like that supposed to turn out to have a normally functioning conscience? He had been a young teenager, emotionally abused, forced into helping to dispose of a body, unpopular at school, and had descended into addiction shortly after.

But that didn't change the fact that he had engineered the murder of his own brother in order to claim the full inheritance for himself. He had tried to kill or scare away Erin by burning down her house. And had tried to kill both her and Bertie Braceling by running them down in his car, succeeding only in killing Bertie.

She knew that he belonged in prison, no matter what trauma he'd had to go through in childhood. He was a danger to others.

And especially to her.

Erin swallowed and turned her head to look up into Terry's face.

"Is that why they came here instead of going to the big city?"

"What?"

"Did Davis and the other man come here because… he wants to get back at me?"

Terry gave her a squeeze. He looked away from her, keeping his face blank. He didn't give any indication of whether he had already thought about this or not.

"You're safe here. You have a good burglar alarm and an on-site cop. You couldn't ask for anything more."

"Things still happen. People can get past alarms. You're not here all the time, sometimes you're on shift. At night, when it is dark and he could get close to the house…"

Erin's chest tightened thinking about it. She tried to take long, deep breaths like she did during her tai chi exercises. She needed oxygen to help keep anxiety at bay. And she needed to breathe out fully to keep from hyperventilating. She was occupied with just breathing in and out for a few seconds. Or a few minutes. She didn't know how much time actually passed while she was stuck in this limbo, unable to talk to Terry or to think about the probability of Davis showing up at her house to take his revenge on her.

Terry's expression was serious. He watched her face, rubbing her back in firm, soothing circles. "I'll ask the sheriff to keep me on days until Davis is apprehended. When you're at Auntie Clem's with lots of people around you. I'll make sure that I'm home nights."

Erin nodded.

"Besides, I'm sure they'll have him in custody very quickly. Prisoners are usually apprehended within twenty-four hours of a prison break."

"Really?" Erin took a deep breath, filling her lungs, wishing that the flashes of light would go away. She didn't want to pass out.

"Really. It's rare that anyone can avoid a manhunt for longer than that. And if they do, it's because they get far away, not because they stick around their hometown looking for trouble. So either he'll get caught, or he'll be far away from here."

"Yeah." Erin nodded. It made logical sense. She just wasn't sure her body would believe it. Her heart was still pounding extra hard and fast, despite her attempts to calm her reaction to the news. "I'm sure everything will be fine."

Terry nodded reassuringly. "It will. And I'll be here with you. Everything will work out."

But why had Davis and Bruel gone to Bald Eagle Falls in the first place, if not to get back at Erin? If Bruel wasn't from there, then he had no reason to show up there. Only Davis. With his immediate family members dead, he didn't really have any other reason to be in town, did he?

Erin gasped suddenly. Terry looked at her, brows down. "What?"

"Melissa."

"What about Melissa?"

Erin thought about her friend with the wild curly dark hair and the generous, laughing mouth. She loved gossip and drama, and she had confided to Erin over the phone that she had liked Davis when they had been in school together. Not only that, but she had also renewed their friendship and had been visiting him in the penitentiary ever since he had been incarcerated.

She had never understood how women could fall in love with men in prison, behind bars, who had committed atrocious acts and would never be released. What would make a woman date someone like that? Other than just the thrill of telling other people about it. And Melissa had not shared that particular information with the church ladies she associated with most often. Melissa was always chattering about information she had learned through her part time job doing administrative work for the police department, but she had managed to keep that little tidbit secret.

"Melissa… she and Davis were friends."

He nodded slowly. "That was a long time ago. You don't think that they would get back together, do you?"

Erin shifted her position, suddenly uncomfortable. With all of the animals and Terry cuddling against her, she suddenly felt hemmed in, unable to breathe. She pulled her feet out from under K9 and tried to convince the cat and the rabbit that she needed some more room. Terry shifted away a couple of inches to allow her more freedom of movement.

"They already were back together. Melissa… she's been visiting him at the penitentiary this whole time. Ever since he was arrested."

Terry stared at her open-mouthed. "Are you kidding me?"

"No. It's true. She goes to see him every few weeks. Writes and phones the rest of the time. They're... quite close."

"Why is this the first time I'm hearing this?"

"Well... it's Melissa's personal life. I expect she didn't want to share it with anyone else in the department. She had to know how you would feel about it, knowing that one of your staff was friends with a violent felon."

He cleared his throat. "Well, it isn't any of our business, of course, and doesn't affect her employment with the department." But he pursed his lips, considering this new information. Thinking, Erin was sure, about how often Melissa ended up sharing information that she had learned through the department. She had been admonished about it more than once, but that didn't seem to stop the flow of information. And what if she had shared with Davis? What information might she have passed on to him that could cause them problems?

"Nothing that the police department in Bald Eagle Falls does would be of any interest to Davis Plaint," she told Terry reassuringly. "What would he care about who you have picked up for shoplifting or public drunkenness? Nothing that happens here really has any impact on him while he's in prison."

"It's not that... though I'm not sure you're right. What goes on on the outside can affect prisoners and vice versa. It's just... well... the appearance that she might have helped him to escape prison. That she might have been able to gather the information he needed to make his escape."

"What would Melissa know about that?"

"Nothing through the department... but there are other places she could have gathered intelligence. A lot easier for her to find things out from outside the prison than for him on the inside. Things like blueprints or inspection reports..."

"They don't make those public, do they?"

"There is a certain amount that is available to the public. Sometimes through things like budget approvals, or annual reports to shareholders, information on living conditions or details on their website about how visits are handled. There's more information available publicly than you would think."

Erin still couldn't believe that anything that was public knowledge would be of any use to Melissa trying to help her friend escape from the penitentiary.

"What are you going to do? You can't tell the sheriff."

"Why not? Why wouldn't I?"

"Well… because it's private information. It isn't any of his business. And Melissa wouldn't want it spread around. The other ladies don't know. At least, I don't think any of them do. If you question her about it, then people will find out about their relationship…"

"We can talk to her discreetly. More easily than the general public, since she's already at the office. No one else would need to know. Not that we're going to make decisions in a manhunt based on whether or not the other gossips are going to find out about Melissa and her boyfriend. That can't be part of the equation."

"But you should try to keep people's private lives private…"

"When they intersect with a police investigation… that can't be one of our considerations."

Erin leaned against him, thinking about it. Her heart had slowed down as she thought about Melissa and her problems rather than about Davis coming back to Bald Eagle Falls to take his revenge on her.

"Maybe that's why he came to Bald Eagle Falls. To see Melissa. Not because of anything to do with me."

"Hopefully, that is the case," Terry agreed. He shifted to get up. "I need to call Sheriff Wilmot and give him an update. We'll want to get someone over to Melissa's place tonight to keep an eye on the place. Then question her when she is away from home, in case he's already there."

No point in allowing him to take a hostage.

"Poor Melissa."

Terry stood, then looked down at her. "Poor Melissa?"

"She didn't ask for this to happen. I'm sure she wasn't involved in anything illegal."

Erin was about to make a further point about Melissa being one of the church ladies, and therefore careful not to do anything illegal or immoral. But she had seen enough of the behavior of the upright women of Bald Eagle Falls in the time that she had been there to know that their idea of what was moral and acceptable was often far different from Erin's or what she would have expected from them according to their Christian beliefs. Things got warped somehow. A person made excuses for her own behavior. It was much easier to say that she followed some generalized principle than to actually live it with exactness.

"Maybe not. Maybe she had nothing to do with the escape. But we still have to make sure that she isn't harboring a fugitive."

CHAPTER 6

*E*rin picked up her phone to look at the time. Terry rubbed the back of his neck. "Are you ready for bed?"

"No. I was just thinking... we should probably tell the neighbors. Not everyone has a burglar alarm, and if Davis is lurking around in the woods back there..."

"We're doing a search of the woods."

"Sure, but it's dark. And there aren't really a lot of you. You could miss him hunkered down somewhere, or he could sneak into someone's house to hide from you." Erin raised her brows. "That's kind of my point."

Terry nodded slowly. He scratched his jaw, nails scratching against the short stubble. Erin gritted her teeth. The noise always made her squirm like fingernails on a blackboard. Not that schools used blackboards anymore.

"It might be a good idea to canvass the neighbors," he admitted. "A few of them have already been by, wanting to know what was going on after hearing the sirens."

"I was thinking that Mrs. Peach might already be in bed," Erin said, thinking about her elderly next-door neighbor. "But I think she would want to know what was going on."

"So, do you think we should contact her tonight or not?"

"Yeah... I think we should. I can go over there. I don't have my jammies on yet."

"Okay," Terry agreed. "You do that. I'll talk to the sheriff about doing a quick visit to the homeowners along the edge of the woods who might not know what is going on yet."

Erin was nervous as she stood on Mrs. Peach's doorstep, waiting for her to answer the doorbell. Informing her neighbors had seemed like a perfectly natural next step. Still, she hadn't been thinking about precisely what she would say. Erin didn't want Mrs. Peach sitting up all night worrying that a convicted murderer might break into her home. Still, she needed to know what was going on. Erin tried to formulate the best way to tell her when she made it to the door.

It had been a few minutes since Erin had rung the doorbell, so she tried again. It might take several times to wake Mrs. Peach up if she had already gone to bed. But Erin knew that it took her a while to get around, too, so she didn't want to keep ringing the doorbell if Mrs. Peach were already on the way there, but just hadn't been able to make it yet. Erin always hated it when someone rang the doorbell two or three times when she was already on her way to answer the door. It was irritating.

A light went on in the front bedroom. So at least she was awake. Erin waited. She looked around, seeing who else still had their lights on. Pretty much the whole block was lit up. Erin normally went to bed before anyone else, but it was getting to be the hour when she would have expected others to be getting ready to retire for the day.

Terry poked his head out Erin's front door. "Okay, Erin?"

"Yes. Just be another minute."

He nodded and withdrew.

Another light went on. Hallway. Mrs. Peach was making her way slowly to the front door. A living room lamp was turned on, and then the porch light, illuminating Erin brightly so that anyone looking out the peephole would be able to see who it was. She covered her eyes for a moment and forced a smile.

"It's me, Mrs. Peach. Erin Price."

The door opened, chain still on. Mrs. Peach peered out at her. "What are you doing here? Is there something wrong? Did you lock yourself out?"

"No. I just wanted to let you know what's going on…"

"What's going on?"

"You might have heard the sirens earlier?"

"Yes. I'm not deaf."

"No, I know that. I didn't know if you might have already been asleep, though. Or you might have had headphones on or been listening to music."

"What did you call the police about *this* time?"

Erin wasn't sure that was very fair. She hadn't been the last one to call the police. And she hadn't made any nuisance calls. Mrs. Peach was the one who was likely to call the sheriff complaining that Orange Blossom was too loud and Erin needed to keep him under control. As if she could stop him from yowling so loudly.

"A couple of men escaped from the penitentiary," Erin informed her, deciding to approach it from that side rather than the fact that yes, she had been the one to call the police when she had stumbled across a body in the woods.

But what would anyone else have done?

Mrs. Peach's eyes were sharp and alert. "An escape? I didn't hear about that."

"I don't know if it has been announced to the media yet." Erin assumed that it had been or would be soon, knowing that two dangerous convicts were on the loose who might cause harm to the public. Although now they were down to just one escaped convict. "But there were, and one of them… was found in the woods," Erin gestured, though of course, Mrs. Peach knew where the woods were and didn't need any explanation.

"My heavens. But he was found. So there is no need to worry about anything."

"One of them was found," Erin confirmed, nodding. "But… there is still one other one on the loose. The police are doing a search of the woods tonight, but it's dark, and… I just wanted you to know.

Put the chains on both of your doors, close any windows, that kind of thing..."

"Yes, I will," Mrs. Peach agreed immediately. "Of all things! Thank you for coming over to let me know."

"I didn't want to wake you up, but I thought you needed to know."

"You did the right thing. I would have been very upset in the morning if I heard what had been going on and no one had bothered to tell me. We're a community here. You are supposed to take care of your neighbors."

"Exactly." Erin was relieved. "I'm glad you aren't upset about me interrupting your sleep." She had another thought as she stood there. Mrs. Peach did not have a burglar alarm to arm, but Erin did. "Will you be okay here? If you don't feel safe, you could come over to my house to sleep. I have a guest bedroom that you could use. Officer Piper says he thinks they'll catch him within a day, so you could come back to your house once the danger was past."

"Oh, but you'll be needing the guest bedroom for Officer Piper, won't you? I know he does stay over sometimes."

"Well, I..." Erin's face burned with embarrassment as she tried to figure out how to tell Mrs. Peach in a way that wouldn't offend her Christian sensibilities that she and Terry shared a bed. "Uh, Terry..."

Mrs. Peach's mouth turned up in an elfin grin. Her eyes sparkled. She reached through the partially opened doorway to pat Erin on the arm, cackling. "Oh, don't you worry. I was once a young person myself," she laughed.

Erin felt herself turning an even deeper shade of red at the thought of elderly Mrs. Peach as a young woman, keeping company with a young man of her own. She coughed and rubbed at her eyes, trying to hide her embarrassment.

"I'm quite happy staying here," Mrs. Peach assured Erin. "This has been my home for thirty years and I am quite all right sleeping on my own. I'll make sure that everything is shut up tight, and the chances that this escaped prisoner would ever come here are..." She shrugged. "Well, why would he? He'll want to get as far away from this place as he can, won't he?"

"I hope so, yes."

Mrs. Peach peered at her sharply through the door opening. "Why wouldn't he? He doesn't have any reason to stay around here, has he?"

"Well… I'm just a little worried that he might… well, he might want to harm me since I had something to do with him being put in prison."

"Who is this man?"

"Davis Plaint. Do you remember Angela Plaint, who had a bakery here before I moved in and opened up Auntie Clem's?"

"Of course I remember. She had two boys and a girl. The girl committed suicide."

"Yes," Erin admitted. "That's right. And her boys, the younger one was Davis, and he… well, he was involved in his brother Trenton's death."

"And Bertie's. Yes, I remember that all right. Well…" Mrs. Peach cocked her head. "All the more reason for me not to sleep in *your* house tonight."

Erin stood there with her mouth open, not sure what to say to that.

"Thank you, dear," Mrs. Peach told her. "I appreciate you taking the time to keep an old lady informed. You take care of yourself."

And with that, she shut the door.

CHAPTER 7

*B*ack at the house, Erin found that Willie and Vic had crossed the yard and were visiting in the kitchen with Terry. Erin nodded a greeting to them.

"You heard?"

Willie shrugged his thick shoulders. "Sheriff would like me to help with organizing and effecting the search."

Erin knew that this was one of Willie's areas of expertise. He had helped to find and rescue her back when she had first come to Bald Eagle Falls. He had helped to organize a search for Roger Cox when he had wandered off from his family.

Only this wasn't a rescue. They would be looking for a potentially dangerous offender.

She studied Willie's face, skin stained dark from mining and processing ores, another of his ventures. He didn't look tired. Even though it was late in the day for Erin and Vic, the rest of the Bald Eagle Falls townsfolk who didn't get up at unearthly hours to bake bread were still reasonably fresh. She was glad about that. She didn't want people searching for a convicted murderer in the dark woods, their reactions too slow, or unable to focus fully due to fatigue.

"I'm glad you're going to be helping them."

Willie nodded his acknowledgment. No false modesty about how anyone else could have done it just as well.

Vic pushed a length of fine blond hair back over her ear, her eyes wider than usual, making Erin think of a deer in the headlights. She hoped that she didn't look just the same. But she probably did.

"If it ain't one murderer, it's another," Vic said flippantly, making light of it. "Just what did we do to deserve this kind of attention?"

"I wish I'd never heard of Davis Plaint," Erin informed them, shaking her head.

"Don't you worry, we'll find him," Willie assured her.

"I hope so. How long has it been since they escaped? He could be far away by now."

"It's been a few hours," Terry acknowledged.

"But he didn't head for the city," Willie pointed out. "If they wanted to get as far away as possible, then why come here? It's the wrong direction. They must have had something that they wanted to do here. Otherwise, they could be a lot farther away by now."

Erin tried to ignore the brick in her stomach. Willie would help. The Bald Eagle Falls police department was small, but they would all help. They were smart. They could outwit Davis Plaint, a dropout with a long history of drug dependency.

"Davis might not have stuck around," Terry pointed out.

Willie shook his head. "You want my expertise? He's here in Bald Eagle Falls. And we're going to find him."

Terry didn't argue the point. He knew it was probably true. Erin suspected that he had only been arguing to make her feel better. But his words hadn't helped.

Willie was checking over the equipment in his multi-pocketed jacket, focused on the job at hand. He flashed a look at Terry.

"Funny how the police department is so quick to try to pin a murder or other crime on me, but when you need my help…"

"It isn't anything personal," Terry assured him. "We have to follow the evidence, and when you have a strong motive and you have been on the scene… it would be negligent for us not to investigate. It isn't because any of us actually thought—"

Willie swore, stopping Terry cold. "Don't expect me to believe any of that crap," Willie growled. "I've been at the other end of inter-rogations often enough to know that you are never going to forget my history with the Dyson clan and are going to assume I'm still involved with them and committing whatever crimes I can get away with."

Erin never could understand how Terry could be so sure that Willie was mixed up in any illegal ventures. From what she knew of Willie, he was kind and helpful. He was keenly protective of Vic, and of Erin too, for that matter.

"I've never said that," Terry said stonily.

"You don't think that I'm still working with the Dyson clan."

"Can you honestly say that you're not? That you haven't had anything to do with Nelson Dyson or anyone else in the clan since you moved back to Bald Eagle Falls?"

Willie stared at Terry, eyes as cold as ice.

Terry nodded as if this proved his point.

But having a business relationship with someone in the clan wasn't the same as being a soldier for an organized crime family or participating in their activities. Willie could provide legitimate business services to someone in the Dyson family without being a clan member or doing anything illegal.

Even Nelson Dyson had not had anything to do with the family crime syndicate when Erin had met him, trying to get Charley out of trouble. People could leave the clan. Just like Vic and her brother Jeremy had both left the Jackson clan. It caused a lot of strain on the relationships with their family, but they had done it, and Erin didn't see any reason Willie couldn't do the same. He had put in the time that he'd been indentured to them for, and then he'd gotten out.

Erin didn't know why Terry and the other law enforcement officers always had to assume the worst of Willie. It seemed like within a system that claimed people were innocent until proven guilty, there should at least be some consideration given for whether a person actually *was* innocent.

She put her hand on Terry's arm, and he shrugged and turned away from Willie, breaking off from the discussion. They both knew that he and Willie were not going to come to some understanding. Not with a five-minute discussion.

"You're not joining the search?" Willie asked, his voice holding a note of mockery as if he thought that Terry might not be up to it.

"We decided that it was important Erin not be left here without protection," Terry said flatly, not rising to the bait. "If Davis is back in town with some idea of revenge…"

Willie nodded. "You going to stay here?" he asked Vic. "I don't want you alone either."

"I can defend myself," Vic reminded him.

"I know you can. But three against one is much better odds than one on one."

Except that Erin had no skills to defend herself against a person like Davis, and might put the other two in danger because she would be so inept in the event of an attack. She was a distraction and a liability.

Vic looked at Erin as if she could hear these thoughts. She put her hand on Erin's arm and pulled her closer. "What was that? Did you say something about ice cream that you needed help eating?"

Erin laughed. "Of course, there's ice cream," she agreed. And she might even have some herself. She'd been really good about watching what she ate lately. She was shorter than Vic and didn't have her high metabolism, which meant that any extra calories showed up on her hips much faster.

Willie snapped down another flap on his jacket and headed out the door. "See you ladies in a couple of hours."

Erin and Vic went to the freezer to make proper arrangements for the disposal of the ice cream.

CHAPTER 8

*E*ventually, Willie and the police department had to suspend the search of the woods and the area surrounding them, conceding that they had done all that they could and that they needed to save their resources for other areas as well. They couldn't tire out all of their law enforcement officers and then expect them to work their usual shifts the next day. They would probably have to call for reinforcements from Moose River, the state police, or the FBI. Erin assumed that with something like a prison break, the FBI would probably be eager to step in.

Willie rubbed his eyes, which were now puffy and showing definite signs of fatigue. He looked Vic and Erin over. They were sitting on the couch in front of the TV, with empty ice cream bowls on the coffee table, but neither of them had actually been paying much attention to the TV programming. Terry was sitting a short distance away, one of the easy chairs placed to have a line of sight with both the front window and the back door. K9 was snoring.

"Did either of you ladies get any sleep?"

"No."

Willie motioned to Vic. "Why don't we hit the sack and see if you can at least get a couple of hours under your belt?"

Vic shook her head. "We're going to go in for the early shift at Auntie Clem's."

"What? You're crazy. On zero sleep?"

"We may as well. We're awake anyway."

"You're going to be dead on your feet by the end of the day."

"We won't work all day," Erin told him. "Just the early shift. We'll have someone else on after the early morning rush. Maybe by then, I'll be tired enough that I can get some sleep."

"You really need to take care of yourselves. Don't kill yourself over…"

"Over my business? It isn't just a job or my livelihood. People depend on Auntie Clem's being open."

"And you could call someone else to open up for you."

"Why bother when we're both awake anyway?"

Willie shrugged and rolled his eyes. "Fine, okay." He directed his comments back to Vic. "I'm going to go sack out for a while. Do you mind?"

"No. We'll be heading over to the bakery soon. Go ahead."

"I feel kind of awkward going to sleep when you two are headed to work."

"You've just been in charge of a big manhunt. We were just sitting here eating ice cream. Who do you think is going to be more tired?"

"Well… I suppose. But be careful. Don't stick your hands in any blenders."

Erin winced. "I promise, no blenders this morning."

"Just be careful," he repeated.

"We will."

Willie nodded, bent over to give Vic a quick kiss, then headed out, punching his code into the burglar alarm before opening the door.

The morning after a shocking or tragic event in Bald Eagle Falls always brought a rush of people to Auntie Clem's Bakery. The women gathered to discuss all of the details available and gossip and speculate on what they didn't know. Business after a murder was always brisk.

So Erin wasn't surprised that when she went out to the storefront to flip the Closed sign to Open that there was already a group of women waiting for her. Not just the usual few with their coffee cups, in for a muffin to eat before work or at their desks, but a wide variety from both Bald Eagle Falls and the surrounding farms.

"Is it true that you found the body?" Cindy Proust demanded before Erin had even returned to her place behind the counter. And of course, Cindy would have heard, even though she was outside the town, since Erin's best employee, Bella Proust, was her daughter. Erin had already contacted Bella to let her know that she and Vic would need someone to fill in for them after the morning rush. Even though she was still in high school, Bella was the one this assignment would come the easiest to. She would make a few phone calls to the other employees and have substitutes set up in no time.

But then there was her mother.

"Yes, I'm afraid so," Erin admitted to Cindy.

Cindy—and everyone else—stared at her expectantly, waiting for the rest of the story.

"I was just out for a stroll," Erin explained with a sigh. "Some fresh air and exercise, and to watch the sunset." She described hearing the birds, seeing the black, skinny cat, and then finding the body.

"Black cats are bad luck," Lottie Sturm pointed out. She and Cindy Prost were good friends and were often to be found together. Egging each other on in subtle and not-so-subtle bullying.

Bad luck for Erin or for the escaped convict?

"I don't think it was the fault of the cat," Erin informed them.

Vic giggled, waiting at the till to ring up the first purchase of the day. Since Cindy was the one making the inquiries and the person that Erin wanted to get rid of the quickest, she aimed her smile at Cindy and raised her brows.

"Now, what can I get for you today, Ms. Prost?"

"Well, those lemon bars look mighty tasty," Cindy pondering them in the display case. "We're having a spring social this week and those would go awfully nicely with some tea or punch."

Erin nodded. "You'd like a full tray, then? I've got a few fresh out of the oven in back."

She didn't stop to worry about why she hadn't been invited to this spring social. It was probably something for the church ladies, and Erin was not part of that group, nor did she aspire to be.

"Yes," Cindy said, after pursing her lips. "That would be best."

"I'll go get them. Let Vic know if you want anything else."

She retreated to the kitchen to package up a tray of the lemon bars and could hear the women murmuring to each other, though she couldn't make out the words. More gossip and speculation, most likely, since they didn't actually know very much about the body that Erin had found in the woods.

"There was a search last night," she heard Mrs. Mans say as she returned to the front with the box of lemon bars. "And since they wouldn't be searching for the dead man that they had already found…"

"There was another escaped prisoner," Vic admitted.

The women gasped and looked around at each other, covering their mouths in shock, eyes excited over the news. They weren't afraid, because whoever would have thought about an escaped prisoner spending any time in Bald Eagle Falls stalking the townspeople? They had no reason to believe that anyone would stick around.

Erin herself was still trying to convince herself that Davis would be far away. There was no need for him to be in Bald Eagle Falls. It was much safer for him to run in the other direction. Escape to Canada and live a quiet life in Toronto or out in the sticks. No one would ever find him if he kept his head down and didn't arouse any suspicions.

"They must have had outside help," one of the women suggested.

Vic rang up Cindy's lemon bars, a loaf of bread, and a muffin. Erin looked at Lottie. "And what can I get you?"

"I heard that it was Davis Plaint."

Erin nodded. "That's what I heard too."

And everyone knew it wasn't just something she had overheard whispers about. Erin was right in the middle of things. She would know directly from the police authorities that it was true. More gasps of shock and making eyes at each other. It was almost comical how dramatic they were.

"I'll have a slice of the chocolate banana bread… and maybe some white rolls for dinner tonight."

Erin nodded and got them packaged up for her. "You have a nice day, Miss Sturm." She hoped that Lottie and Cindy would leave quickly and not hang around trying to get more information or to stir everyone up. Things could get nasty when the two of them were around.

Surprisingly—or perhaps not so surprisingly—Melissa Lee was not one of the early visitors to Auntie Clem's. She was usually one of the much-sought-after sources and put in a showing early in the day to impart whatever information she had been able to discover. Working for the police as a part-time office assistant, Melissa was privy to information that was not public and often imparted tidbits to the public that the police department would have rather she kept quiet. But so far, it had not cost her her job, and she kept showing up with new information every time there was a major crime to talk about.

But this time, Melissa had reason not to show up at Auntie Clem's Bakery.

After the initial wave of women had been served and were on their way, Erin looked at the clock. "I'm going to take some muffins and coffee over to the police department," she informed Vic. "Bella said that she'd have someone here by nine to help out, so you should have someone here soon. And I won't be long at the police department. Just taking them some treats after their long night. I don't imagine things have settled down for them much today."

Vic nodded her understanding. "They'll be happy to get something sweet to fill the empty spaces. And I'm sure the coffee won't be turned down either. They're going to need something to get them going."

"Maybe I should start a line of energy bars." Erin thought about the possibility. Something quick and portable that could be eaten on the run. Lots of protein and something for an extra kick of energy. "Maybe with ginseng?"

"That's a good idea," Vic approved. They had a very good supply of ginseng, and its merits were well-known by the townspeople, many of whom had grandmothers who had gathered and sold "sang" in the old days, trying to save their farms or mineral claims from bankruptcy. "Good for the student athletes too." They often came in for a muffin or other snack between school letting out and practices. "And hikers."

"Yeah. There might be quite a market." Erin made a mental note to look into it more later, checking out recipes on the net and researching who to target in her ad campaign. "But in the meantime, muffins will have to do."

After packing a few muffins in a box and filling a carafe with fresh coffee, Erin made her way down the street to the police department offices in the town hall building. She stopped at Clara Jones's desk at the front of the offices, knowing that Clara would not let her just walk in to say hello to Terry and possibly overhear conversations about things they were not ready to release to the public.

"Hello, Clara. Are these boys giving you any rest?"

Clara smiled in appreciation. She didn't actually look too harassed, but Erin imagined that there was a lot to do with the ongoing manhunt. She was probably fielding a flurry of calls from the Bald Eagle Falls public wanting to know what was going on and perhaps to report sightings of the missing prisoner.

"It has been a mighty busy morning," Clara admitted. "You've brought us some supplemental energy?"

"Solid and liquid," Erin agreed. She opened the muffin box and offered it to Clara. In former days, she would have been able to walk around the office, giving Terry and the other law enforcement officers their choice as well. But she had taken a few too many liberties, and Clara was now tasked with ensuring that Erin did not have free run of the offices.

Clara selected a blueberry muffin and put it on a napkin on her desk. Then she stood up to take the box and carafe from Erin. "I'll put these in the kitchenette."

"Is Terry around? Or are they out looking for Davis?"

"Everyone is out at the moment. They searched the woods last night, but a lot can be missed in the dark. They'll go over everything with a fine-tooth comb today."

Erin nodded. "Well, tell him I said hello." She hesitated. "And what about Melissa? Is she in today?"

CHAPTER 9

*C*lara raised a penciled eyebrow, considering Erin.

"She was supposed to be in, but she called in sick today." Clara gave a little shrug, her brows coming closer together. "I don't know when the last time she called in sick was. She only comes in for a few hours, so she can usually manage that, even if she feels a little under the weather. Sometimes she'll call in and say that she'll come by later in the afternoon when she's feeling better…"

"But today, she just said she wouldn't be in at all."

"That's right," Clara agreed. "Said she was puny."

"Well, maybe I'll give her a call later on," Erin said. "See if she's feeling any better."

"I'm sure she'll be just fine."

"Say hello to everyone for me. Hopefully, they'll stop by at some point to refuel." Erin nodded toward the box of muffins and coffee carafe.

"Oh, I'll put this out on an All-Points Bulletin. They'll stop by." Clara gave Erin a rare smile. "They always do."

Erin was glad that her gifts were appreciated. Even if she did have an ulterior motive, she liked the opportunity to serve the police department in her way.

~

Erin didn't usually take a nap in the afternoon, even if she hadn't slept well the night before, for fear that it would wreck her sleep that night too. Or that she would wake up with a headache or grumpy. Or all three things. She had to be really tired for it to feel worth it to take that nap, however much she wanted one.

But she knew as the hands of the clock moved closer and closer to noon that she wasn't going to be able to make it through the day with her tank on empty. And who knew how long Terry would be with the manhunt? She didn't like his working too long either. Ever since the head injury he had sustained during the Bo Biggles investigation, he had been susceptible to migraines and other issues if he didn't get enough sleep. Even though it had been months since he had been hurt, he still didn't have the energy or attention span that he'd had before the incident. He would crash when he got home, whenever that was.

Cheyenne and Charley arrived just before the lunch rush and pulled on their aprons. "Never fear," Charley announced, "your favorite sister is here!"

Erin smiled at her half-sister, younger by eight years, who she hadn't even known had existed until after her arrival in Bald Eagle Falls. Erin hadn't known that her mother had been pregnant at the time of the accident and the doctors had kept her alive until her baby could be delivered safely. Erin had never seen Charley or been told about her by her social workers. They had all pretended that she didn't even exist.

And now Erin had the opportunity to know her. Though they were not very much alike and Erin hadn't even liked her very much when they had first met, Charley grew on her. She had put her inheritance into the pot to help save Auntie Clem's Bakery. Even though she couldn't keep baker's hours, she was there to help out with the bakery when she was needed. Preferably in the afternoon. As different as they were, Erin was glad to have her sister around.

"Thanks for coming in," Erin told the two women. She smothered a yawn. "Vic and I didn't get any sleep last night. I'm starting to feel it."

"Me too," Vic admitted. "I'm slap wore out. Time to go home and lie down."

"I think I will too. Feels weird to sleep during the day, but I don't think I could stay awake if I tried."

"You okay to drive home?" Charley demanded, leaning closer to look at Erin's eyes.

"Terry dropped us off this morning, so Willie is going to drive us home. If he wasn't… yeah, I might have walked instead of driving. Even though it is only a few blocks, I'm not sure I could keep my eyes open the whole way."

"Wasn't Willie up all night too?"

"He was, but he's been sleeping since we came in this morning. So he'll be fine."

"Okay." Charley nodded her approval. "Good. I don't want you plowing into a fire hydrant or something."

It was funny to have Charley mothering Erin and making sure she was acting responsibly. Usually, it was the other way around.

"We're being careful," she laughed. "We had to promise Willie this morning that we wouldn't use the blenders. Everyone seems to think that we might be too impaired to work."

Charley nodded. "If it was me, I'd probably need more than a little caffeine jolt to keep me going."

But she didn't say what she would have taken instead. Erin didn't want to think about what illicit drugs Charley might rely upon. Charley had been pretty responsible since she had moved to Bald Eagle Falls after her fall-out with the Dyson clan in Moose River. She had been something of a party girl before that, so Erin had to allow her a little leeway. It took time to overcome a background like that. Charley wasn't going to settle down to be like one of the staid Baptist ladies.

~

Erin climbed down from Willie's truck. It seemed like a long trip from the gravel parking pad across the backyard to her door. But at least she didn't have to go up the long flight of steps to the loft apartment over the garage like Vic did.

"Okay," she said, covering a yawn. "See you guys later."

"Have a nice nap," Willie laughed.

Vic murmured something sleepily, but Erin couldn't make out what it was.

"You too," she told Vic, returning whatever it was.

She had to focus on finding the right key to open the back door and then punching her code into the burglar alarm so that it wouldn't blast the whole neighborhood. So far, that had only happened a couple of times, but if she were going to do it again, then it would be when she was so tired.

"Hello, sweeties," she told Orange Blossom and Marshmallow as they hurried out to the kitchen to greet her. "Yes, Mommy is home. I know it's weird to see me this time of day, but…" She trailed off, not sure what she had intended to say. The animals certainly wouldn't be upset that she had come home early. They would be happy to cuddle up with her and have an afternoon nap.

She didn't have the energy to get them treats, so she ignored Orange Blossom's loud demands and headed straight for her bed.

"Anybody home?" she called out, in case Terry had gotten off of work. But she didn't expect him to be there, and he wasn't.

Erin dropped her purse beside the bed and climbed in. She closed her eyes and was asleep before her head hit the pillow.

CHAPTER 10

*E*rin awoke, her head feeling thick and heavy. She wasn't sure how long she had been asleep, but she could tell that the sun was low in the sky. She lay still for a while, just thinking about whether she had the energy to get up and make herself some supper. She should get up so as not to mess up her sleep schedule. But she couldn't quite convince herself to get out of bed. Her body still wanted to sleep more, even if the logical part of her brain kept telling her that she had to get out of bed and not sleep the day away.

She felt around for her phone, eventually finding it in the purse that she had put down beside the bed. She hadn't missed any important calls as she had feared. Everything must be going smoothly at Auntie Clem's. She played around with her phone for a few minutes to wake her brain up. Orange Blossom stirred beside her. He stretched his front legs out in front of him and blinked at her, kneading the bed with his claws.

"Comfy?" Erin asked.

He purred.

Erin heard a bang at the side of the house. She listened for a minute, trying to figure out what it might have been. Houses made noises. And sometimes, she heard noises from the neighbors or other houses in the neighborhood. People made noise. She wouldn't like it if everything were always as silent as a crypt. She liked some noise and activity around her, often turning on the TV if she were home alone and it was too quiet, even though she was doing something else— working through her plans for the week or poring over one of Clementine's thick genealogy books or files.

But the noise was strange enough that she got up and went to the window to see if she could see the source of it. She heard another noise, and it seemed to be closer to the back of the house, not the front. Erin walked across the hall to the other bedroom, the one Clementine had used as a sewing room or crafting room and looked out the window into the back yard.

The noise was coming from Mrs. Peach's house or yard, not her own. At first, Erin simply turned away, figuring that it was none of her business. But then she turned back. Mrs. Peach was an older lady, she didn't get around very well, and she wouldn't be in her yard lifting furniture or taking a big bag of garbage out to the bins. Erin never heard anything from her unless she called on the phone.

She looked out the window again, trying to see what was going on. She could just barely see a shadow, but couldn't tell whose shadow it was or what they were doing in Mrs. Peach's yard. It could very well be the utilities guy. Or the police.

There could be a hundred different reasons for someone to be in Mrs. Peach's backyard.

Erin walked through the house to the back door and walked out onto the porch, where she had a better view of Mrs. Peach's backyard. But her view was still hampered by the tall fence. She stood on her tiptoes and tried to see what was going on. There was bound to be a good reason for someone to be in Mrs. Peach's backyard.

She caught a glimpse of the man. Not someone she recognized.

Not Davis.

She hadn't realized until then that it was Davis she was expecting to see. And the fact that it wasn't him was a huge relief. She let her breath out.

He was an older man. Lots of salt in his salt-and-pepper hair.

Fairly tall, for her to be able to see him over the fence. He didn't seem to be sneaking around, his movements not furtive. She watched him move around the yard for a minute, but he seemed to just be doing chores. Maybe Mrs. Peach had hired him to clean up her yard. Erin couldn't stay out there watching him the whole time he was there. He would eventually feel her gaze on him or turn around and catch a glimpse of her. She went back into the house, frowning to herself.

It wasn't anything to worry about. Mrs. Peach could hire someone to take care of her yard or some work on her house. There was nothing suspicious about that. It definitely wasn't Davis Plaint.

She paced around for a while, fed the animals, and watched and listened for the man. He must have finished with the yard work, because she couldn't see or hear him anymore. He had gone back to his own home, or out for dinner, or on to the next job on his list. Erin wasn't usually home during the day. He could have been coming around weekly for months; she wouldn't know it.

But eventually, Erin couldn't stand it. She tapped Terry's picture on her phone, dialing through to him. It rang a few times before he picked it up.

"Erin. Hi, sorry I haven't called today. Things have been pretty busy."

"That's okay. I know you're working hard on this prison break. I wasn't expecting a call."

"But I should have at least touched base with you. Checked in to see how you are."

"I'm fine. You don't need to worry about me. Just worked the morning and then went home for a nap, so I probably would have slept through your call anyway."

"Good. I'm glad you got some sleep."

There was a question in his voice. If she was okay with his not calling her and she was fine and didn't need anything, why had she called him?

"I just wanted to make sure... there wasn't anyone else involved in the prison break, was there?"

"What do you mean?"

"I mean, it was just Davis and that other fellow, right? No one else escaped with them?"

"No, no one else escaped with them."

"Okay. I just wanted to make sure."

There was a short pause while he considered this. "Uh… why? It's sort of a strange question to ask."

"I just… there's someone over at Mrs. Peach's house. I don't know who he is. Never saw him before. I just wanted to make sure that you weren't looking for anyone else."

"No. Plenty of investigating to do, but we're not searching for anyone other than Davis Plaint."

Erin opened her mouth to ask whether they had seen Melissa and whether Melissa had been in contact with him, but decided it wasn't even worth asking. Terry wasn't going to tell her any details of an active investigation.

"What's this guy doing over at Mrs. Peach's?" Terry asked.

"Oh… I think… maybe just some yard work. He was back and forth a few times. I didn't want to be too obvious about watching him… Sorry, I wish I knew more."

"Did you talk to Mrs. Peach?"

"No."

It would be the perfectly logical thing to do, but Erin didn't want to look like a nosy neighbor. Mrs. Peach was entitled to have whoever she wanted over to the house. If she had relatives or friends or people she had contracted to do work for her, that was fine. She certainly didn't need to report it to Erin.

"I'm sure it's nothing," Erin said. "I don't want to be a busybody."

"You're not."

"I don't think he was doing anything wrong. I don't want to be throwing accusations around. He's just helping her out with something. It's none of my business."

"Okay. But we can look into it if you think it might be something to be concerned about. There's nothing wrong with one neighbor saying to another, 'I saw a man in your yard today, just wanted to make sure he was someone you had invited over.'"

"I know. It's okay. I don't need to follow up. Just wanted to make sure that there wasn't another escaped convict out there."

"Not that we are aware of."

Erin's chest tightened and her heart gave a hard throb. "They *would* tell you, wouldn't they?"

"It was a joke, Erin! Yes, of course they would tell us if they had another escapee. They wouldn't be keeping it a secret!"

"Okay. You scared me for a minute."

"Sorry. It was just meant to lighten the mood."

Even knowing that Terry had only been teasing her, she still felt like someone was nearby, watching her. The feeling of reassurance she had called for was gone. Despite Terry's words, she couldn't believe him. Davis could still be out there sneaking around, checking out her house and seeing how easy or hard it would be to break in and take his revenge on her.

"Erin?"

"Yeah, sorry. I was just watching the cat. You'll be back tonight, won't you? They can't keep you working all day and night and not give you time off to sleep."

"I'll be home tonight. Of course. I just have a few more things to wrap up here, then I'll be back."

"Okay. Thanks." She bit her lip to keep from saying anything about how he needed to take care of himself to make sure he didn't trigger a migraine or experience other negative consequences due to not getting enough sleep. He already knew that. She didn't need to nag him about it. "See you later, then."

After hanging up with Terry, Erin wandered the house for a few minutes, unsure what to do with herself.

Thinking about Melissa had reminded her of talking to Melissa on the phone shortly after Erin had moved to Bald Eagle Falls. Melissa had initiated a video call, and Erin took it while sitting in the little book reading nook in the attic. She hadn't used the space regularly for a while. It was a nice place to curl up when she was alone, but she often had company and visited in the living room or watched TV. There was no TV in the attic nook.

The other problem was the animals. Although Orange Blossom

had eventually figured out the fold-down stairs, he didn't like to use them. He would most often just crouch at the bottom of the stairs, giving loud, distressed meows like he was stuck in a tree instead of having all four feet on the ground. Marshmallow, on the other hand, couldn't or wouldn't use the stairs. So spending time by herself in the attic really did mean that she was by herself, without even the animals there to keep her company.

Erin pulled down the little-used staircase and climbed up to the airy attic room. She turned on the light, walked over to the window seat and sat down, looking at her phone.

She wasn't even aware of her intention to call Melissa. Her mind was on all of the other events and the danger that lay ahead if they didn't find Davis.

But maybe Davis had never intended her any harm. Maybe he didn't resent the fact that her testimony had put him in prison and he had returned to Bald Eagle Falls for another reason—to see Melissa.

"Hello?" Melissa's voice sounded far away. "Erin?"

"Hi, Melissa." Erin's mind raced as she tried to think of what to say. "I heard you were sick today. So I just wanted to check... see if you're okay. If you need anything."

"Oh, that was very kind of you. Just a bit of a stomach flu, I think. Nothing too serious. But I don't think they would have wanted me at the office, spreading germs to everyone else."

"No, probably not," Erin agreed with a laugh.

There was an awkward silence.

"So... everything is okay?" Erin asked.

"Yes. Of course. Why wouldn't it be?"

"I know that Davis was one of the men who escaped from the penitentiary."

"Oh, was he?" Melissa's voice was deliberately light.

"I figured... he might have come to Bald Eagle Falls to see you."

"Hmm. No, I haven't seen him around. He must have gone to see someone else."

"Melissa..."

"I'm really not feeling well, Erin. I need to go back to bed."

"Were the police by to talk to you? I'm sorry, I didn't want to break any confidences… but I thought that if anyone knew where to find him, it would be you."

"Well, you were wrong. I have to go." Melissa gave a fake cough. "I really do."

She broke the connection.

CHAPTER 11

$\mathcal{I}$t's amazing how much better you feel after a good night's sleep," Erin told Vic the next day as they started to put fresh baking out in the display case before opening.

"I feel like a whole different person," Vic agreed.

"Yesterday, it felt like everything I did was ten times as hard as it should be. And I was jumping at shadows. Today… it's all so much easier. I'm alert and focused and calm. It really is hard to believe how much of a difference there is."

"I still think we made the right choice coming in yesterday, though. We were up anyway, so it saved someone else from having to get up early. And you know that the business wouldn't have been nearly as good if someone else had been managing things. People want to talk to the lady who found the body, not a substitute."

Erin cleared her throat. "I think I've had enough of being the lady who found the body now. Maybe someone else could take over that job."

"Not me," Vic declared. She'd been too close to a number of the investigations recently. And she had been the one to find Rip Ryder's remains. That had apparently been enough for her.

"Maybe I could retire, and all of the bodies could show up somewhere else. Moose River? The city, where they've got lots of cops? I don't think I want to do it anymore."

"Well, as you've observed in the past, there is nothing that brings more business to Auntie Clem's than the discovery of a new body or some other disaster. The ladies will always come out to discuss something shocking. If you're not going to find bodies, you're going to have to find another way to create scandal."

"I could probably think of a few ways," Erin laughed.

Vic giggled at the thought. "Until you do, we're just going to have to take advantage of all of the bodies we can. Upsell, upsell, upsell!"

"I do my best. Maybe we can arrange for some promotional events during the year that would simulate finding a new body. What about Day of the Dead? We could celebrate that."

"You're not going to get very many people in the Bible Belt to celebrate Day of the Dead. It's a pagan holiday. Other gods, and all that."

"Hmmph. Well, there must be something we can celebrate here. Or make up."

"Halloween was initially Christian. All Hallows' Evening. I mean, it's Catholic, so I'm not sure how the Baptist ladies would react. But at least it's Christian."

"We already do stuff for Halloween. But it's hard when you can't include witches and ghouls."

Vic shrugged. "I know."

In a few minutes, Erin flipped the front sign over to Open and unlocked the front door. A few people drifted in. The regulars, not a big crowd like the day before. There would still be some discussion of the body and the still-missing Davis Plaint, Erin knew, but things would be a lot slower. And though she appreciated the days that brought in extra money, she didn't mind a slower day to allow her some recovery time.

"Good morning," Erin greeted and took her place behind the counter.

The customers looked at each other, and Mrs. Peach stepped forward with her walker. Erin was glad for Southern hospitality that inspired the other customers to allow her to go first instead of everyone trying to be first in line. It wouldn't take long to serve Mrs. Peach, and then they would have their chance. A few minutes. Not a bad length of time to wait in line while they chatted or checked their social media highlights.

"Good morning, Mrs. Peach," Erin greeted her cheerfully. "What can we get for you today?"

"Oh, I don't know…" Mrs. Peach studied the goods in the display case more intently than usual. She generally knew what she wanted and was ready to order as soon as she was asked. Her eating habits were pretty routine, so Erin generally knew what she would want even before she opened up her mouth.

She hovered with her hand over a seeded loaf of bread, but Mrs. Peach didn't nod or ask for it. And she didn't pick something else out right away. Erin waited. There was a pause in the murmured conversation between Mary Lou Cox and Betty Thompson. Then they resumed as if they weren't paying any attention to Mrs. Peach's order. Or lack of one.

"I just don't know," Mrs. Peach dithered. "What do you have that is special today?"

"What is special?" Erin repeated, and pondered. She knew Mrs. Peach's usual preferences, but this was different. She obviously wasn't asking about the baked goods she usually bought. "Do you have something in mind? An event? Or just looking for something new? Do you want sweet or savory?"

"Well, it's for Mr. Peach. I want to make a nice dinner, and I'm just not sure what to have with it and for dessert."

Mary Lou and Betty Thompson stopped talking. Everyone in the shop stared at Mrs. Peach. Erin was glad that she was not the only one who was startled. She cleared her throat, glanced aside at Vic, frozen at the till, and then back into the display case.

"For dinner, it really depends on what else you are serving, but we have white or whole grain rolls, Or these herbed ones, with rosemary. They're quite nice to go with anything from pasta marinara to roast beef dinner."

"Yes, those would do nicely. I'll take half a dozen of those."

"And for dessert… what does your husband like? Is he a pie or cake guy? Or cookies, ice cream, biscotti with coffee…?"

"I remember he always was partial to a chocolate chip cookie…" Mrs. Peach trailed off uncertainly.

"These chocolate chunk and white chocolate cookies are pretty popular. They're a bit of an upgrade from the usual chocolate chip cookie. Great by themselves or with some ice cream."

Mrs. Peach nodded again. "I'll take a dozen of those."

Erin went to work packing the rolls and cookies for Mrs. Peach. "Is there anything else?"

"No, that should do nicely. I'm sure I'll be needing something else in the next few days, but I'm not sure yet what he'll want. We'll just have to play that by ear."

Erin nodded obligingly. "Of course. We'll see you in a couple of days, then. And you know that if you ever change your mind or need something last minute, you can just call and let me know, and I'll bring it home with me."

Normally, Mrs. Peach would roll her eyes at the offer and tell Erin that she could get around just fine and wasn't as infirm as Erin seemed to think. But this time, she just nodded in agreement. "It's very nice of you to offer. Maybe…"

Erin smiled. "Just give me a call. It isn't like you are out of my way!"

Vic gave Mrs. Peach her total, and she paid for it, then placed her purchase on the platform of her walker and made her way slowly out of the store.

Erin waited a few seconds, until she was sure that the door was shut and Mrs. Peach was out of hearing range. She looked at Vic and the other customers. "I had no idea that there even *was* a Mr. Peach."

Vic shook her head. Mary Lou looked at Betty Thompson. "I remember hearing something years ago, but it was too long ago to remember the details. Was she married?"

Betty nodded. She moved forward to look into the display case and pondered the possibilities as she considered her answer. "She was married years ago. There was quite a scandal. They had been married for years… maybe twenty. No children. Other than that, nothing really remarkable about them. People didn't pay much mind. And then… he left her."

"After twenty years?" Vic gasped.

"Yes. It was shocking. As far as anyone knew, they had not fought. Some couples squabble all the time and you wonder why they didn't break up sooner. But Gladys and…" Betty strained her memory, closing her eyes. "Gregory? Maybe? They had never seemed like the kind who fought or had major differences. Both were quite quiet and kept themselves to themselves."

"Was there another woman?" Vic prompted. "Someone he'd been seeing on the side or had just met and ran away with?"

"No, not as far as I know. But people didn't talk then like they do now. It was all pretty hush-hush. Gladys didn't say anything about it. So we didn't ask a lot of questions."

Betty Thompson was someone who always asked Erin a long list of questions about the baking and the ingredients before making a purchase, so it struck her funny bone that Betty wouldn't ask her friend about what had happened to her marriage.

"He just… took off one day?"

Betty nodded. "Yes, as far as I know. For a while, she said she thought he would come back to her one day. But after a while… well, obviously he wasn't."

"Until now," Vic pointed out.

"Thirty years later! What kind of a man comes back to his wife after thirty years?"

Erin shook her head. "And what kind of wife takes him back?"

Betty nodded slowly. "It's a puzzle, all right. I never expected it."

"I can't help thinking about Angela Plaint and her husband taking off," Erin said, a slight shudder raising goosebumps on her arms despite the Tennessee heat. Adam Plaint had not actually run away as people had supposed at the time. He'd been killed.

"Don't think about that," Vic advised, reaching over to put a hand on Erin's arm.

"It wasn't the same," Betty said. "When Adam Plaint disappeared, he was just gone. No one had seen him go or ever heard from him again. But it was different with Mr. Peach. He didn't… disappear."

Erin blinked at her. He *hadn't* disappeared? She had assumed it had been the same as Adam Plaint's case, where they all just woke up one morning and he was gone, and no one ever knew what had happened.

Or almost no one.

"What happened, then?" Vic asked. "What did he do? Where did he go?"

"He left town, but he didn't go far. The first few years, he lived in Aspen Ridge. Then... I think there was somewhere else. And eventually, Moose River. We all knew where he was. We just didn't know... why he had left, if he and Gladys had a fight, or he decided he was a homosexual, or decided that a barren marriage wasn't for him. Maybe he got tired of her. But she never got a divorce, even though she could have. But she never talked to him again, as far as I know."

"How bizarre," Vic observed.

Mary Lou cleared her throat, reminding them that she was patiently waiting for Betty to place her bakery order so that Mary Lou could be served, and whoever else might come after her.

"Oh, I'm sorry, Mary Lou," Erin apologized. "Betty, have you decided what you want? Or do you want to let Mary Lou go ahead while you think about it?"

CHAPTER 12

*E*rin didn't know what time Mrs. Peach usually ate supper or whether she would continue with the same routine now that Mr. Peach was home and his preferences needed to be considered, but she decided to take something over to them anyway. Despite the churning of her gut and her inability to decide what to say, she marched next door, knowing that she would be forced to say something once Mrs. Peach's door opened, whether it was coherent or not.

"Erin?" Mrs. Peach opened the door a few inches and looked at her. "Is everything okay?"

"Yes. Everything is fine. I just thought…" Erin displayed the bottle in her hands. "I thought that since Mr. Peach has returned home, you might like to celebrate…"

Mrs. Peach's face tried to arrange itself into a pleasant expression. Still, Erin could see her uncertainty with how to deal with this intrusion. Erin could understand that.

"I don't know whether you are a drinker or not, so it's just sparkling grape juice." Erin tapped the label and held it closer to the older woman. "I wouldn't get alcohol for someone I didn't know…"

"Oh. Well, thank you." Mrs. Peach reached for the bottle, then stopped, her fingers an inch from it. "Would you… like to come in for a moment?"

"No, no," Erin said quickly. "You probably want some time alone together. I don't want to interfere. I just wanted to give you something that might… mark a special occasion."

Mrs. Peach's expression softened. "You must come in and at least say hello. So Mr. Peach knows who you are."

"I could meet him another time. I don't want to crash your party."

Mrs. Peach opened the door wider. "Come in, come in," she urged. She took the bottle of sparkling grape juice from Erin and escorted her into the house.

Mrs. Peach's house was the reverse floor plan from Erin's. Mrs. Peach walked slowly and Erin was careful not to walk too close on her heels.

"Gregory? Gregory, we have a guest," Mrs. Peach called out.

Mr. Peach stood up from an easy chair in Mrs. Peach's dimly lit living room to greet her properly. He was the man who had been in Mrs. Peach's backyard the afternoon before. That was one mystery solved, at least.

"This is Erin Price, the baker. She lives next door. She's brought us some sparkling grape juice to have with supper," Mrs. Peach showed him the bottle.

"Oh, how thoughtful," Mr. Peach said gravely, reaching out his hand to shake Erin's. "It's good to meet you, my dear."

"Thank you. It's lovely to meet you too. Mrs. Peach is such a good neighbor."

"Erin lives in Clementine's old place," Mrs. Peach informed her husband and motioned in that direction.

Erin glanced around the living room. It was furnished similarly to hers. Erin had kept the furnishings that Clementine had picked out. Two old ladies with similar tastes probably shopping at the same stores or ordering from the same catalogs. It just made sense that their tastes would be similar.

She could see no imprint that Mr. Peach had left behind when he had left. Either it had never been there, or Mrs. Peach had eventually erased every sign of him in the intervening thirty years. There were no pictures of him, no masculine chairs, no sports memorabilia. Anyone looking at it would assume that Mrs. Peach was a spinster or a widow who had lost her husband many years before. And in a way, she had.

"I don't want to keep you from dinner," she told Mr. Peach. "This is probably a really bad time of day to show up on the porch uninvited."

"You could sit and visit," Mr. Peach invited, motioning to one of the other chairs. "Gladys is still working on supper."

"Oh." Erin shook her head. "I should help in the kitchen."

"Nonsense," Gladys said. "I don't want anyone messing around in my kitchen. I'm too set in my ways. Dinner is not on the table yet, so you may as well set a spell."

Erin could tell them that she had her own dinner to get ready. But she was too interested in hearing what the two of them had to say to take her leave immediately. She made an uncertain gesture. "I don't know, are you sure? The two of you must have a lot of catching up to do."

She winced and bit her lip. That was a tactless thing to say. She hadn't intended to make a big deal of the fact that Mr. Peach had returned after such a long absence. Though she supposed that showing up with a bottle of sparkling grape juice did that without words. You didn't buy champagne or sparkling juice for someone to celebrate an absence of a week.

"Sit down," Mrs. Peach insisted, giving a bark of laughter. "You may as well have *something* to tell all of the old biddies at the bakery."

Erin sat in the chair, her face burning. Smooth, Erin. So very smooth.

Mr. Peach was smiling as well. Neither of them seemed to be very awkward about the situation. If it were Erin, she would have been mortified to have to explain where her husband had been and why he had suddenly shown up again. She remembered how Adele had reacted when her husband had made an unexpected appearance, hiding from him and not wanting to talk to anyone about what was going on. That was how Erin would have reacted. Or maybe she would have just fainted. Repeatedly. Any time anyone asked her about her estranged husband's reappearance.

"So you are a baker?" Mr. Peach asked politely. "Gladys has been catching me up on the new specialty bakery in town. You make gluten-free bread?"

"Yes, everything gluten-free."

He raised his brows. "Everything in the bakery? That seems… needlessly difficult."

"Some people are very sensitive to wheat or gluten. I won't have any in my bakery. Then there is no chance of cross-contamination in anything I make, unless it was contaminated at the supplier's end. So far, we have not had any incidents where someone has reacted to the baking."

She swallowed the guilt over this not being entirely true. There had, in fact, been a couple of deaths from her baking. But those had not been cases of accidental cross-contamination. They had been premeditated murder. So they didn't count.

"Is it very difficult baking gluten-free? I have always been under the impression that it is hard to make gluten-free bread and other things."

"It can be. There is a lot of experimentation involved to figure out the right blend of ingredients and procedures that will work the best. Most of my customers will tell you that they can't tell that my products are gluten-free. I've worked very hard to come up with recipes that work."

He nodded his understanding. "That's very thoughtful of you. You're gluten-free yourself? You have this… celiac's disease?"

"Actually, no. I was inspired by one of my foster sisters when I was younger. That was when I started baking gluten-free. Back then, it was almost impossible to find good gluten-free baking. There is a lot more variety out there now, but most people who have celiac disease or are allergic to wheat are still pretty limited in their choices, especially in rural areas like this."

"So you provide a service," Mr. Peach offered, sounding more interested. "This is your way of showing love for others."

"Uh… yes, I guess one way," Erin agreed uncertainly. She didn't really like the framework that he put her in. She wasn't limited by having celiac disease herself, but she also wasn't an unselfish purveyor of gluten-free goods to all who needed it. Auntie Clem's was a business. A venture that was supposed to make her money while doing something she enjoyed.

"I am a pastor," Mr. Peach told her, leaning forward to be closer to her. "I am also involved in providing a service to those less fortunate."

He smelled faintly of mint and Old Spice aftershave. Erin rubbed her nose, willing herself not to sneeze as it tickled the inside of her nostrils.

"That's very interesting," she said neutrally. "Where do you... work?" Work was undoubtedly the wrong word. Serve or preach or something else that related more closely to being a minister. But it was already out of her mouth.

Mr. Peach smiled. "I am the pastor for the penitentiary."

CHAPTER 13

*E*rin was glad that she wasn't drinking the sparkling grape juice. She would have either choked on it or sprayed it across the room. As it was, she coughed and tried not to give away to Mr. Peach how much his words had startled her.

He was the pastor for the penitentiary? The one that had just had two prisoners break out? And one of them had ended up dead practically in his wife's backyard? Erin cleared her throat and tried to talk in a natural voice.

"Really? How long have you been doing that?"

He scratched his chin. "Almost thirty years."

"Wow. What's that like?"

"It has been very rewarding." He smiled and sat back in his chair. "Are you a Christian, Miss Price?"

It was clear from his tone of voice that it was a rhetorical question. He didn't have any doubt that anyone living in Bald Eagle Falls would be a Christian, even if she didn't go to church regularly. Erin knew that even those who rarely darkened the doorstep of one of the local churches, even for Easter or Christmas, still considered themselves Christians. It was what they believed, not whether they attended an organized congregation or not.

"Actually… no."

His eyes widened. He raised his brows and opened his mouth, but for a few seconds, no words came out.

"You're not. I just assumed… well, of course not everyone is Christian. We had a number of men find the Lord while in prison who were not previously of the faith. And there are always those who are wandering… still seeking the truth."

"Doesn't a pastor in a place like a penitentiary have to serve all different religions? Muslims and Jews and Buddhists and all that?"

"Well, yes, of course. We've had a few men who were of other faiths. But most were Christian. Are you… Jewish?" Mr. Peach took a stab at it.

"No. I'm an atheist, actually."

"Ahhh." Mr. Peach stared off into space, his expression sad. "There is an old saying that there are no atheists in foxholes. I can tell you for a fact that the same is not true of prison. We did have our lost sheep." He nodded slowly. His eyes went to Erin. "I always pray for the lost sheep."

Erin shifted uncomfortably. She looked around the room for an excuse to leave. Mrs. Peach would be serving her husband dinner before too long. Erin could say that she needed to go home to prepare her own. But it seemed like an awkward time to end the conversation. He would think she was leaving because of what he had said. Which seemed rude, even if it was true.

"Did you know the men who escaped?"

Mr. Peach's mouth tightened. He looked toward the kitchen for Mrs. Peach. Now they were both uncomfortable and wanted out of the conversation. How much more did Mrs. Peach have to prepare?

"Yes, I did know both of those poor souls," Mr. Peach admitted. "I only hope that Davis—Mr. Plaint—can be brought back into custody without mishap. There has been enough loss of life already."

"Poor souls?"

"I can't give you any information about them, of course. Priest-penitent confidentiality. But I can tell you that they both very much regretted the choices that led to their incarceration. If they could go back in time to change those decisions, I am sure they would. But unfortunately, that is not an option we are given in this mortal coil."

"I know Davis. Not well, but… we talked a couple of times."

"Then I am sure you know he had a very difficult childhood. A lot of things happened that would have been obstacles in any person's life. The loss of his father as a young man. Addiction. Other family circumstances. It is tragic when a person's circumstances and decisions lead him to make the decisions Davis did."

Erin couldn't help feeling sorry for Davis despite the things that he had done. Yes, he had done terrible things in his desperation. But she had seen other people driven into bad choices by circumstances. Erin had never tried to harm anyone, but she had still made choices that were not the best. When a person was fighting for her—or his—life, it was hard to do anything but live in the moment and disregard the long-term consequences. There would not be a long-term if she didn't make survival-driven choices.

Mr. Peach was watching Erin. "I see that you understand what I am talking about."

She nodded. "I don't know what I would have done if I'd been in the circumstances he was in. When he was a kid, I mean. And those choices all impacted on what would happen later in life."

"Yes. Exactly. And it is a story that you hear over and over again in prison, unfortunately. Our justice system does not allow for much mercy for those who have fallen by the way."

"And the other one? Mr. Bruel? What was he like?"

Mr. Peach pursed his lips. "Like Davis, Mr. Bruel was in the section for violent offenders. He regretted the things he had done in his youth that had resulted in him being incarcerated there. Like with Davis, there is little hope for release. *Was*." He sighed and looked down at his hands, folded in his lap. "I guess he's been released now."

And in his mind, where had Bruel been released to? Erin didn't believe that there was a soul to go anywhere after death, but knew that the Christians believed that the souls of people who had committed such great sins in their lives would be tortured for eternity. That didn't sound like much of a release to her.

Erin scratched at the arm of the chair she was sitting in, unable to sit without fidgeting. "Why do you think they came to Bald Eagle Falls?"

It was Mr. Peach's turn to fidget. He cleared his throat, looked again toward the kitchen, hoping for a call to dinner.

"I would guess that they must have family or other contacts here. I know this is where Davis came from. Maybe it was his suggestion."

"He doesn't have any family left. So I don't know why he would come here."

Erin hoped that Mr. Peach would know a little more about it, but he didn't mention Melissa or any other reason Davis would have to come to Bald Eagle Falls. Or any reason Mr. Bruel might have picked Bald Eagle Falls.

But she didn't want to probe too much. She already felt herself on thin ice asking him about the escaped prisoners.

"Well…" She tapped her phone. "I think I'd better be going. I don't want to monopolize your time. You and Mrs. Peach must have —" She caught herself before saying again that they must have a lot of catching up to do. How many times did she have to point out that Mr. Peach had been absent from his wife's life for thirty years? She changed tack, not even trying to finish the sentence she had started. "You have a nice supper. I hope you enjoy the baked goods and sparkling grape juice."

Mr. Peach stood up to bid her goodbye. "Yes, we shall have quite the feast tonight. Thank you very much for your gift. You take care of yourself, now."

Erin nodded. "Thank you, you too." She raised her voice slightly to call toward the kitchen. "Goodbye, Mrs. Peach. Have a nice dinner!"

"Oh, we shall. Thank you for stopping by."

Erin headed to the door to let herself out. She stopped, looking at it for a moment before turning the doorknob.

"You might want to get a burglar alarm," she told Mr. Peach in a low voice. "I worry about Mrs. Peach being alone during the day, with Davis out on the loose…"

"I can't see how Davis would be any danger to my wife."

"Well… I don't know either. But he tried to burn my house down and to run me down with his car, so I don't exactly trust him. I don't know why he would come back to Bald Eagle Falls, but if it has anything to do with me or you... Mrs. Peach could be... in the way."

He shook his head. "Davis wouldn't do anything to harm anyone. I've counseled with him numerous times since he was incarcerated—"

"And he escaped and killed Bruel, his partner. You can't trust that he won't do something to one of us. You just can't. He's not a stable person."

CHAPTER 14

$\mathcal{T}$erry had promised to get off work in good time so that he would be able to catch up on his sleep. Neither of them wanted a setback in his recovery from the head injury. Nor, Erin assumed, did the police department. Terry was a vital part of the department. If he weren't available because of his health, it would cause hardship for the rest of the law enforcement officers. Things weren't quite as sleepy as one would expect in sleepy little Bald Eagle Falls.

Erin made a salad and some sandwiches, working slowly, hoping that Terry would arrive home by the time she was ready. She was just trying to decide whether to wrap the sandwiches in plastic to keep them from drying out or to put them out on the table when she heard the jingling of dog tags and keys at the front door. On the table, then! She set out the plates and put the finishing touches on the meal as Terry walked into the kitchen.

"Looks like my timing was good!" Terry observed.

"Perfect," Erin agreed. "Wash up and grab a chair."

The animals, who had been remarkably quiet while Erin had been in the kitchen, decided that if Terry was home, it must be time to eat. Orange Blossom yowled loudly to let her know his opinion. She fed the beasties while Terry washed up, then sat down with him.

"You could have eaten without me," Terry said, glancing at the clock on the wall. "You usually eat earlier than this."

"I was over at Mrs. Peach's."

He raised his brows while putting a clump of salad on his plate. While they were friendly with their neighbors, Erin didn't usually call on them. Especially at suppertime.

"Visiting with her husband, Mr. Gregory Peach," Erin told him.

Terry put his fork down with a clank. "What?"

Erin nodded, glad that she wasn't the only one who had been in the dark about Mr. Peach.

"Yes. Apparently, he left his wife thirty years ago but now has returned."

"That's... astonishing. I've heard some bizarre things, but that takes the cake."

"And do you know what Mr. Peach does for a living?"

"I have no idea. What?"

"He is a pastor."

Terry shook his head. "A pastor who walked out on his wife? Seems a little hypocritical."

"The pastor at the penitentiary."

His fork was already down, so it didn't clatter to the table or floor when she informed him of this detail, but he gaped at her just the same.

"He is the pastor at the penitentiary? That Davis Plaint and Christian Bruel escaped from?"

Erin picked up her sandwich to eat. "Exactly."

"Well... that's an interesting development. I think we are going to want to talk to him."

"He said he doesn't have any idea why they would come to Bald Eagle Falls unless it was for Davis to see his family. Which we know he didn't do. And he doesn't think that he or Mrs. Peach are in any danger from Davis. I suggested that they should get a burglar alarm, but he wasn't concerned."

Terry picked up his fork and started to eat again. "You just took it upon yourself to go over there and question him about it?"

"No..." Erin tried to frame it differently. "I just took over some sparkling grape juice for Mrs. Peach. I thought it would go nicely with their dinner. Sort of a celebration. I wasn't expecting her to invite me in. And I *didn't* know that Mr. Peach was the pastor at the prison until he told me that."

"So this just happened to come up in conversation."

"Yes."

Terry raised an eyebrow skeptically but didn't voice his doubts.

"Mr. Peach was who I saw in the yard," Erin told him, in case he hadn't picked up on that part. "I just didn't know who he was. Or that there even *was* a Mr. Peach. I always thought that Mrs. Peach was a widow. She never talked about her husband and certainly never told me that he'd walked out on her. I found that out from Betty Thompson."

Terry chewed and swallowed. "I assumed the same. I'm not up on my gossip about things that happened thirty years ago."

"I guess not!" Erin laughed.

"That was before my time. And you didn't come across anything about it in Clementine's journals?"

Erin thought back. She was sure she would remember if she had read that Mrs. Peach's husband had walked out on her in one of the journals. It would have jumped out at her.

"No. I didn't read anything like that. Most of what I've been reading was a lot later than that. I don't know if it would be in the earlier journals, back when it happened."

She made a mental note to see if she could find Clementine's journal for the time around when Mr. Peach had pulled his disappearing act. Except according to Betty Thompson, he hadn't just disappeared. They had known where he was.

"You don't think that Mr. Peach could have had anything to do with the prison break, do you?"

"The FBI is still investigating how it happened. They say that the men must have had help from someone on the outside, but we don't know whether they had direct contact with someone or if there was also someone on the inside facilitating communications. It's going to take some time to sort out who all was in on it."

"Mr. Peach seems nice. I hope he wasn't involved." Erin took another bite of her sandwich, pondering the possibility. "He wouldn't have wanted them to come right to his backyard, right? If he was helping them, he would have directed them somewhere else."

"That would be the logical thing to do. To be honest, I don't see why either of them would want to come to Bald Eagle Falls. Even if Davis wanted to meet up with Melissa… it would make more sense to hook up in the city, where they were less likely to be spotted and had better access to highways or places to hide out. And why would Bruel come along with him? So far, we haven't been able to find any connections between Bruel and Bald Eagle Falls. Not even an uncle or cousin."

"Someone he worked with? How long had he been in prison?"

"Quite a while. He was convicted at least twenty-five years ago."

"Mr. Peach said that he was in the violent offenders section and that he didn't expect him to ever be released."

Terry gave a brief nod of agreement.

"So he must have been in for murder."

"Murder isn't the only charge that will get you twenty to life. Especially if they are stacking charges."

"But if he's a violent offender… it's not just fraud or grand theft."

"No."

She had hoped to squeeze a little more information from Terry about Christian Bruel. What he was in for, what kind of person he was, whether he had any visitors…

Why had Davis killed him? Why not just separate and go their different directions? Did Bruel know something that Davis felt could be used against him? Too much about his past or about his plans for the future?

Or maybe he had some other beef, something that had happened in prison. An insult or slight that Davis had pretended to forget but took his revenge for once they were free.

Terry picked up his sandwich. "Someone will have to have a talk with your Mr. Peach."

Erin did not see Mrs. Peach the next day at the bakery. But then, she didn't usually come in every day, and she had bought baking for a couple of meals, so Erin hadn't really expected her.

It was early afternoon when she answered a soft knock at the back door of the bakery. She knew who to expect and wasn't surprised to see Adele waiting there.

"Hi, Adele. What can I get for you today?"

Erin had instituted a program offering free day-old baked goods to the residents of Bald Eagle Falls or the surrounding farms who were in need. While most of the rural homeless that Erin had offered to help had turned her down, Adele collected food every few days for some family. Erin didn't know who the bread was for, but she had promised "no questions asked," so she stayed in the dark and was just grateful that someone had taken her up on the offer.

Adele asked for a few loaves of bread and some muffins. Erin added a couple of pizza shells and some cookies. They would be a treat for someone. Adele smiled and nodded her thanks but didn't leave immediately. Erin waited to see if there were something else.

"I found your cat," Adele offered.

"My cat?" For a moment, Erin thought she meant Orange Blossom, but then realized what Adele was talking about. "Oh, the skinny black cat in the woods?"

Adele nodded. "He's a pretty sorry-looking thing, but I've got him in the cottage and I'll get him fed up and on his way to good health."

"Poor thing. He did look pretty sad. Do you want to take him to Doc Edmunds? I'll cover the cost."

"Not yet. Maybe later, when he's doing better, to get his shots and dewormed."

And neutered. Erin didn't want an intact male running around in the woods or the neighborhood making trouble for everyone. He wasn't her cat, but she had some responsibility in looking after it and looking out for her neighbors' pets.

"I'm so glad you found him. I was worried. I would have tried to catch him the day that I saw him, but with everything else that happened, I couldn't."

"No. And you don't want to be wandering around in the woods

right now. Until they find that other escaped prisoner and take him back where he belongs."

"What about you? You probably shouldn't be wandering around there alone either."

"I don't go alone," Adele advised, and Erin knew she was talking about her shotgun. Adele would be armed, and Davis Plaint, just escaped from prison, would be unarmed. Or would only have whatever knife he'd used to stab Bruel. Erin didn't know if he had left the weapon behind or taken it with him. It would make more sense to take it with him rather than wandering around completely unarmed. But that was assuming that the stabbing of Christian Bruel had been premeditated or that Davis had at least been composed enough afterward to think to take it with him.

"Would you like to come to see him?" Adele asked.

Erin looked at her blankly.

"The cat. Would you like to come to the cottage and see him?"

Adele didn't normally invite people to her cottage, so it was quite a compliment that she had asked Erin. And, of course, the answer would have to be yes.

"Of course. I would love to see how he is doing. Should I come over after work today?"

Adele nodded. "That would be convenient."

Erin smiled. "Okay, I'll see you then."

Adele got on her way, and Erin locked the door behind her, pondering the invitation.

CHAPTER 15

*E*rin invited Vic to go along with her to see the cat, but Vic shook her head. "Adele didn't invite me. She only invited you. And she's still not comfortable with me around, so I don't want to put a damper on things. I'm sure I'll get a chance to see this kitty later if everything turns out."

Erin sighed. "Okay. But I wish she would get over it. It isn't like she did anything to you personally. It was her husband. We both know that she didn't have anything to do with the kidnapping. She didn't even know."

"I don't know if it's as cut and dried as that," Vic said slowly. "She says that she didn't know until after… but what if she did? Or what if there were things that she thought she should have understood but didn't until it was too late? She might blame herself for not figuring it out sooner. And for that matter, when *did* she figure it out? Not until you guys found me? Or did she figure it out before that and didn't tell anyone because she didn't want to get her husband in trouble?"

"You don't believe that, do you?"

"I don't know. I don't know what happened. I don't know what she knew or who else was involved. I'd never accuse her of anything. I don't have any evidence that she had anything to do with it. But the way she acts when she's around me? So guilty?" Vic shrugged. "I'm not supposed to think that it means anything?"

"It doesn't."

"Maybe not. But I don't know that."

Erin looked at Vic for a few moments, thinking about it. She had never known that Vic had any doubts about Adele's innocence in the kidnapping. And she had hoped that everyone would just get over it and be able to go back to normal. But apparently, that wasn't going to happen. Maybe Vic might always harbor doubts about Adele's loyalties.

She enjoyed walking through the woods for the first couple of minutes. The air was clear and there was a gentle breeze blowing, which helped to keep the temperature down. That, combined with the canopy of leaves that blocked out the direct sun made it quite pleasant to walk. Erin knew the various tracks through the woods now and could find her way around pretty well, as long as it wasn't nighttime.

But then she started to think about Adele's warning that she should not be wandering around in the woods alone.

Why would Adele warn her not to be in the woods alone and then invite her over to the cottage to see the cat? Maybe she had assumed that Erin would bring Vic or Terry along with her. Or that she would be armed. Though *that* was doubtful; Adele knew that Erin didn't carry a weapon.

Maybe she had just thought that Erin would be safe as long as she stuck to the direct route to the cottage and didn't wander anywhere else.

Adele's warning and trying to untangle all of the different reasons Adele had invited her to the cottage kept her brain whirling and anxiety building all the way to the cottage.

She had a pretty good idea that Adele hadn't just invited her over to let her see the cat. She had something else on her mind. Something she had wanted to be alone with Erin to discuss, despite the risk of walking through the woods while Davis was still at large.

It was a relief when Erin finally saw the cottage up ahead. She quickened her steps and was nearly at a run when she stepped into the clearing and across the few paving stones to Adele's door.

"Adele?" Erin knocked on the door.

It was a tiny place. The cottage didn't have a doorbell, but it was only one room. Adele couldn't miss hearing Erin's call and the knock on the door. She opened the door a moment later. Erin felt a rush of relief.

"Thank you," she murmured to Adele's welcome and hurried into the cottage.

"Everything all right?" Adele asked.

"Yes. Just spooked myself thinking about what you said about not walking through the woods alone."

"Oh. I'm sorry. Well, here you are, safe and sound."

"Yes." Erin blew out her breath and gave a little laugh. "Like I said, I just scared myself. I'm sure there was nothing to be worried about."

"More than likely, Davis is far away from here by now."

"Do you think so?" Erin grasped at this hopefully. She wanted to be told that Davis was no longer a threat.

"He doesn't really have any reason to stay around here, does he?" Adele asked, raising her brows. "And he has to know that everyone is looking for him here, especially after that other fellow's death. It would be stupid for him to remain in the county. Even in the state. If I were him, I'd get as far across the country as I could."

"Yes! Me too! I couldn't understand why he even came here in the first place. It doesn't make any sense."

Adele shrugged. "I'm sure he had his reasons."

She looked away from Erin and around at the interior of the cottage.

It was spare, just one room with a bed, a table and chairs, and a cookstove. Somewhere to eat and sleep and have a visit. She could do her handicrafts at the table. There were no electronic distractions, except maybe her phone. She spent most of her time outside. Erin wasn't quite sure how she filled her time; it seemed like there was a lot of it to fill and Erin would have been bored. But it was the life Adele wanted.

"Over here," Adele directed Erin's attention to a box near the stove. Erin took a couple of steps closer and could see the black cat curled up in the box, which had been lined with a small blanket or towel.

"Oh, there's the little fellow. Hi," Erin got closer, watching the cat carefully to make sure she didn't scare it. He opened one green eye to look at her, but otherwise didn't move, continuing to breathe just as deeply as he had been.

She could tell that he was still pitifully thin. It probably wasn't fair to assess him against Orange Blossom, an indoor cat with all the food he needed and a commanding voice to encourage his people to obey him. But if she were to compare the two, Orange Blossom probably made up at least three of the little stray.

Then again, when she had found Orange Blossom, he had been tiny. Barely old enough to have left his mama cat. The black cat was probably an adolescent, no longer a kitten. Outdoor and feral cats did not get as big as coddled indoor cats. Nor did they live as long.

Erin got closer so that she was within arm's reach of the cat. He kept watching her with his one open eye, but did not get up or growl at her. She could see where his fur was patchy and matted from the birds' attack. Had he been hurt before they had attacked him, and that's what had attracted them to him? Or had they just seen a creature that was smaller and could be disabled or driven away from a nest?

"Have you seen Skye with the magpie before?" Erin asked. "Was it even Skye, or was it another crow?"

"It was Skye. I have seen him with the magpie a few times. They seem to have become friends."

"Is that normal? I thought that birds only made friends with their own species."

"I don't know how usual it is. Skye is very intelligent. Maybe the magpie is too."

"Can they communicate with each other? Don't they speak different languages?"

Adele approached and, bending down, reached out her hand and touched the cat's dark fur. His back twitched and he turned his head toward her. Adele scratched his ears.

"I thought you came to see the cat, not to talk about the birds."

"I can do both. Do you think he would let me pet him too? Or should I not?"

"You might not want to, since you have a cat at home. You wouldn't want to spread any vermin he might be carrying. But you're probably fine if you wash well afterward."

"He's very nice. He's calm, I thought he would be really jumpy, having been an outdoor cat and now he's trapped inside. Do you think he is feral? Or raised by people?"

"He probably had people around him," Adele said. "He isn't as wild as I would expect a feral cat to be. But sometimes they can surprise you. Some cats just seem to be open to humans. Maybe that's why they became domesticated in the first place."

Erin couldn't resist reaching over to pet him. His fur was rough and coarse, not like Orange Blossom's fur, soft and clean from constant grooming or being brushed by his humans. Blossom didn't have to go out to fend for himself, so he had more time to spend on personal hygiene.

But she had to admit that she was still attracted to the new little cat. He was so defenseless, even against the birds. She just wanted to hold and protect him.

"Are you going to keep him? Make an indoor cat of him?"

He lifted his head and nosed at her fingers, giving her a brief lick.

Adele looked pointedly at the interior of the small cottage. "There isn't much *indoor* here. I'm more of an outdoor creature myself. I don't know if I could force another being to stay cooped up inside all the time."

"You could take him out on a leash."

Adele's nostrils flared, clearly not approving of this idea. "I've never seen you take Orange Blossom out on a leash."

"No, but sometimes I take him and Marshmallow out in the yard without one."

It had actually been a while since she had done so, making Erin feel guilty. But Adele didn't need to know how long it had been. She had seen the animals in the yard before, so she knew it to be true.

"And if I took this fellow out to my yard for a bit of exercise, do you think he would stay?"

Of course, it was a ridiculous question since Adele didn't even have a fence around the cottage. Her yard *was* the woods.

"I just don't want him to get hurt. Outdoor cats don't have long lifespans."

"We'll see," Adele said. But it was clear that she had already made up her mind not to force any animal to stay in her cottage.

For a few minutes, they were quiet, Erin just silently stroking the cat and letting him nuzzle and lick her fingers.

The silence grew. Erin knew there was more to the invitation to come to the cottage than just to see the cat.

"What's going on?" Erin asked finally. "Can I help with something?"

Adele looked at her, eyes half hooded, deciding what to tell her.

CHAPTER 16

*Y*ou know that Rudolph… my husband… is in the penitentiary," Adele said.

"Yes. Of course."

"In the same section as those other men escaped from."

"Oh?" Erin nodded politely. "I didn't, but… I'm not surprised. It's not really that big of a prison, is it?"

"No. Not compared to some. I'm worried… about whether he might have been involved in all of this…" Adele made a gesture toward the place in the woods where Erin had found the dead body.

"Really? Why? Did he say something to you about it?"

Adele's answer was sharp. "I thought it was pretty obvious by now that my husband doesn't tell me any of the things that he is involved in. Why would he start now?"

"Why are you worried, then? Just because two men escaped… that doesn't mean everyone in the prison was in on it, or everyone in the section. I'm sure it came as just as much of a surprise to the other prisoners as it did to us. If they had known about it, wouldn't they all have wanted in on it?"

"Prison breaks of more than one or two people are rarely successful. The smaller the breach of security, the better."

"Okay… so what makes you think that your husband might have had something to do with it?"

Adele reached over to stroke the cat with a couple of fingers. The little black cat was purring away happily, unaware of the tension around him.

"The man who was killed. Christian Bruel. He was Rudolph's cellmate."

Erin's eyes went wide. She started making connections immediately. Christian Bruel had shared a cell with Rudolph Windsor. Rudolph Windsor was married to Adele. Bruel had been killed practically on Adele's doorstep.

She could see why Adele would be concerned. Had Rudolph told Bruel where to go? How to escape? Was Rudolph supposed to be in on the prison break too, but through some stroke of bad luck, hadn't managed to get out with them?

Adele didn't look at her. Erin thought through the various scenarios. She couldn't get away from the thought that someone had told Christian Bruel to go to Bald Eagle Falls, and that was where he had been killed. Was he supposed to meet someone? Take a message to Adele? Rudolph had been working with one of the clans before he had been arrested. Was he trying to get back to them? Was one of them supposed to be waiting for him when he made it away from the penitentiary?

"Do the police know?"

"I keep expecting them to knock on my door. So far, no one has. I think they must not have put it together yet."

Erin nodded slowly. "The Bald Eagle Falls police department is not involved with the investigation of the prison break. That's being done mostly by the FBI, I think. The FBI wouldn't necessarily know that Rudolph's wife lives in Bald Eagle Falls. You're kind of off the grid."

Adele nodded. "Even if I was on county records somewhere, they wouldn't necessarily connect my name with that of Bruel's cellmate, just because we have the same last name."

"So, what are you going to do…? Do you want to tell them?"

Adele shook her head. "I don't want to get him in hot water, especially if he didn't have anything to do with it. I do want to talk to him, though."

"That makes sense." Crouching down to pet the cat was beginning to make Erin's legs hurt. She stood up, stretching them. The cat yawned and looked up at her, wondering why she had stopped.

"You must think me very silly," Adele said, her face getting pink.

"No, I don't. I think you're a very wise woman. I always have."

Adele gazed at her skeptically. But it was the truth. Erin admired Adele for knowing how she wanted to live and going after it. She admired her knowledge of nature and herblore. Her kinship with wild animals. Her maturity and how she always considered a question or situation before answering or acting, rather than running headlong into things.

"I don't want to go to the penitentiary alone," Adele explained, clearly pained by the admission.

"Oh!" Erin was surprised. Had Adele never visited her husband while he'd been in prison? She knew that they were estranged. Rudolph had turned out to be a con man and Adele hadn't wanted any part of that life. But Erin had assumed that Adele would still feel compelled to visit her husband in prison, even if it was only a brief visit once every few months. "Did you want someone to go with you?"

Adele nodded slowly. "I think that would make it easier for me."

"I'd be happy to go with you, if you like. I'll just need to set up my shifts at Auntie Clem's so that I can join you. When were you hoping to go?"

"I suppose that tomorrow would be too early. What about Saturday?"

"If you want to go tomorrow, I can probably get someone to cover me in the afternoon. I can put in my morning hours and still get off in time for a visit at the penitentiary."

"It's a couple of hours of driving. Each way."

"I know."

At Adele's look of surprise, Erin reminded her. "I visited Charley there when she was arrested."

"I forgot that the county jail is there too."

"I assume that both will have the same visiting hours. Maybe we'd better check, just to be sure. You wouldn't want to get out there and then find out that you weren't allowed to see him for some reason."

Adele nodded. "Then… we could leave at about noon?"

Erin nodded. "Sure. I'll make sure the bug is gassed up and ready to go."

Adele looked at Erin with an odd expression on her face as if expecting Erin to say something else. To give an excuse and say she couldn't go after all, or to drill her with questions about why she wanted to talk to her husband and why she hadn't done it before.

Erin shrugged. "I'm happy to help a friend."

"It won't be a pleasant place to visit."

"No. But that doesn't matter." Erin turned her attention to the practical. "The penitentiary should have a website online with all of the rules for visitors, so we can make sure it goes as smoothly as possible." Erin sat down on one of the chairs at the table and pulled out her phone. There was, luckily, good cell reception even in the woods. She tapped in a search and looked down at the list of results. "Here… it looks like this covers everything"

She read the rules. Everything from not wearing flip-flops or revealing clothing to leaving their personal items locked in the car and bringing in federally recognized picture identification. A list of what forms of ID were recognized.

"Do you want me to go all the way in to talk to Rudolph?" Erin asked. "Or just drive with you there? If you want me to be part of the visit, you'll need to get him to put me on his visitor list."

Adele nodded. "I'll submit a request. They told me how to do that before."

"Will they do it in a day?" Red tape meant that seemingly simple requests could be held up for weeks or months while the prison went back and forth on approving form after form. Or rejecting them.

"Yes, they're supposed to. They are piloting a new streamlined process. Rudolph has a lawyer that I can get to call them if they don't."

"Okay." Erin looked at the time on her phone and then at the window. It wouldn't be long before the sun set. "I'd better get back before dark. I will make sure I can get off at noon so that we can go. We'll meet… at my house?"

The summer cottage wasn't exactly accessible by car. Erin could park on a nearby street, but it would be easiest to meet at the house.

Adele nodded. "I will be at your house at noon. In prison-appropriate footwear."

CHAPTER 17

*E*rin was glad that Terry wasn't yet home, even though it was getting late and she wanted to spend some time with him. She preferred not to explain to him why she was taking time off from Auntie Clem's. After the visit, maybe she would talk to him about it, but she didn't want to try to explain to him why Adele wanted company for her visit to her husband.

Adele had her reasons, and it didn't really matter to Erin what they were. She was happy to help a friend, and Adele was someone who never asked for help. If Terry knew, he would demand an explanation and would have to be told about Rudolph being Christian Bruel's cellmate.

Erin had the arrangements all made by the time Terry got home. Dinner was on the table later than usual for the second night in a row, but Terry didn't remark on it. He probably assumed that she wanted to eat with him instead of the two of them eating separately at different times of the evening.

"It's nice to have you on days right now," Erin commented. "It's easier for us to see each other."

"It is nice," Terry agreed. "But it won't last forever, so don't get too used to it."

"I know. How is the manhunt going? Do you have any leads? Any sightings?"

"The problem with a hunt like this isn't that there aren't any sightings, but that there are too many. And you have to check out each one to see whether it is legitimate."

"And are any of them legitimate?"

He gave a shrug and a brief nod, head tilted sideways. "That is the question."

"A lot of police hours without getting anywhere."

"Yes."

"And the investigation at the penitentiary? Have they found out whether there was an inside man? Or an outside man?"

"Pastor Gregory Peach? They're looking into it. It is rather suspicious, him showing up on his wife's doorstep after thirty years, right after the prison break. His preliminary statement is that he was worried about her. Having Bruel show up here, dead, prompted him to take action when up until now, he felt like he had let too much time pass for him to talk to her. But he took this as… a sign from God that he needed to go home and fulfill his family responsibilities."

Erin raised an eyebrow. It seemed like a stretch. A statement that was almost believable, but not quite. Mr. Peach making an excuse that he hoped sounded like the truth.

But then, religious people did illogical things sometimes. They saw miracles in coincidences and signs in natural phenomena. So maybe the pastor had seen God's hand in Bruel ending up on his wife's doorstep.

"Huh. Well, I don't know if I would believe that. Is there anyone else they are looking into?"

"There will be a lengthy investigation into all of the circumstances and people surrounding the two men. These things can take years. They will be identifying all of the weak points in the penitentiary's security, every failing that allowed the men to escape, and investigating the backgrounds of every person in the section, both staff and prisoners. Anyone with connections with Bruel, Davis Plaint, or Bald Eagle Falls will be thoroughly investigated."

So sooner or later, they would get to Rudolph Windsor and

discover his marriage to Adele, and eventually track Adele to Bald Eagle Falls. Even if Adele's name wasn't on any landholdings or utilities in Bald Eagle Falls, she had to file tax returns and probably had a driver's license. Something official would eventually place her in Bald Eagle Falls, and the feds would come knocking on her door as she feared.

It was probably a good idea to talk to Rudolph first and get his story.

"But so far, nobody," Erin summarized to Terry.

"Not yet. But that doesn't mean that nobody else was involved in the escape. Just that they haven't been able to identify him yet."

"Yeah. Well, hopefully, they'll be able to identify everyone involved and to figure out where Davis disappeared to."

Vic expressed doubts as to why Erin would choose to go to the penitentiary with Adele, especially on such short notice, but Erin had covered her shift, and she was the boss, so Vic accepted it. Erin had gone with Vic to Moose River when Vic's father had been ill and possibly dying, so she knew that it was the kind of thing Erin did. She wanted to help her friends and she just volunteered, even though sometimes it was inconvenient. Hadn't she helped Charley by feeding Iggy when she had been arrested? And that was no small feat with the travel time between Bald Eagle Falls and Moose River. At least Iggy hadn't needed to be fed every day. Erin could stock his reptarium and then leave him to his own devices for a few days.

She picked Adele up at the house and they headed out to the highway.

"I really appreciate this," Adele said, twisting her hands in her lap. "I didn't know who to ask."

"Well, I'm glad you asked me. I'm happy to help you out."

"You're a real friend."

Erin shrugged. She watched the highway, letting Adele relax and not have to feel like she was under a microscope. As curious as she was about Adele's and Rudolph's relationship—how they had gotten together and what had gone wrong, and when Adele had realized he was running illegal ventures—she wasn't going to put Adele on the spot and insist on answers. If Adele felt like talking about it, she would.

"How are you doing?" Erin asked after a while. "Are you nervous?"

Adele nodded. She was watching out the side window, her face away from Erin and her handsome red hair hanging down, smooth and sleek. "More nervous than I should be, going to talk to my own husband." She shook her head. "What a situation to be in. I would never have thought, when we first met…" She trailed off and didn't finish the sentence. But Erin understood. Things didn't always turn out the way a person expected them to. She was sure that Adele had no idea when she had first met Rudolph that he was such a scoundrel. For sure, she wouldn't have married the man if she'd had any idea the way things would turn out.

And now she had to worry about the possibility that not only was he ripping people off, but that he might have known about or been involved in a prison break that had gone very wrong.

They worked their way through other polite topics of conversation. The weather, other things that had been in the news lately, the black cat, any issues that Adele had experienced in the woods, making the occasional suggestion of things that Erin might want to improve to make it a nicer, safer place for them both to enjoy.

Eventually, they turned onto the long road that approached the prison. All of the trees in the acres around the prison had been clear-cut, leaving only bare ground and nowhere for an escapee to hide. The long road meant that they could see anyone approaching the penitentiary from a long way off. And of course, there were high fences around the compound, with curling razor wire along the top. Erin remembered the security measures from when she had visited Charley there; gates and guardhouses as she entered, having to go through a metal detector, an interview with someone from the security staff making sure that she understood the rules. She didn't know how anyone could get in or out without being caught.

Adele stared at the buildings. Her face was very white.

"It looks scary, but it's not so bad," Erin assured her. "Everyone I dealt with was really respectful and told me everything I had to do. No yelling or violence or anything like that."

Adele nodded. "Thank you," she said faintly.

Erin was stopped at the gate and showed her ID. They waited while someone walked around her car, looking in all of the windows. The uniformed man called out to her to pop her trunk, and Erin obeyed. She was glad that she had cleaned it out recently so that it was neat and tidy. Not that there had been anything illegal in it before, but the guard seeing her trunk messy would be like his seeing her underwear. And she wouldn't want a rice flour spill to make them think even for an instant that she'd been transporting illegal drugs.

Eventually, the guard returned to his booth, hit the button to raise the gate, and motioned her through.

"Y'all have a nice visit."

Erin nodded and continued on her way. She followed the signs and eventually reached the lot for the high security prison in a different part of the compound from the county jail where Charley had been held. Erin hoped that all of her reassuring words to Adele applied to the higher-security area as well.

A man in an orange vest motioned her to the parking stall she was supposed to take and then stood there as they got out of the car. He looked them over. "Is this your first time visiting?"

Erin nodded, since it was their first time in that part of the penitentiary.

"Take your picture ID with you, one key, no more jewelry than just a single ring. Lock everything else in the car. Wallets, phones and other devices, handbags, everything. If you have a gift for an inmate, it needs to be checked in."

"No." Adele shook her head. "No gifts."

He stood watching while Erin and Adele stripped off any personal items and left them in the car. They had both been careful to follow the written rules regarding dress and makeup, and he was apparently satisfied.

"Go straight in those doors." He pointed. "Take a number. Line up along the wall. You will be called in and someone will walk you through the check-in procedure."

"Okay." Erin swallowed and forced a smile and a nod. "Thank you for your help."

"Yes, ma'am. Y'all have a nice visit."

Adele and Erin headed for the visitor doors.

"You're right," Adele said, "they're all very nice."

"It's probably better for them if they keep everyone calm and happy. You don't want a bunch of visitors who are anxious or angry. That would wind up the prisoners."

CHAPTER 18

The check-in procedure for the high-security building was more involved than that in the county jail section, but it wasn't too onerous. The woman CO who checked them through was sour-faced and brusque, but she wasn't abusive and didn't expect them to know everything they were supposed to do without being told. Eventually, they were escorted to the sort of open visiting area that Erin had seen on TV. That was a little surprising. Erin had expected to be put in a booth with bulletproof glass separating them from Rudolph, and maybe a phone handset to communicate with him.

"Adele!" Rudolph held out his arms for her. He was a good-looking man, but no longer had the playboy look he'd had the first time that Erin had seen him, strolling into Auntie Clem's Bakery to ask where to find his wife. He did still have smile lines around his mouth and eyes. There was already a hint of five o'clock shadow around his jaw, but maybe he hadn't shaved that morning.

Adele took Rudolph's hands in hers rather than allowing herself to be hugged by him. He bent in for a kiss and she gave him her cheek. Undeterred, Rudolph gave her a peck, then motioned to one of the tables as if it were the prime table in a fancy restaurant. "How is this?"

Adele sat down across the table from him, still holding both hands. Erin went around to Adele's other side and sat down. Several placards were posted around the room with the prison visitor rules on them, but Erin didn't need to be told that everyone had to sit down and not remain milling about. She hoped that Adele didn't regret having brought her along, now that she was sitting with her husband with no chance of a private conversation.

"And you're the lady baker," Rudolph said, looking at Erin. "In that specialty store."

Erin nodded. "My name is Erin Price. Yes, I own Auntie Clem's Bakery. Gluten-free and special diets."

"The place that burned down."

Erin swallowed. She wondered whether he was the one who had torched Auntie Clem's 1.0. Or had it been one of the Jackson boys? Or someone else from the clan?

"Yes, it did. We were able to reopen at another location."

"I heard about that. The Plaints' old bakery."

With Davis Plaint in the same section, Erin imagined that Rudolph had probably heard a lot about Erin taking over the old bakery. Some of it true and some not. She nodded politely and didn't ask him what he had heard.

Rudolph turned his attention back to Adele. "I'm so glad that you came to visit. You can't know how lonely it gets here."

"I suppose it probably does," Adele agreed, but didn't look too sympathetic. It was his own fault that he was there, after all. If he'd been willing to stay with her and fly straight, things could have been very different. But leopards like Rudolph didn't change their spots. Once a scam artist, always a scam artist.

Erin thought for an instant of Reg Rawlins, one of her foster sisters, a girl who had always been looking for the next big con. People like Rudolph and Reg could be great fun to be around. But eventually, they conned and stole from the ones closest to them, or got arrested, or had to go on the run. And that was no fun. Being victimized or left alone were not nice situations to be in.

"How have you been? Are you still in Bald Eagle Falls?"

"Yes, for the time being," Adele told him. "I have not, as yet, been run out on a rail."

Rudolph gave her a grin, like being run out of town would have been a big joke. "We were always on the move," he confided to Erin. "Between her being a witch and my... *business ventures*, it didn't seem like we were ever in a place for very long."

Erin nodded. "We've tried to keep that from becoming public knowledge."

"Her being a witch or married to me?"

"Both." Erin tried to give him a withering stare, but his grin made it impossible to keep the appropriate expression in place.

"You *knew* I was still in Bald Eagle Falls, though, didn't you?" Adele asked.

"Well..." He gave an offhanded shrug. "I hadn't heard that you were anywhere else."

"And you told your cellmate, Christian Bruel, that I was in Bald Eagle Falls. In the woods."

Rudolph's smile faltered. "Why would I do that?"

"How am I supposed to know how your brain works? You told him, or he wouldn't have shown up on my doorstep when he escaped."

"On your doorstep," Rudolph repeated. "Bruel showed up... on your doorstep?"

"Well, not literally," Adele admitted. "But he was pretty close. In the woods where my cottage is." Rudolph had visited her there when he had been in town. "That's where he was killed. Erin found his body." Adele nodded in Erin's direction.

Rudolph shook his head and brought his hands up in front of himself in a "stop" gesture. "No, no. I never told him where to find you." He looked at Erin. "Or you. I wouldn't do that. He's a violent offender. I wouldn't want him anywhere near my wife."

"Then why did he show up there?"

Rudolph frowned, thinking about it. "I might have mentioned Bald Eagle Falls. But just in passing, you know, like you do in conversation. 'Where were you arrested?' or 'Where was that operation?' Or just saying, 'I've got a wife just over in Bald Eagle Falls, but she never comes to visit me.' You say things. You live with a person for a while, and you talk to each other, learn things about each other."

"That doesn't explain why he would go to Bald Eagle Falls when he broke out. Why wouldn't he go the opposite direction? To the city? Or out of the state? There's no reason for him to go to Bald Eagle Falls."

"I swear. I didn't send him there. I wouldn't send him to you. You would never help out an escaped felon. Unless maybe it was me." He said this last without any wink, nod, or innuendo. Not flirting with Adele, just stating a fact. He was still her husband, and she might help him if he escaped.

Adele shook her head automatically. "I wouldn't suggest that you test that theory."

He leaned back in his chair, the charming grin back in place. "I don't plan to. I'm not like some of these other guys here. I'm not a lifer. I sit quiet and do my time, and I'll get out. Then I don't have to spend the rest of my life looking over my shoulder. Doesn't make sense for a guy like me to try to break out. The lifers, that's different. They know that the only way they are ever going to get out is to break out. Unless they get one of those innocence projects working for them." He nodded and tapped his finger on the table. "Now those places, those innocence projects. They do a lot of good in a place like this. Help get people off when they shouldn't be here in the first place. Or when they got life when they should have only got five years. Those guys are gold if you can get them on your case."

"Did you ever try to get one of them to help you out?" Erin asked curiously.

"Me? No. Like I said, no point in it. By the time they could do anything, I'd be out anyway. And there's no point in chasing reparations. Uncle Sam never gives you what he really owes you anyway. But the lifers, they need someone like that to keep hope alive." Rudolph looked at Adele. "Did you bring me anything? Some gum? I'd really love a pack of gum."

"No. I didn't bring you anything." Adele gave no indication that she would consider it. Just a closed door.

"You could put money into my commissary fund. Just twenty bucks, honey. That would go a long way to being able to get ramen and deodorant and other necessities."

Adele shook her head. Erin admired her for being so tough. There was no way Erin could have stood up to a husband who wanted her to put money into his account for such little luxuries. She even felt like *she* should give a little something to Rudolph, and he was nothing to her. She just felt sorry for him, having to be there and to be so limited in his daily pleasures. Long, tedious days with no reprieve.

"The guy who roomed with Bruel before me, Hatch, he got help from one of those innocence projects. Amazing to hear about it. They proved how he'd been set up. The cops and the prosecutor and even his own lawyer, they were all involved, making sure he got put behind bars. Messing around with the evidence to make it look like an airtight case against him. When he was innocent!"

"What did he do?" Erin asked. "I mean—what was he convicted of doing?"

"Killin' a girl. His own girlfriend. But he didn't do it," Rudolph emphasized. "They proved that all of the evidence was fabricated, those innocence guys. Amazing work. Just amazing."

"How long was he in prison?"

"Here? Thirty years. And transferred here from the federal pen, where he served ten years or more. They put a man in prison for forty years. An innocent man. Can you imagine that? Imagine them putting someone behind bars when they knew that he was innocent. Knew that he was innocent because they had fabricated all of the evidence. What kind of monster does something like that?"

"Not someone you want to know," Adele said dryly.

Rudolph laughed loudly, attracting looks from several other visitors and a stern glare from one of the supervising Corrections Officers. Rudolph subsided into a quiet chuckle. "No, sir. Not someone you want to know," he agreed with a nod.

"Did he get any reparations?" Erin wondered.

"None. Not a plug nickel. For forty years or more in prison. No one deserves that."

"Not if they're innocent," Erin agreed.

"Forty years for another man's crime. And that man, whoever really did it, free as a bird. Unless he got caught killing another woman later on. Maybe a whole series of 'em like you see on TV. And old Hatch, he does the time for it. And what do you think it is like when he gets out? Everybody assumes that if he wasn't guilty of that, he must have been guilty of something else, or he never would have gotten scooped up and sent to the pen. And even if he was innocent, he's tainted now. He's got the prison stink on him. He's lived like a criminal, so he's become one of them. Just as likely to kill you as look at you."

Erin shuddered at the thought, imagining some of the other criminals she had faced. Rudolph was as charming as could be, acting like he had just come off a yacht or out of a country club. But others that she had faced—men in organized crime, men who had grown up hard and saw killing as nothing more than removing an inconvenience—those men were scary. Far scarier than Rudolph Windsor, who gave every appearance of simply having been swept up in something that got out of his control. Of course he had never set out to hurt anyone or break any big law. He had just been running another scam. Like a hundred others he had probably run before, always trying for the big pay-off.

"Is that what he was like, this Hatch?" Adele asked. "As likely to kill you as look at you?"

"No!" Rudolph recoiled at the thought. "A real gentleman. He was a bit of a jailhouse lawyer himself. That's how he got hooked up with these innocence people in the first place. He filed his own appeals, helped others out with theirs. There is always some kind of motion to file, even if it doesn't get you anywhere. Helps the time go by. Gives you a little bit of hope for a reprieve, even if it's just a transfer to a better prison or more yard time. You know, anything to break the monotony."

"A real gentleman?" Adele repeated, lifting one eyebrow up high.

"Well," Rudolph rocked back and forth in his seat, readjusting in the hard chair. "What passes for a gentleman in here. You know, a guy who would never stick a shiv in you unless he was provoked." He gave a shrug. "A man has to protect himself and his property, after all. If you don't do that, you're likely to get killed, not to last forty years in a max."

A gentleman.

Adele shook her head. She looked around the visitor room at the other women visiting their husbands, sons, or fathers. There were a few children sitting at the tables, looking bored but sitting quietly. Familiar with the rules of the visiting room. There had been times listed on the penitentiary website. Lengths of time that a visitor's privileges would be repealed if they allowed their children to be disruptive or out of their control. Six months. A year. A stiff penalty for not keeping your children under control during a visit.

CHAPTER 19

S o, are you in a cell by yourself now?" Adele asked. "Since your cellmate broke out?"

"Maybe I would have been if Plaint had been killed and Bruel was still on the run. But the authorities know that Bruel isn't coming back here again, so they put me in for a new cellmate right away. There's always a bunch of shuffling around whenever anyone is released. Everybody wants something. You can go crazy in here if nothing ever changes. You gotta be able to shuffle things around. Like getting a new cell or cellmate."

"What do you know about the prison break?"

"Nothing. You think the CO's are going to tell us how it was done? They block up the hole and make sure it's never used again. I got no idea how they managed it. Probably had help, but danged if I know from who."

"Someone inside or outside?"

"Both, probably. Someone has connections to a CO or drives a truck or works in the laundry or the shop. Plenty of guys have been around long enough that the administration trusts them. You get help from one of those guys and have someone waiting for you on the outside, who can get you away and drive you somewhere they won't look for you."

"Like Bald Eagle Falls?"

"I told you, I don't know why anyone would have taken them to Bald Eagle Falls. That Plaint, he had family back there, didn't he?"

"No. Not anymore. His whole family had been killed, one way or the other."

Murder and suicide, mostly.

"It must have been his idea. Take Bruel to his home ground, get rid of him, meet up with someone who can put him up for a while without anyone noticing."

Bruel's murder had been reduced to an offhanded "get rid of him," as if it were something that hadn't mattered or had any impact. Erin looked at Adele, who gave a slight shake of her head.

There wasn't much more that could be achieved by talking to Rudolph Windsor. Adele didn't seem to have anything personal to discuss with him. There was no asking after family members or discussion of hobbies. Rudolph asked a couple more times about her putting money into his commissary account or bringing him a gift, but Adele was firm. She didn't make very much money and lived a low-cost lifestyle. And she'd probably lost enough money to her husband in the past to know not to trust him with anything or to know that once she fed him once, he would keep making demands for more. Like feeding a stray cat. Do it once, and you were their new source of food, whether you wanted to be or not.

Eventually, Adele noted the time on the big clock on the wall and got to her feet. "We need to go if we're going to get back to Bald Eagle Falls in good time. Erin has done all of the driving and I don't want to keep her up late. Baker's hours, you know."

Rudolph stood up and gave Erin a little bow. "We are both very much obliged for you taking time out of your busy schedule to bring Adele here. It has been nice to get caught up." He eyed his wife as if trying to decide whether to ask her one more time for a favor, then made up his mind that it was not in the cards. "I do hope this won't be your only visit. You will come back, won't you?"

Adele gave her head a little shake. "I don't have any plans to. We are not *together* anymore. I only… wanted to make sure that you didn't have anything to do with the prison break and the men coming to Bald Eagle Falls."

"It isn't like the feds haven't been by to check things out," Rudolph said cheerfully. "They are being very thorough. If there had been any sign that I was the one who helped those cons, they would have turned it up. But I'm pure as the driven snow."

"On that one count."

He laughed, nodding his agreement. "On that one."

"I still had to be able to look in your face and hear your answer."

"Well, if I knew that all it would take is one little prison break to get you to come to visit me, I would have arranged one."

Adele shook her head at him, not amused. She and Erin began to walk away.

"Oh, one other thing," Erin said, looking back at him. "Do you know Pastor Peach?"

He raised his brows. "I know of him. I'm not religious myself."

"Did he have anything to do with it?"

"With what?"

"With Davis Plaint and Christian Bruel breaking out."

"The pastor?" His voice was incredulous. "No, not that I heard."

Erin nodded. She turned back to Adele, who had paused to wait while Erin asked her questions. Then they walked toward the well-marked exit.

A man stood up from one of the other tables, stepping directly into Erin's path.

"It's the baker."

CHAPTER 20

*E*rin stopped, frozen, and looked at him.

Daniel Jackson.

One of Vic's older brothers.

He and Joseph had pled to some lesser charge in the attempted poisoning of their father. They were now serving the shortened sentence they had received from a plea bargain. Erin hadn't even thought of their being there, but of course she should have. Where else would they be serving their term?

"Excuse me," Erin murmured, hoping he would just move out of the way and she would be able to get past him.

He put a hand on each of her shoulders and shoved her back. Not hard. Just enough that she had to step back and felt thoroughly intimidated.

One of the CO's was immediately there, motioning to the chair that Daniel had been sitting in. "Sit back down with your visitor," the heavyset woman ordered sharply. "Or you're done."

"Just saying hello to an old friend," Daniel growled. He still blocked Erin, and she didn't want to make him angrier by speaking to him. She was one of the reasons that he was in prison. It had been her efforts to figure out who was trying to kill Pa Jackson and her connections with Terry Piper and Jack Ward that had put him in prison.

Even a mention of her friendship with Vic, Daniel's younger sibling who had strayed from the family values, would probably be enough to make him explode. She didn't want to trigger his anger. She only wanted to get out of there as quickly as possible.

"What are you doing here?" Daniel demanded. "Don't you think there are enough people here because of you? You have to come here to taunt us? Rub our noses in the fact that you're free and we're not?"

Erin shook her head but couldn't find her voice.

Daniel drew back his arm to push her again or to hit her. Erin flinched back. But she didn't need to worry. The female CO and the others who were on duty in the visitor room were ready for anything. The woman grabbed his arm and twisted it around behind him. She shoved him into the wall with a shouted order to stay still. Several others crowded around to help handcuff and shackle Daniel.

His face was red as she pulled him back from the wall. He opened his mouth to sneer something further at Erin. The CO pulled a canister of pepper spray from a loop on her belt. "If you think you're going to say something else to this visitor, you'd better think about how sore your throat and eyes are going to be the instant you draw breath," she warned.

Davis closed his mouth with an audible clack of his teeth.

The woman nodded. "Good choice," she approved. "Let's go."

She pushed him in front of her and he went without further protest.

The visitor room was silent, everybody watching Erin. She would have been embarrassed by the display if she hadn't been so scared. As it was, she stood there frozen until one of the other CO's caught her attention.

"I'll walk you ladies out?" he offered, gesturing for them to go ahead of him.

"Thank you," Erin said faintly.

She and Adele headed toward the door once more. Erin looked around, watching for anyone else she knew. It never occurred to her until then how many people she had helped to put in prison in the short time she had lived in Bald Eagle Falls. She had never considered that the penitentiary might be a dangerous place for her to visit.

Adele had needed her, and she had just agreed without thinking of any of the ramifications.

The CO escorted them back to the entrance they had come in, but another uniformed man was waiting for them. "The warden would like to see you."

Erin looked at Adele, anxious. Adele didn't look nearly as panicky as Erin felt. She gave a nod of agreement, looking tall and stately and regal, like a queen who deigned to see a subject for a favor. The new CO took them to an office. Small, with plain white walls, sparsely furnished. They were not invited to sit down.

The man behind the desk was portly, with a round, sweaty face and head and little hair. He pushed away the stack of papers he was signing and looked at Erin and Adele.

"I understand there was an incident in the visiting room?"

"I'm sorry," Erin apologized. "I didn't mean to cause any trouble."

"What is your name?" He looked away from her to tap some commands into his computer. Looking at the admitting log?

"Erin Price."

"And you were here to see Rudolph Windsor. What is your relationship with him?"

"I don't have one. I've only just met him before." Erin motioned to Adele. "Adele is his… wife."

She looked at Adele to see whether she said "ex" or "estranged" or some other qualifier. Adele merely nodded. "Erin came along at my request. I didn't want to come by myself. She's…" Adele gave a dry smile, "my wingman."

The warden allowed himself a small smile of acknowledgment. "I see. And the incident involved what prisoner? Not Windsor."

"No, Rudolph isn't the kind to cause problems," Adele said, then watched him for his response. Agree or disagree? Was he still the man she knew or was he different on the inside?

The warden didn't disagree with her assessment. He nodded an acknowledgment.

"It was Daniel Jackson," Erin said. "I'm really sorry. I didn't even think about him being here. I just came along to support Adele, like she said. That's all."

"We will ensure that he is not in the visitor room the next time you visit," the warden said, ignoring her apology. "Do you have plans to come back in the near future?"

Erin looked at Adele and, when she shook her head, Erin did as well. "No, not planning to come back any time soon. Thank you. I'm really not the kind of person who is disruptive…" She remembered the rules on the penitentiary website, with how long a person would have their visiting privileges revoked if they caused problems. Six months, a year, permanently. She didn't plan on returning, but she wanted to be able to if Adele needed her again. She couldn't see any other reason to visit the prison again. She didn't expect Charley to be accused of another crime and incarcerated. She'd had a couple of overnight stays with the Bald Eagle Falls police department for being drunk and disorderly, but that wasn't something that would land her in the prison.

"You are not the one who will be disciplined for what happened," the warden said firmly. "Mr. Jackson will have his privileges revoked until I am persuaded that he is not going to be a disciplinary problem. That has nothing to do with you."

Erin let out her breath slowly. "Oh. Okay."

The warden looked away from his computer, studying Erin and then Adele in turn.

"You are Windsor's wife?"

She nodded.

"I wasn't aware that he had a wife. This is the first time you have visited?"

"Yes. And probably the last."

"Was he a problem during the visit?" the warden asked sharply.

"No. I only wanted to ask him a few questions. We don't… we are separated. We don't usually have anything to do with each other."

"I see. The two of you are aware of our recent escapees? You are from Bald Eagle Falls?" His eyes went to Erin.

She was about to say, "Both of us are," then thought better of it. Adele was off the grid and probably preferred to remain that way. So Erin just nodded and told the warden, "Yes. And I did hear about your escapees. It's all been pretty scary."

He nodded, glancing at his computer screen distractedly. "I'm sure it won't be very long until the police or feds get Plaint rounded up and he returns to us. As you can imagine, things have been quite tense around here. People are wound up. Even prisoners who are normally well-behaved may react unpredictably. Did Windsor have anything to say about the prison break?"

His eye moved back and forth between them, watching for their reactions, waiting for their answers. Erin remembered the big red letters on placards around the visitor room. *Visits may be recorded.* Did they have the ability to pinpoint the discussions at each table in the visitor room and separate out the other conversations and background noise to get a clear recording of each visit? Had the warden or someone else been listening in the whole time?

Erin looked at Adele for her answer. It was her visit. Erin had just been along for the ride.

"I asked him whether he knew anything about it or had anything to do with it," Adele said. "He didn't seem to."

He studied her for what seemed a long time with watery blue eyes, then nodded. "That will be all. Please give us a heads up if you do plan to come back for another visit, and we will ensure that there isn't any trouble."

Erin and Adele took this as their dismissal and turned back to the CO who had escorted them in. He led them back out to the main doors.

"Y'all have a nice day."

CHAPTER 21

*E*rin was not expecting Terry to be home already when she returned. As she stood outside the garage saying goodbye to Adele, she saw him on the back porch waiting for her, standing with his arms folded across his chest. Erin gave Adele a wave and met Terry on the porch, forcing a smile despite his grim look. As if it had been a perfectly normal day and she was just returning home from Auntie Clem's.

"Hi! You got off in good time."

"I was informed that there was an incident at the penitentiary."

Erin gulped. "Oh? What did they say?"

She really hoped that it wasn't anything to do with her visit. There had been a fight, or someone had confessed to being involved in the prison break. Something that had nothing at all to do with Erin and Adele.

Terry's lips pressed together. "Why didn't you tell me you were going to the penitentiary today?"

"Adele asked me to go with her to see her husband. I just made arrangements at Auntie Clem's… I didn't think it would affect our schedule."

"You figured I would try to talk you out of it."

Erin sighed. "Wouldn't you?"

He looked at her for a moment, then turned and walked back into the house. She followed him in. She didn't know if he was finished with the conversation and would give her the silent treatment or whether they were going to discuss it further.

Terry grabbed a beer from the fridge, popped the top, and turned to face her. He took a couple of swallows. "Yes. I would have. Because it isn't a safe place for you to be. How many people do you think there are at that prison who have a grudge against you?"

Erin looked down at the floor. Orange Blossom padded into the room and started meowing when he saw her. She bent over and scratched his ears, which quieted him a bit, but he still wanted food.

"I didn't think that we would have contact with any of the other prisoners. I thought we would be in those little booths, talking over a phone. I didn't think it would be an open visiting room."

"You didn't bother to find out."

"No. I just assumed. I thought that in a high security section, with violent offenders, it would be stupid to have everyone together in one room."

Terry made a grimace and a movement that was half shrug, half nod. "I would expect them to be more concerned with liability issues."

"But nothing happened," Erin assured him. "I'm not hurt. There were guards right there. And you know those Jackson boys, they're just full of hot air."

She regretted it as soon as the words left her mouth. Terry shook his head vigorously. "They are not in prison for being full of hot air. They are in prison for trying to kill their father for the clan. And also for trying to kill you because you were too close to the truth. They are dangerous, violent offenders. Don't downplay that. Daniel Jackson is not a child having a tantrum."

Erin nodded. He was right. She breathed long inhales and exhales, counting the seconds, hoping to loosen the knot of anxiety in her gut.

"I never thought I would see him. But nothing happened. I'm fine. There were lots of guards right there to take care of things. And the warden says if I ever go back, to give him a heads-up first, and he'll make sure that Daniel isn't anywhere close to me."

"And did you give him a list of all of the other people you have helped to put into that prison?"

"No. I guess if I go again—and I don't plan to—I could ask if I could see someone in a private room, so I'm not around any of those others."

"But you're not going back," he said firmly.

She didn't like his dictating what she could or couldn't do. She immediately rebelled against his putting any restrictions on her, even though she had no intention of going back. What if Adele wanted her to go along another time, a year down the line? What if Vic needed a ride to go visit her brothers? Though Erin couldn't imagine she would want to. She didn't see herself going back there again, but she still wanted to argue with Terry and tell him that he couldn't tell her what to do.

But she'd had a lot of practice in keeping her mouth shut and her thoughts to herself. So she zipped it and didn't engage with Terry.

He looked at her for a minute, waiting for the blow-up. Waiting for the argument. Then he shrugged it off. "And what were the results of this visit? Did you learn anything?"

"I don't think Rudolph Windsor had anything to do with the prison break. I don't know if he knows who did, but I don't think he had any involvement."

"But you can't prove that."

"No, of course not."

She couldn't prove a negative and she couldn't prove what was in anyone's head. Erin didn't have any evidence one way or the other, but she believed what Rudolph had said. That he didn't have any reason to send a violent felon to see his wife and would have done whatever he could to prevent the two of them from meeting up. She couldn't fathom why he would have told Bruel about her intentionally.

Terry nodded slowly. "What are your plans for the night?"

Erin was surprised. "I don't know. Nothing special. Supper, plan, watch TV. Make sure everything went okay at Auntie Clem's today. I have some accounting to do too." Erin rolled her eyes. "I *love* doing accounting."

"That's the life of a business owner. So you're not planning any other adventures tonight?"

"No."

"I have a few loose ends to tie up at the office." Anticipating Erin's objections, he held up a finger to stop her. "Like you with your accounting, there are things I would prefer not to have to spend my time on, but personal preference doesn't come into it. I still have to get it done. I came home to meet you and make sure that everything was okay. If you're just going to be doing the usual stuff tonight, I'll sneak out for an hour after supper. That's all it will be. Just an hour. Then I'll be here for the night."

Erin sighed. She did want him to be there for the evening. Davis Plaint was still out there somewhere, and who knew what he was planning to do? Maybe he had escaped from prison for the sole purpose of getting back at her.

"Okay. After supper, you do your paperwork and I'll do my accounting, and we'll cut it off after an hour. If it's not done, we work on it again tomorrow."

"Deal," Terry agreed. "And if anything happens to concern you, you know how to get me." He took a few more swallows of his beer. "You will tell me if you're worried about anything, won't you?"

"Yes. Of course."

He didn't point out how she hadn't told him about going to the penitentiary with Adele. But Erin hadn't been worried about that. It wasn't something she had needed to talk to him about. It was just something she was doing on her own time, just like he could do what he wanted when he wasn't with her or on shift. She didn't track everything he did, and she didn't expect him to track everything she did.

But she knew it bothered him. He had left work earlier than he should have, just because he wanted to check on her. She wished that the grapevine in Bald Eagle Falls wasn't quite so active. She didn't know who had called him to tell him about what happened at the prison, but it was irritating not to be able to go places without people reporting back to him. Maybe it had been the warden, or maybe one of the feds working on the prison break. Or perhaps someone else she hadn't even thought of. She didn't know of anyone in Bald Eagle Falls who worked at the penitentiary, but there were probably a few of them. Or a connection in Moose River. Jack Ward, for one.

Erin went to the pantry cupboard to get food out for the animals. Orange Blossom, instead of being satisfied that she was doing what she was supposed to and quieting down, began yowling even louder, encouraging her to fill his bowl before the others. Marshmallow and K9 both entered the kitchen at the noises indicating food was being prepared. K9 went up to Terry and nuzzled his hand for attention, and Marshmallow waited patiently. Orange Blossom was the only one who freaked out every night like Erin might forget to feed him if he weren't loud enough.

"See what's in the fridge," Erin told Terry. "I probably need to go grocery shopping. I'm not sure there's much of anything right now."

She fed Orange Blossom and he finally stopped yowling and began to snarf his food down as if one of the other animals might try to steal it. Then K9, and last of all, Marshmallow.

She rubbed her eyes, feeling the fatigue of the day setting in. Was she really going to get any accounting finished while Terry did his paperwork? She might have to bow out and admit to him that she hadn't been able to face it and had procrastinated for another day. She didn't have a hard deadline, after all. It was just something that needed to be done. Someday.

Erin tried. She made a go of it, but her brain did not want to do accounting and her heart was not in it, even when she told herself that she only had to work on it for an hour and then could put it aside. She and Terry could enjoy the rest of the evening together.

Vic called a "Yoo-hoo!" and came in the back door. She walked through the kitchen and stood in the doorway, surveying Erin working on the laptop with papers spread out around her.

"Uh-oh. You look busy."

It wasn't Erin's fault that she had a visitor. She hadn't asked Vic to come over. She clicked the Save button and put the computer to the side.

"It can wait. How did the rest of the day go at Auntie Clem's?"

"Everything was smooth as silk. No problems."

"And we're all set for tomorrow? We didn't run out of anything? You had enough time to prepare the batters for tomorrow morning?"

"Yep, all fine, ma'am. You have that place running like a well-oiled machine."

Erin's face warmed. It was nice to see her business doing so well. Running her own business was nerve-racking, and there were many days that she felt like there was so much she didn't know. She was bound to run into disaster at any moment.

"Sooo..." Vic dragged the word out expectantly.

Erin looked at her. "What?"

"Are you going to tell me how things went with you?"

"Oh... well, just fine..."

"Come on, Erin. I want the scoop. The story. Tell me all about it."

Erin hesitated. She didn't really want to recount the whole thing for Vic for more than one reason. It was Adele's business, not Erin's, and she shouldn't be talking to anyone else about it without Adele's approval. But Adele knew how close they were and that Erin would probably talk to Vic about it. If she didn't want her to say something, she would have told her so.

And she didn't want to tell Vic the part about running into Daniel there. It would undoubtedly upset Vic that her brother had been such a jerk toward Erin, but she wouldn't be able to do anything about it. Daniel was in prison. Not exactly someplace Vic could go and slap him across the head like Erin had seen her do when her brothers were arrested and in handcuffs for their attempt to kidnap and murder Erin.

"I don't know if I should tell you anything. It's not really anything to do with me..."

"Tell me," Vic insisted. "I want to hear everything."

"It's Adele and her husband. Isn't that kind of... privileged? Something I'm not supposed to talk about?"

"You were right there. You can tell me what happened. They can't stop you."

"I just don't want to upset Adele."

"Come on. Spill. Did she tell you that you couldn't tell me about it?"

"No."

"Then she knew that you would," Vic told her, coming to the same conclusion as Erin had herself. She sat on the other end of the couch, folded her arms, and raised her brows, waiting.

CHAPTER 22

*E*rin had managed to tell Vic about the visit with Rudolph Windsor without any mention of Daniel. She was winding up her story when she saw Vic's eyes shift to the front window.

Erin turned to look into the front yard, wondering if Terry was home already. The time had passed quickly, but then it would pass quickly while talking to Vic. Not like it would if she had been working on the accounting. Accounting hours were at least three times as long as visiting hours.

But Terry hadn't pulled to the curb in front of the house. His parking space was still unoccupied. Instead, Mrs. Peach was making her way slowly up the sidewalk.

Erin had an urge to hurry out and help her up the walk, but she knew that Mrs. Peach would just shake her off and say, "There's nothing wrong with my legs, you know."

Instead, Erin pretended that she was still talking with Vic and not watching Mrs. Peach's progress through the window. When Mrs. Peach reached the front step, Erin got up and opened the front door for her.

"Mrs. Peach! Hi, how are you?"

"Just peachy," Mrs. Peach joked breezily.

Erin's jaw nearly hit the floor. She had heard Mrs. Peach make dry or witty remarks but never something silly like that, smiling and laughing at herself. Erin laughed and shook her head. "Well, I'm glad to hear that. Come on in. Can I help you with those steps? They are a little steeper than they should be."

"Just give me your hand." Mrs. Peach grasped Erin's offered hand strongly. "It's my balance, not my legs. If I just have something to hold on to, I'm fine."

Still, it was an obvious effort for her to get up each of the stairs. She nodded to Erin at the top, smiling and puffing a little bit. "There, you see? Nothing to it."

"Come in," Erin guided her into the house. "Come sit down and have a visit."

Mrs. Peach looked around the living room and made her way over to one of the chairs. "I noticed at Easter—it still looks just like it did when Clementine lived her."

"Maybe one or two little changes," Erin said. "But I like things the way she had them. I didn't want to bring a bunch of modern furniture in here to ruin the look."

"It's very nice. Comfortable to walk back in here, like I never left."

"Good. I'm sure that would have made her happy. Were the two of you close friends? I never asked."

"We were neighbors. Not as close as we should have been, maybe. The last few stragglers of our generation, it should have drawn us closer together. But it's hard… getting old made me feel disconnected. Like… not even I was the same person as I had been. That a person like me didn't belong in this new world."

That made Erin sad and sorry she had asked. She nodded but didn't say anything else to fill the silence. Mrs. Peach had never come over uninvited for a visit before. She had made an obviously difficult journey. It wasn't just a whim or stopping by Erin's on the way home from something else.

"This is silly," Mrs. Peach said, with evident embarrassment and anxiety. "But I was just wondering if you had seen Mr. Peach."

"Oh… no, not since I saw him at your place. Is he missing?"

"No, I'm sure not… I just don't know where he was going. He's not used to living with someone else," Mrs. Peach excused him, "having to account for himself. A man who's been living as a bachelor for thirty years can't suddenly be expected to act like a married man."

"How long has he been out?"

"All day. I thought... maybe he had work today and just didn't tell me that he went in to the penitentiary. I thought he was going to stay home until things had settled down; that was what he said, but maybe he got called in. Things like that do happen, you know... maybe someone had a spiritual crisis and needed him there..."

"Did you call the penitentiary?"

"Oh, I couldn't do that. Checking up on him? Like I didn't trust him?"

If he were Erin's husband, she certainly wouldn't have trusted him. This was a man who had abandoned her decades ago and never bothered to call to explain himself or to apologize. Who just showed up again one day and expected to be treated as the man of the house as if he had never left? She wouldn't have trusted him one inch.

"Do you know what his usual hours at the prison are?"

"No. But... it's getting dark. He was gone when I got up this morning. I've waited all day, thinking he just went out for a coffee and would come back... or that he'd gone for a walk and would be right back... or that he ran some errands... got a flat tire... or went out the prison to deal with someone who was in trouble..."

"If he was gone that early, then he should definitely be back by now," Vic agreed. "Maybe it would be a good idea to make a few phone calls. Just in case something happened to him."

"No, I couldn't do that to him. I don't want to be a nag."

"You didn't nag him for thirty years. I think it's time," Erin told her. "He could be in the hospital with amnesia. Not even know who he is and how he got there."

Mrs. Peach rolled her eyes. "That kind of thing only happens on TV. In real life, people don't go around getting amnesia and forgetting who they were or how they got there."

Erin thought of Willie, who had done just that after getting hit over the head. "Well... it's pretty rare. Not like on TV where it happens all the time," Erin temporized, "But it does still happen now and then. Or he could be unconscious or have had a stroke. We just don't know if we don't look into it. Not to be nosy, just to make sure that everything is okay."

Mrs. Peach pursed her lips, considering it. Then she slowly nodded. That was probably why she was there. She knew that was what she needed to do, but she needed someone else to tell her so and to talk her into it.

"We can call the penitentiary first," Erin suggested. "It shouldn't be hard to find out from them whether he was working today or not. They have to log everyone in and out." Erin didn't mention that she had been there herself earlier in the day. If she said that she had been there but hadn't seen Mr. Peach, it would just make Mrs. Peach more anxious. It was a big prison. Mr. Peach could have been in any number of places and Erin would never have seen him.

"I don't have the number of the prison. I have an old phone book back at the house. The number probably hasn't changed since they stopped printing a new phone book every year…"

"It's on the website," Erin said, pulling out her phone and doing a quick search. "Here it is…" She waited for Mrs. Peach to take out her phone and, eventually, the older woman did. It wasn't an old flip phone version like Erin had half expected. It was a large screen, fairly recent edition. Erin would have thought that her kids or grandkids picked it out for her but remembered that she didn't have any children. Mrs. Peach launched the phone app and looked at Erin, waiting. Erin read the number to her a few digits at a time.

"I don't know what to say," Mrs. Peach said nervously.

"Just tell them that you wanted to see what time he left," Vic said, "so that you can have dinner ready for him when he gets home."

Mrs. Peach looked taken aback by this suggestion. She opened her mouth to argue with Vic, probably to tell her that she had already made and eaten dinner and anyone at the prison was bound to know that most people in the area didn't wait until late in the evening to eat their final meal of the day. But then someone answered and she was put on the spot.

"This is Gladys Peach," she said in a wavering voice. "I'm Pastor

Peach's wife. I was just wondering what time he left there… so I know when to expect him home… he forgot to call."

Though if he really had forgotten to call, Mrs. Peach would undoubtedly have called his cell, wouldn't she? Most people around Bald Eagle Falls, even the elderly, had cell phones and would not consider getting into a car for a long drive without having it on them.

"Oh, let me see…" Mrs. Peach had put the phone on speaker, whether intentionally or unintentionally, so Erin and Vic could hear the penitentiary receptionist's pleasant voice as she tried to help. "I didn't realize that Pastor Peach was married. I'm just pulling up his check-out time…" She trailed off. Erin pictured her looking at the screen, discovering that there was no check-out time. "Maybe he is still here. Let me just put you on hold for a minute while I try to track him down."

There was a click and then dead air. No easy-listening music while they held for her. Mrs. Peach looked at the phone, waiting for the voice to come back. Erin was sure that she understood what was going on just as well as Vic and Erin. Mr. Peach wasn't at the penitentiary.

A good ten minutes passed. Erin tried not to time it, not to watch the clock. She tried to think of things to say, but Mrs. Peach didn't engage with her, made no effort to pick up the conversation to keep herself busy while they waited.

Erin thought of her waiting for thirty years for a man who was never coming home. All of those lonely evenings, wondering why he had left and when or if she would ever see him again.

What had Mr. Peach been doing during that time? Had he had another woman? A mistress or second wife to keep him company? Did he prefer to live like a bachelor? It was a long time to live on his own without anyone else. Surely, he had sought out company at some point.

"I'm sorry to keep you waiting." The woman's voice finally came back. "I wish I could help you, but… Pastor Peach wasn't here today. Do you think you might have misunderstood? Maybe he was going out somewhere else?"

"Yes, that must be it," Mrs. Peach agreed. "Thank you for your help."

So he hadn't gone to the prison. But maybe he had gone back to his other home. Or maybe he had gone into the city, or was a gambler, or any one of a hundred other things. There was no saying how he might have spent his day and forgotten about the wife waiting for him.

Mrs. Peach sighed. "I guess all I can do is wait," she admitted. "Sooner or later… I'll hear something. I don't want to chase him."

This time she didn't sound like it was because she didn't want to be a nag or frighten him away by being too possessive, but to protect her own pride. She didn't want people to think that she would let him play with her heart like that. Not again.

"I thought things were different this time," Mrs. Peach said. "I thought… he's an old man; he's ready to settle down now." She shook her head. "He seemed so sincere. He told me that he was going to make things right. He was going to get all of our affairs in order. Pay off the mortgage. Sign a new will. Make things right with me. He said that he saved his money all that time, that it was mine as much as it was his, and he wanted to give it to me." Mrs. Peach patted at the corners of her eyes. "He said the things I wanted to hear, so of course I fell for it all." Her voice was hoarse.

Erin looked at Vic.

"I'll put the kettle on," Vic suggested. "We'll have some tea."

CHAPTER 23

*T*erry was surprised when he returned home to find Mrs. Peach and Vic there, instead of Erin alone. Of course, he was used to Vic often being over visiting while he was out. They were so close, both as friends and geographically, that Vic was there almost as much as she was in her own apartment. Mrs. Peach, on the other hand, had only been there once before, for Easter dinner.

And it was clear when he walked in that he had interrupted an emotional scene. The tissues, red-rimmed eyes, and tea testified to that.

K9 went to Erin for some ear scratches and petting, whining a little as he looked at Mrs. Peach. She reached over and petted him as well. "It's been a long time since I had a dog. We always had them on the farm growing up. But I haven't had one of my own for a long time." She scratched K9's ears and jaw. "And K9 is such a nice boy."

K9's tail waved back and forth happily and he licked her hands.

Terry shut the door and looked around at the ladies, unsure how to deal with the tea party in his living room. He cocked an eyebrow at Erin, querying what he was supposed to do.

"Terry, come talk to Mrs. Peach for a minute. Maybe you can give her some advice…"

He took a seat and gave Mrs. Peach a reassuring smile. He was good at that, always very kind and reassuring to victims. Women were always drawn to the handsome officer.

"Hi, Mrs. Peach. How can I help you?"

Mrs. Peach related her concerns about Mr. Peach's disappearance once more. Terry nodded and scratched his jaw, thinking about it.

Mrs. Peach dabbed at her eyes and wiped her nose. "What do you think I should do, Officer Piper? I don't want to make a big stink. It would just embarrass both of us. But... I am concerned. I'm trying not to think that something could have happened to him, because he's probably just taken off again, right? He thought he could make married life work, but after making all of those promises, he decided it was just too much for him, and he ran away again." She shook her head, tears running down her wrinkled cheeks. "That's how he deals with his problems. He runs away."

"I can understand why you wouldn't want to file a missing person report and start a full-scale manhunt," Terry agreed. "He does have a history and a logical reason for leaving again. I'm sorry that he did that. He obviously has no idea how to treat his spouse."

She gave an unhappy little laugh.

"So what do you think I should do? Just go back to the way things were, and maybe he'll pop in for another visit in ten or twenty years?"

"Well... despite his history of disappearing on you, there are a couple of other things to consider. One is that Davis Plaint is still on the loose. Despite our efforts to find him and take him back into custody, we have not been able to track him down. He knew your husband, I assume?"

Mrs. Peach nodded. "Yes, of course. He said so."

"He said he didn't know Davis well, but had talked to him a couple of times," Erin confirmed, remembering her visit with Mr. Peach while Mrs. Peach made dinner to celebrate his return home. How could he turn around and leave her again so quickly?

"So there is the possibility that Davis had something to do with him disappearing again. Either voluntarily or non-voluntarily."

"I... suppose. But why would Davis want anything to do with

him? Why would he be sticking around Bald Eagle Falls and what would he want with my husband?"

"I don't know. They might have had more of a history than your husband was willing to say. Being a spiritual advisor, he had a duty of confidentiality. So he couldn't tell you everything."

Mrs. Peach nodded slowly. "I suppose that is true." She shook her head. "It's so strange to think of him being a pastor. He *used* to be a car mechanic."

"It's possible that Davis contacted your husband to say that he needed him, that he wanted advice or to turn himself in. Or he may have taken him unaware. Either way, we know that Davis Plaint is a violent offender and, because of his connection with your husband, we have to consider the possibility that he intended him harm."

Mrs. Peach sniffled. "Yes," she said stoically.

"And there's always the possibility that he had an accident or a medical emergency. He is not a young man. I don't know what kind of health he was in."

"No. I don't know either. He didn't say that there was anything wrong with him, but we had just barely met again... we were just getting to know each other."

"So I think that at a minimum, we should check with the hospitals and let the police department know to be on the lookout for anyone matching his description. We don't have to go with a full-on missing person report, just to keep an eye out for him or for any trouble." He looked toward the backyard. "And maybe when the sun comes up, we make another sweep through the woods to look for any sign of him or Davis again."

Mrs. Peach nodded. "Yes... and you can keep it quiet? So everybody doesn't have to know?"

"Sure. We don't have to say that we're looking for anyone other than Davis. Nobody outside of the police department has to know anything different."

Erin leaned forward. "Is Melissa still home sick?"

Terry rolled his eyes. "Yes. Which is probably a good thing. I wouldn't want to have to put her on leave."

Mrs. Peach looked bemused by this but didn't ask anything about it.

"We don't have any indication of foul play at this point," Terry told her reassuringly. "As you say, he might have just gotten overwhelmed with responsibilities and high-tailed it out of here. He might be back at home—at his other house—and just not want to answer your phone calls. We'll get Moose River to do a welfare check and see. I know Jack Ward over there. He'll handle it discreetly. And would it be okay if I walk you back and take a look around your house and yard? Just to see if there is anything out of place or something that might indicate where he went?"

"Yes… of course. I don't know what you're going to find there, though."

"Probably nothing. But with missing persons, it's always best to check the house first. There have been many cases, especially with children, where they were in the house all along."

Erin thought of several cases she had heard of in the media. Sometimes it was just a child who fell asleep in a cupboard, but all too often, the results were far more tragic.

She hoped that Terry wouldn't find Mr. Peach in the basement or the shed in the backyard. She didn't suspect poor Mrs. Peach of disposing of her husband, of course, but Terry was right about Davis. Who knew just how much Mr. Peach had known about Davis that he might not want to leak out?

erry walked Mrs. Peach back home and did a quick search of her house and yard, but returned to the house shaking his head.

"No sign of him there," he confirmed.

"Good," Erin said. "I really didn't want her to have killed him and stuffed his body in the basement."

Terry rolled his eyes. "You've been watching too much TV."

"It does happen in real life," Erin insisted.

"Yes... but not very often. And I didn't think that old Mrs. Peach was the type to have killed and disposed of her husband."

"No, I didn't either. But it's the ones you don't suspect, isn't it?"

He shrugged his shoulders and spread his hands apart. "Not in my experience."

"Well," Vic looked at her phone. "I guess I should leave you guys with a little bit of alone time tonight. See you in the morning."

Erin nodded. "Thanks for helping out with Mrs. Peach. See you tomorrow."

Vic took the tea things back into the kitchen and let herself out. Erin saw her in the backyard a few minutes later with Nilla, taking him out for one last walk before beginning her bedtime routine. Terry snuggled up to Erin on the couch.

"Sorry, I was a bit longer than I expected to be."

"You have to take care of yourself. You don't want—"

"I know," Terry agreed, interrupting her. "I don't want to trigger a migraine or crash and not be able to make my regular shift. I know. I'm tired, but I'm not exhausted."

"Okay."

There was a tap at the front door. Erin looked at Terry and he looked back at her, both of them tired of company and wanting to unwind and get ready for bed. Eventually, Erin put her feet on the floor and went to the front door to see who it was. After looking through the peephole, she turned the lock and opened the door.

"Beaver. Hi."

Rohilda Beaven, better known as Beaver, slouched into the room. She was blond, a darker blond than Vic, and around Erin's age, though by the adventures she recounted, she should have been much older. She'd packed a lot into her adult years. Her ponytail hung out through the back of a camouflage ball cap, and she was in her usual outfit of an army-green halter top and camouflage cargo pants, topped with a hunting jacket, too warm for the weather. It had a lot of pockets and Erin had no idea what they all housed, but she knew it was heavy with the weaponry and equipment she carried.

Beaver billed herself as a treasure hunter and, on her vacations, she did go on trips all around the world hunting for lost and hidden treasures. But the rest of the time, rather than being a bum, like she said she was, she worked for one of the federal agencies, though Erin wasn't sure which one. It was all hush-hush, and Beaver didn't share those details with anyone. A few people in Bald Eagle Falls knew about her real work, including Erin and the police department, but the rest believed the fiction that she was an unemployed bum, living mostly off of her boyfriend Jeremy, her junior by a number of years. Jeremy Jackson, Vic's other brother.

Beaver looked around the room and nodded at Terry, her hands in her pockets. She chewed a thick wad of gum, as usual. She didn't take a seat.

"Sorry to disturb you. I know that your guests just left, and you probably want some time to yourselves."

Erin blinked at Beaver. "What? Were you watching the house?"

She gave a brief nod and shrug. "What's up with Mrs. Peach?"

Erin looked at Terry. He didn't indicate that she shouldn't talk to Beaver about it or that he intended to recount the story to her.

"She's worried about her husband."

"The pastor?"

"That's the only one she has!"

Beaver chuckled. "She could have had another. I doubt I would have stayed married for thirty years after some scoundrel left me."

"Well, it sounds like you know that she did."

"What is she worried about?"

"He's disappeared. She wants to know where he is and if he's okay, but she doesn't want to draw attention to the fact that he's disappeared and maybe left her again."

"He's missing?"

"She doesn't know where she is. He might not be missing. Terry is going to check with Moose River to see if he went back home." Erin looked at him.

Terry nodded. "He's not in any of the local hospitals and hasn't been identified by any of our police department. He didn't work at the penitentiary today. It's entirely possible that he just went home without telling Mrs. Peach and isn't returning her calls."

"But that would be a complete reversal." Beaver frowned. "Why would he come here in the first place if he was just going to turn around and go back? Why go to all of that effort and humiliation?"

"Maybe it wasn't like he imagined it would be," Erin offered. "Maybe he was expecting his welcome home to be… bigger. His wife isn't the person that he left thirty years ago. Maybe they didn't get along."

Beaver pursed her lips. She chomped on her gum and shook her head. "I don't think it is a coincidence that he came back here after the prison break and he works for the prison. He came to protect her or to make contact with one of the escapees. So if he's left, then either he thinks the danger is gone, or he did whatever he came here to do."

"You don't think *he* killed Bruel, do you?"

"Don't know. Within the realm of possibility. Or he came to

make contact with Davis Plaint, and despite the failure of the police department to find him, he did make contact and is now on his way… home or somewhere else."

"Or he thinks the danger is gone," Erin repeated the other possibility Beaver had suggested. "Because he knows that Davis Plaint has left Bald Eagle Falls?"

"Or because he took care of the risk," Beaver said.

"Killed Davis?"

"Maybe."

"Did you already know that Mr. Peach is missing?" Terry asked, frowning at Beaver.

"I knew he wasn't home." She chewed her gum vigorously, apparently enjoying his consternation.

"Because you've been watching the house?"

She shrugged, not answering.

"You know, it's the polite thing to let the local police know when you're conducting an investigation in their area." Terry raised an eyebrow at Beaver.

"You already know about the investigation."

"Which investigation? Is this part of the investigation into the prison break?"

"There are clear connections."

"So, is this something else?" he persisted.

"Don't know yet." Beaver chewed her gum. "There is a lot to be investigated."

"You're not exactly being open. If you're expecting us to answer your questions…"

"It's 'need to know,' Officer Piper. I *do* expect you to cooperate with a federal officer during an investigation."

"Without filling us in on what you know."

Beaver glanced at Erin. "Us?"

"I meant the police department, not me and Erin"

But neither one of them was telling Erin she had to leave. Which meant that neither was going to give the other classified information.

"I've told you what I know," Terry said. "And that is that Mr.

Peach isn't home and his wife doesn't know where he is. We will look into it further but, for now, that's all the information we have."

"You'll keep me apprised?"

Terry shrugged. "If I find out anything of note."

Beaver narrowed her eyes. "We need to know where he is."

"And I'll do my best to find out."

Beaver chewed, studying him, then finally nodded. "Look forward to hearing from you." She nodded at Erin. "Miss Erin. Enjoy the rest of your evening."

CHAPTER 25

*E*rin was getting ready for the day, tidying up a few things that had been left out when they had headed to bed the night before. It had been later than Erin's usual bedtime, and Terry had insisted that she was too tired to do anything else and that he would put things away when he was up. But he had not picked anything up when he had gotten up later to watch TV for a while. He couldn't always get to sleep as early as Erin had to so, after cuddling for a while, he would get up and do something relaxing before going back to bed.

But apparently, that did not extend to cleaning up after himself. Erin picked up another small plate and cup and took them into the kitchen to put them in the dishwasher. The animals had been fed, so Orange Blossom didn't start making noise every time Erin entered the kitchen. Sometimes she wondered why she needed the burglar alarm when he was so loud.

She walked back into the living room and did one last scan for dishes, food wrappers, or anything else that should be picked up. A movement outside caught her eye and she looked out the window to see what it was.

A man was walking down the street, very slowly, lurching with every step. A little late to be coming back from a night of drinking, as the bars had been closed for a couple of hours, but he might have been drinking with a friend or might have been so drunk that he'd been passed out in an alley up until then.

It was rare to see someone so drunk on the streets of Bald Eagle Falls, especially in the residential area. But Bald Eagle Falls wasn't immune to the problems of alcoholism and addiction.

The man lurched again and fell to his hands and knees. Erin winced. At least he hadn't done a face plant on the concrete. She stepped closer to the window to study him, wondering if it were a neighbor she knew or if she should call the police department and tell them that he needed some help.

He was an older man. Tall. Salt and pepper hair. Erin almost pressed her nose against the window in shock. Mr. Peach! Not missing after all, just out on a binge. Well, Mrs. Peach would be pleased.

She slipped on a pair of sandals at the front door and let herself out, hurrying down the sidewalk to help Mr. Peach up.

"Who is it? Who's there?" he murmured, twisting his head around to see her face.

"It's me, Mr. Peach. Erin Price. Next door, remember? In Clementine's old house?"

"Clementine?" He looked around.

"Right," Erin agreed, though she didn't know if he had understood what she said about Clementine's house or if he thought that Erin was Clementine. It didn't really matter, as long as he trusted her and didn't fight back against her attempts to help him. Some people were like that; they would swing at anyone while they were drunk. "Here, give me your arm. Let's get you up."

She'd had a couple of foster fathers who were drunks. She'd learned when to stay out of the way and how to help someone bigger than she was. Mr. Peach was quite a bit taller than she was, but luckily not portly. It wasn't that hard to lean him on her shoulder and get him back up on his feet. He wasn't actually as unsteady as she had expected. His face was white rather than flushed, and he didn't wobble when he stood still.

"Good, good. Now let's get you home. You're almost there. Just take it slowly, one step at a time."

He staggered forward again, taking mincing little steps instead of the wide-legged gait most of the drunks she knew adopted. He kept holding on to her and, even though he staggered a few times, he managed to stay on his feet and didn't wipe her out.

"Is she okay?" Mr. Peach asked anxiously. "No one can hurt her. No one can touch her."

"Mrs. Peach?" Erin asked. "Do you mean Gladys? She's just fine. She was over earlier. Worried about you, but she's just fine."

"She's just fine," he repeated, slurring a little. Erin shook her head. Mrs. Peach was fine, but Erin suspected she wouldn't be happy about her husband coming home in the condition he was in.

"And how about you?" Erin looked Mr. Peach over as they walked. There was a large blotch of blood on his shirt, probably from a nosebleed. By the look of his split lip and a cut over his eye, he'd either fallen and hit his face or had gotten into a fight at the bar.

She tried to avoid breathing too deeply. The stench of spilled alcohol hung over him, as overpowering for Erin's sensitive nose as if someone soaked a rag in gasoline and held it over her face. Behind it, she could detect other scents. The blood on his shirt. The odor of a public men's room. The clean scent of soap and something else that might have been cat food. But Mrs. Peach didn't have a cat. Had he been somewhere there was a cat? Or maybe had fish for dinner at some point during his bender?

She breathed through her mouth and tried to avoid getting too close to his face and his breath. A good whiff of his breath might be all it would take for her to lose what little breakfast she'd gotten down.

"Here's the turn." Erin guided Mr. Peach from the city sidewalk to the private sidewalk that led to the door. "Slow, take it easy." He stumbled again and almost took Erin down with him. "Just a little farther, then you'll be able to lie down and go to sleep," she promised.

It seemed like the sidewalk was a lot longer than the one to Erin's door, though it must be exactly the same. As she tried to get Mr. Peach up the steps, she remembered helping Mrs. Peach up her steps the previous evening. It took a good deal more strength to keep Mr. Peach upright and to get him up the stairs one step at a time. As he was struggling to shift his weight to take the last step, she leaned forward and managed to get her finger on the doorbell, holding it in for half a second to make sure that it made a nice clear ding-dong for Mrs. Peach. She would be in bed, of course. No one got up as early as the bakers.

Eventually, Mr. Peach was on the top step. He put both hands against the door to hold himself up.

"Where is she?" He raised one hand and pounded it against the door before Erin could stop him. She didn't imagine that Mrs. Peach would be too impressed by his behavior. He would be lucky if she didn't turn him away or tell him to sleep it off on the back porch.

"Open the door!" He called out, smacking it again.

"Behave!" Erin told him. "She's coming. You have to give her time. She's not a young woman anymore, you know."

"My wife," Mr. Peach babbled. "Take me to my wife."

"She's coming. But you have to wait patiently. Quietly."

"Where is she?"

Erin shook her head and didn't try to reason with him. She couldn't exactly protect Mrs. Peach from finding out that her husband had just been out on the town on a drunken binge when she had been so worried that something might have happened to him. If he was an alcoholic, it was best she knew.

The door opened and Mrs. Peach was staring out at them, her eyes wide and round in the light from the streetlights.

"Erin? What happened? Where was he?"

"Sorry. I just saw him when he was in front of my house. He fell, and I came out to help him the rest of the way. Didn't want him to get hurt." Erin's eyes fell on the blood again. "Any more than he already is."

"Is he drunk? He never used to get drunk! Neither of us drinks."

"Well… I guess this time…" Erin shrugged. "Maybe things have changed in the thirty years that he was gone."

Mrs. Peach sighed. "I suppose they have."

"You're safe," Mr. Peach declared, looking at her. "Thank goodness you're safe!"

"Of course I'm safe, you silly old man," Mrs. Peach snapped. "I'm at home safe and sound. You're the one out there drinking yourself to death, getting in fights."

"Can we get him in?" Erin suggested, conscious of the amount of time that was passing. Vic would be wondering where she was and why she wasn't ready to go to Auntie Clem's like she always was. "I wouldn't take him all the way to the bedroom. Maybe on your couch? With a basin, in case he gets sick?"

Mrs. Peach stared at her for a moment as if she were speaking another language. Then she nodded slowly. "Yes, okay. Let's do that." She leaned closer to Mr. Peach to make sure he heard her. "You're sleeping on the couch tonight!"

Erin chuckled silently to herself. Mrs. Peach really did take the cake. Imagine welcoming her estranged husband back into the home and then finding out he was a raging alcoholic. Trying to adjust at seventy—or however old Mrs. Peach was—to living with someone again and figuring out how to deal with his addiction.

Erin assumed that the drinking was new. Betty Thompson hadn't mentioned it when she'd been telling Erin Mrs. Peach's history, and Mrs. Peach herself had said that they didn't drink. Though that might have been a lie told to cover her embarrassment.

"Come on, then," Mrs. Peach invited. She grasped her husband's arm and gave it a little tug. "Come inside."

Erin helped him navigate the step up over the doorstep and into the house and guided Mr. Peach toward the couch even though he kept trying to break off and go in the direction of the bedrooms. Eventually, they reached the sofa and Erin helped him sit down in the middle of it, then gave his shoulders a little press to get him to lie down. He resisted and felt his pockets.

"No, no. I have to…"

Erin watched while he fumbled around, eventually finding an envelope in his pants pocket. He handed it, slightly crumpled, to Erin.

"This…" he said, tapping the envelope after he had handed it to her. "This is…" He trailed off, obviously losing the thought in his drunken haze.

Erin put the envelope on the coffee table. On one end, in neat handwriting, was Mrs. Peach's name. "Gladys." She helped Mr. Peach to recline and put his feet up for sleep. Of course he was too tall for the couch but, as far as she was concerned, he deserved to be uncomfortable. Though he would probably pass out and not even know how uncomfortable he should be.

Mrs. Peach had gone into the kitchen to get a bowl, as Erin had suggested. Who knew whether Mr. Peach would make it until morning without throwing up. Erin pulled the ends of the shoelaces on Mr. Peach's shoes and prepared to pull them off.

"No!" Mr. Peach shouted, lurching upright again and reaching for his feet. "No, don't touch them!"

"I was just going to help you get ready for sleep. You don't want to wear these while you sleep."

"Don't. Don't touch," Mr. Peach pushed her away with surprising strength. "Leave me alone!"

Erin looked at Mrs. Peach as she came into the living room with a large bowl. Mrs. Peach shrugged. "Just leave it, then, Erin. He'll be fine here."

"Okay. He'll probably go to sleep. He's pretty… impaired."

"No," Mr. Peach murmured and lay back down again. He closed his eyes.

Erin and Mrs. Peach both stood there for a moment, watching him and listening to him breathe. It wasn't quite a snore, but did sound labored. Maybe he had sleep apnea. Something that was obstructed when he lay down.

"Maybe we should turn him onto his side," Erin suggested.

Mrs. Peach nodded. Probably something she was used to. Or had been used to when he had still been living with her. But maybe it was a recent development or only happened when he was drunk.

The two of them together managed to get him readjusted. Erin listened closely. She thought his breathing was better in that position.

"Do you need anything?" she whispered to Mrs. Peach. "I'm sorry to wake you up so early."

"It isn't your fault. We'll be fine. I'm going to go back to bed. He'll probably sleep for hours, and I can get a couple more in."

Erin nodded. "Okay. Call me if you do need something, okay? I can pick something up for you at lunch, if you need…" Erin tried to think of what she might want. "Bottled water or anti-nausea meds. Maybe some ginger tea."

"A frying pan to hit him over the head with," Mrs. Peach intoned.

Erin giggled. "Good luck."

"Thank you for your help, Erin."

CHAPTER 26

*E*rin walked through her house, quickly locking the front door, turning off a couple of lights, and grabbing her purse as she headed out the back door.

"There you are!" Vic shook her head. "Where were you? You weren't in the house, but your things and the car were still here. I thought that someone had come along and kidnapped *you!*"

"No, I'm okay, I'm sorry." Erin hurried toward the garage. "Let's get on our way, and I'll tell you about it while we get ready for the customers."

She was later than usual, but there would still be plenty of time to bake and set up before they opened the bakery and the first customers arrived. Erin got busy pouring batters into baking tins and told Vic about Mr. Peach's arrival that morning.

Vic's eyes were wide. "Why, that scoundrel! She was crying and so worried about what had happened to him, and he's out on the town? Someone should give him a good talking-to." Vic changed what she was going to say at the last minute.

"Yes," she agreed. "Someone certainly should. I felt so sorry for Mrs. Peach, spending all of that time worrying, and then him showing up like that on her doorstep in the wee hours of the morning. So disrespectful of him. If he was going to stay out drinking, he could have at least slept it off somewhere else and gotten home at a decent hour."

"Unbelievable. And she thought he didn't drink?"

"Yes! And when I took them over the sparkling grape juice, I definitely got the impression that they were not drinkers. But I guess he is."

"Some things are bound to change over thirty years. Especially when he doesn't have a wife looking after him and making sure that he behaves himself."

"Yeah. Poor Mrs. Peach."

They worked in silence for a while. Erin was so comfortable working alongside Vic, they could talk or not talk, and either was just as comfortable. She didn't feel like she had to keep Vic engaged with interesting conversation like she sometimes did around other people.

The morning progressed without incident. None of the busybodies said anything about Mrs. Peach and her wayward husband, so they must not have heard about him carousing the night before. That would be a relief to Mrs. Peach.

It was over their early lunch, before the actual noon-hour rush, that Erin's phone rang and, looking at the face, she saw that it was a call from Mrs. Peach. Maybe she had decided to take Erin up on her offer of picking something up for her.

"Good morning, Mrs. Peach," she greeted pleasantly.

"Erin!" Mrs. Peach sounded as if she had been crying again. Erin's stomach tightened.

If that bounder had been giving his wife more trouble…

"Yes, I'm here. What is it?"

"You need—I need—can you come here?"

"Of course," Erin agreed, already reaching for her purse and digging into it to retrieve her keys. "I'll be right there."

Nothing in Bald Eagle Falls was very far away. The house and Auntie Clem's were only a few blocks apart, so Erin was at Mrs. Peach's in a few minutes. She knocked on the door and then turned the handle.

Mrs. Peach had sounded very upset. She might not be able to make it to the door. It was unlocked, so Erin pushed the door open.

"Mrs. Peach?"

Mrs. Peach's voice answered from much closer than she had expected, the other side of the dimly lit living room. The blinds were still closed. To give Mr. Peach the sleep he would need to recover from his binge, Erin assumed.

"In here," Mrs. Peach's voice was as gravelly as a long-time smoker. "Oh, no, no…"

Erin didn't hesitate, but walked into the room and over to Mrs. Peach's side. She was sitting on one of the chairs. Mr. Peach was still lying on the couch asleep, his legs hanging off the end. Erin blinked, trying to hasten her eyes adjusting to the poor lighting. She put her hand on Mrs. Peach's shoulder.

"What is it? How can I help?"

"It's Gregory." Mrs. Peach motioned to him. "You can see. He's…"

Erin turned her eyes to the sleeping pastor. He was quiet, the snoring of the earlier morning having passed as he slept off the effects of the alcohol. He hadn't woken up at Erin's entrance.

In fact, he was so still and quiet that Erin couldn't detect the rise and fall of his chest as he slept. She stepped closer, dread growing from a hard knot deep in her stomach to a tightness that seized her whole chest and kept her from taking in air. She held her breath, waiting for Mr. Peach's next inhalation, but it never came.

"He's dead," Mrs. Peach wept.

CHAPTER 27

*E*rin forced herself to take another step and examine him more closely. His face was very pale in the light that leaked in through the blinds. The split lip and the cut over his eye that she had noted when she brought him home looked black. He was very, very still.

Hesitantly, Erin reached out and took Mr. Peach's wrist to feel for a pulse. His skin was cool to the touch, stiff and waxy. She dropped his wrist without trying to pinpoint the pounding of his heart.

"I'm so sorry, Mrs. Peach. Is there someone I should call?"

"I don't know. Who do you call? I've never had a dead husband before!" Mrs. Peach's voice had jumped to a higher pitch. She sounded frantic, almost hysterical.

"It's okay. I'll take care of it. You just sit down…" Erin realized that Mrs. Peach was already sitting. "Try to take a few deep breaths and relax. I know this is a shock, but it will be okay."

"How can it be okay? He was back. He was loving. He was everything I dreamed of for all of those lonely years. How can you say it will be okay? It will never be okay again."

Erin pulled out her phone, considering whom to call. The emergency dispatcher? Terry? The doctor? The funeral home? As a care worker, she had reported natural deaths before. But usually, she'd had the number of a family member to call.

She decided that Terry was the best bet. He would know the proper protocol to follow and was someone Mrs. Peach knew and could trust. She tapped his name and waited for him to answer. She really hoped that he wasn't on another call but just walking his beat, keeping his eyes open for anything out of place.

"Erin. Hi, how has your morning been?"

"Umm…" Erin didn't answer, and tried to think of the best way to introduce the problem. "I'm at Mrs. Peach's. Terry… Mr. Peach is dead."

"Are you kidding me?" His voice was sharp. "How do you know that?"

"He's here. I… touched him. He's dead."

"He's home? When did he get home?"

"Oh. Early this morning." It hadn't occurred to Erin that no one had called the police department to let them know that Mr. Peach was no longer missing. She probably should have done that herself. "He came home drunk. I helped to get him up the steps and into the house."

"Why didn't you tell me?"

"I… it was early. You were still sleeping. I went to Auntie Clem's and never thought about it. Just dealing with the usual baking and customers, you know, I didn't think to call you and let you know that he had shown up."

"You're sure he's dead?"

"Yeah. I am."

"I'll be right there."

Erin patted Mrs. Peach on the shoulder again and went over to the window to open the blinds and keep an eye open for Terry. He pulled his police car in front of the house a few minutes later. No light or siren. She was glad that he'd kept it quiet instead of attracting the attention of the entire neighborhood. She opened the door to let him in.

Terry and K9 walked through the door and looked around, taking everything in. He went over to Mr. Peach's body on the couch and felt for a carotid pulse. He withdrew his hand almost immediately, as Erin had done.

"Mrs. Peach. I'm so sorry. Are you okay?"

She just shook her head and cried.

"Erin, do you want to make some tea for her?" Terry suggested.

"Yes, of course." Erin went into Mrs. Peach's kitchen, the same layout as hers, and quickly found everything she needed. She didn't hear the two of them talking and, when she took the tea back out to Mrs. Peach, Terry was sitting on the chair next to hers, just sitting with her. K9 lay on the floor beside him.

"Here, take it slowly. Don't burn yourself," Erin instructed, handing over the cup of hot tea.

Mrs. Peach took it automatically and had a sip. She rubbed at one eye, smearing away tears. Terry waited until she'd had a few swallows, then began.

"Erin told me she helped Mr. Peach home early this morning. Can you tell me what happened after that?"

Mrs. Peach shook her head. "I went back to bed. Got up like usual this morning and... just went about my daily chores... I wasn't very quiet," she admitted, "and I thought that he'd wake up on his own. But it got late, and I wanted him up off of my couch. I shook his arm... and that's when I realized." She tried to suppress a sob. "My Gregory was gone."

"It appears he went peacefully in his sleep," Terry consoled. "He didn't suffer."

Especially since he'd already been three sheets to the wind.

"I don't know what to do," Mrs. Peach said.

"I'm going to call for someone to transport him to the city. The Medical Examiner will need to have a look at him. Then he'll be released to the funeral home and you can make arrangements."

Mrs. Peach sniffled and nodded. "Okay."

Terry withdrew to the kitchen and made a call on his phone, speaking in a low voice that they could not overhear. Erin sat down in Terry's vacated seat. She couldn't very well sit on the couch with Mr. Peach.

"Can I get you anything else?" she offered. "Or call a friend? Someone from your church?"

"No. I don't want anybody yet. I just want... I can't believe this is real. It seems like a dream, him coming home after all of this time. But then this... my life is going to go back to just the way it was, as if nothing had even happened. How do I know it was real?"

Erin rubbed Mrs. Peach's back soothingly.

Terry returned. He had out his notepad. "Can I ask you a few more questions, Mrs. Peach? Are you up to it?"

She nodded and dabbed at her watery eyes with a tissue. "Yes. I'm fine. I don't know why it has affected me this way..."

"Did Mr. Peach have any medical conditions that you are aware of?"

"No. He seemed perfectly fine. He didn't take any pills. He wasn't diabetic. No pacemaker or asthma inhaler. He was old like me, but... to just go like this." She shook her head, trying to make sense of it.

"And when he lived with you before, you weren't aware of any congenital disease or defect, something he was supposed to be careful of?"

"No. Nothing like that."

"Erin says that he appeared to be drunk when she helped him up the steps."

"I can't understand it. He never used to be a drinker. I would have known. He never gave any indication when he came back that... he was an alcoholic."

"Some people just binge every now and then and seem fine the rest of the time. I'll try to find out where he was drinking, if there were any witnesses. He must have had old friends in town."

"I guess. But I don't know who. I didn't keep his friends in my address book. He had his own."

"Of course. And these injuries..." Terry looked at Erin. "You saw them this morning when you initially helped him home?"

Erin nodded. "Yes. I noticed then. And blood on his shirt. I guess he got in a fight."

"People who get that drunk sometimes do," Terry admitted.

"I never knew him to get drunk or to be violent," Mrs. Peach protested.

"I know. But it's been a lot of years since you knew him. Things do change."

She shook her head sadly.

Eventually, an ambulance pulled up in front of the house. As with Terry, they didn't have on the siren to notify the entire block that something was going on. Though Erin figured that with a marked police car and ambulance in front of the house, people would be wondering what was going on anyway.

The paramedics were kind and gentle with Mrs. Peach, sympathetic to her plight and assuring her that Mr. Peach had not suffered but had simply died in his sleep. It happened sometimes, and it was in no way her fault. They reiterated what Terry had said, that the funeral home would be able to pick up his body once the medical examiner was finished with his review. It would be quick, just a formality.

Terry walked outside with the paramedics, making sure of all of the arrangements.

With Mr. Peach's body removed from the house and his crumpled blanket left behind on the couch, the room felt strangely hollow and expectant. Mrs. Peach reached over to the coffee table to straighten a couple of books that had been bumped out of place by the paramedics and saw the envelope lying there with her name on it.

"What is this?"

"Oh, yeah," Erin nodded at it. "That was in his pocket this morning. He wanted me to give it to you."

"What is it?" Mrs. Peach examined the sealed envelope as if there might be something on the outside that would answer her question. But as Erin had seen that morning, there was only Mrs. Peach's name. Gladys.

Mrs. Peach turned it over in her hands, but no new information appeared. "Do you think I should open it?"

"I think that's what he intended. He said to give it to you."

Mrs. Peach still hesitated. But eventually, she slid a nail under the flap and carefully tore it open. Erin saw a sheet of white copy paper with lines of handwriting scrawled across it. A love letter to Mrs. Peach? An apology and explanation for his behavior?

Mrs. Peach gasped. "His will!"

"Oh." It was probably a shock for Mrs. Peach to see it right after he had died. As if he had known that he would. "You said that he was going to write a new one," she reminded.

Mrs. Peach nodded, her eyes skimming over the page. "Yes. He did. But… what is this?"

Erin couldn't see what was written from where she was sitting. "What's wrong?"

"He said he was going to leave his money to me."

CHAPTER 28

*E*rin leaned closer. Of course, it was none of her business, but she was curious, and Mrs. Peach seemed to want her to see it. Maybe she had misunderstood the wording of the will.

Mrs. Peach stabbed her finger at the middle of the page. "Who is this?" she demanded, her tone furious. "Who the—who did—he said he was leaving it to me. All of it, all of the money he'd saved while he was gone. He said that I deserved it."

> *I leave the residue of my estate to the Willie Nelson Partnership*

Erin frowned. Was that some kind of joke? She looked at Mrs. Peach. "The Willie Nelson Partnership?"

"He didn't even like country music!"

Things could change over thirty years. But a complete turnaround in his music preferences?

"That's kind of weird," Erin admitted. "Is it a charitable foundation or something? Maybe they give money to… up-and-coming musicians. Or maybe it's nothing to do with music."

Mrs. Peach stared at her. "He said he was going to give it to me. He said he was going to make a will and make sure that everything was all in order and that all the money he's earned over the past thirty years would come to me, because I was the one who deserved it!"

"And why would he turn around and do this a few days later?" Erin said. She looked for the date on the will. Maybe it was from years ago and he wanted to burn it in front of her as part of his bid to be reconciled. Show her that he really had turned over a new leaf.

But the date on the will was that day. He must have signed it just before returning home.

It didn't seem like he had turned over a new leaf at all. Disappearing without a word, coming home so drunk, changing his will to make sure that his wife was cut out of it instead of being his sole beneficiary. If he'd turned over a new leaf, it had been in the wrong direction.

"This is some kind of joke," Mrs. Peach said, echoing Erin's thoughts. "It's some kind of cruel joke. It can't be real. Doesn't a will have to be signed before two witnesses?" She gave a single, bleak laugh. "That's it. It isn't even a valid will. It's something he made up. He was going to show me this one, and then laugh, and show me the real one that he had a lawyer draw up."

"I don't know." Erin shrugged. "I *think* that wills have to be witnessed."

Mrs. Peach nodded. "I'll call Betty Thompson. She used to work for a law firm. She'll know."

Erin nodded.

Terry returned to the house, K9 panting at his side. Terry's eyes were sharp as he took them in, both gaping over the paper.

"What's that? What's going on?"

"Oh…" Erin wasn't sure she wanted to involve him in it. Did it make Mr. Peach's death look suspicious if he had just signed a new will that day? Even if it was a fake one? She didn't want to cause any complications for Mrs. Peach. "It's just… something that Mr. Peach left for Mrs. Peach. When I helped him in this morning, he said to give it to her…"

"Is it a letter?" Terry asked, stepping closer to them. "Please tell me it wasn't a suicide note. If I missed something about the scene…"

"No, it's not a suicide note," Erin said. "Just a legal document she needed."

"It's a will," Mrs. Peach told Terry, sabotaging Erin's attempts to make it look innocent. "He signed a new will. He said he was going to, but he said that he would leave everything to me! And this..." Mrs. Peach shook the piece of paper and made a hissing sound. "This is *not* what he said!"

"A will. Could I see that, please? Maybe put it down on the table. We should not touch it if it might be evidence."

"Evidence of what?" Mrs. Peach's voice rose in a shriek. "What are you saying?"

"I'm not saying anything," Terry's voice stayed calm and even and reassuring. "As I told you, we are required to investigate any unattended deaths. I just want to make sure that all aspects are considered."

He looked down at the will, his eyes going back and forth as he skimmed through it.

"Hmm. That is odd, isn't it?" Terry took out his phone and snapped a picture of it. "I am going to take it now, as evidence but, of course, you will get it back when we are finished. And I'd better take a closer look around here. Maybe also the room he was sleeping in? Not last night, obviously, but the night before?"

He looked at Mrs. Peach, and she grew red in the face. "Of course that's my bedroom, Officer Piper, and you don't have any right to search my personal things."

"I will not snoop. I'm just looking for anything he might have brought with him. Other clothing, a suitcase or briefcase. He must have brought a couple of things with him if he intended to be back here for any length of time."

Mrs. Peach shifted from foot to foot, wringing her hands together. "I don't have... he just had one bag with him."

"If I could just look at that, please."

"Well, I suppose."

She was lucky that Terry wasn't demanding to go through the entire room looking for anything shady Mr. Peach might have hidden. If he deemed Mr. Peach's death suspicious, Erin was sure he could have gotten a warrant to do so.

Terry nodded and headed toward the bedrooms with K9. Mrs. Peach got up immediately to direct him to Mr. Peach's bag. Erin waited for them to return, left stranded in the living room by herself. But at least Mr. Peach was no longer lying there.

The air was stale. She could still smell the liquor he had spilled. But it did not smell like the room a drunk had slept in for hours. That was a very different smell, traces of alcohol that had been sweated or breathed out into the air. Something about the whole thing just did not seem right. Mrs. Peach would agree with that, of course. She had not expected to lose her husband again so soon. She'd been ready to try again, to get accustomed to each other once more and start living their lives together again. Erin didn't know if she could have been so brave or forgiving. If a man walked out of her life for thirty years, she would not be quite so quick to welcome him back.

CHAPTER 29

*M*rs. Peach seemed okay with being left alone, since her husband's body had been removed from the house. Erin had the distinct impression that Mrs. Peach wanted to finish her cleaning for the day, which included the living room and the couch. That was why she had been unable to let Mr. Peach sleep any longer and had tried to wake him up. Now that they were out of there, Erin was sure she was going to be vacuuming the living room and the crevices of the couch and making sure that everything was crisp and clean and tidy.

In a similar vein, Erin didn't want to stay home, but wanted to finish out the day as she had planned, back at Auntie Clem's Bakery. Terry offered to drive her even though she had her car. Erin suspected it was because he wanted to talk to her on the way over. It meant that he would need to pick her up again after work if he didn't want her to walk, but then he would be home in good time, despite the investigation into Mr. Peach's death.

"She's a tough old bird," Terry told Erin in the quiet of the car. "She'll be okay."

"I know. She's used to living alone; I would be more worried about her getting used to living with someone else than I am with her being by herself. And she has friends she can call on."

"I want you to tell me everything you can about what happened this morning. From the time that you saw him to the time that you left the house. And anything else that might be related."

"Well…" Erin thought back to tidying up that morning and seeing Mr. Peach on the sidewalk. Had it really all just happened in one day? It seemed like a week ago. "I was getting ready for work when I saw someone stumbling along the sidewalk."

"Stumbling?"

"Yes. He was tripping and lurching and having a hard time keeping his balance. Then he fell right down. Then I could see who it was, and I went out to help him up."

Terry nodded, his eyes on the road. He didn't tell her that she should have been more careful, that she might have been putting herself in danger helping a man she didn't really know. She could have woken Terry up and gotten him to help.

But he didn't. He just listened. Erin went on, telling him how she had helped Mr. Peach to his feet, walked him to the door, and woken Mrs. Peach up. Then she had helped to get him settled for sleep and returned home.

Terry was nodding. "What did he have to say? Did he talk about where he had been or anything like that? Did he talk about the will?"

"He seemed to be worried about Mrs. Peach. Whether she was okay. He asked me that more than once. And he wanted me to give her the envelope. I didn't know it was his will. He never said."

"He didn't say anything about where he'd been drinking or who he had been drinking with? Nothing about where he had been the last twenty-four hours?"

"No. Nothing like that. I could tell he'd been drinking… you know, because he was walking so unsteadily, and he'd been in a fight, and had spilled alcohol on his clothes."

"What kind of alcohol?"

"I don't know," Erin said automatically. Then she paused, thinking about it. She wasn't much of a drinker herself, but she had known enough people over the years to know something about how the different drinks smelled. "Whiskey."

"For sure whiskey rather than beer or wine?" Terry checked.

Erin nodded. "They smell quite different."

"Okay. So he'd been drinking whiskey. Falling down drunk. Worried about his wife. Wanted to give her his new will that *excluded* her from inheriting from him."

"I don't understand that part at all. Why would he write a will that said that? Mrs. Peach says it was probably a joke. Do you think it could be?"

"No... not from what I saw. It looked like... it had been planned and written out to cover all of the legal requirements. If it had just been a joke, I don't think he would have gone to the trouble to put payment of debts or any of the other stuff in there."

"All of the legal requirements? You think that... it could be legally enforced?"

"I'm not an expert. We'll have to have a lawyer who knows all of the rules look at it to be sure. But yes... they call a handwritten will a holographic will. I have no idea why. But it is legal in most places. Certainly Tennessee allows holographic wills."

"But it wasn't witnessed. They have to be witnessed, don't they?"

Terry shook his head. "No, I don't think so. Just everything in the person's own handwriting, signed and dated. No witnesses required."

"Then how can we know it is even his handwriting? If no one saw him write it, how will they prove that?"

"They'll compare it to other samples of his writing. See if he was planning to make changes to his will. If he talked to people about it or mentioned what he planned to do."

"Mrs. Peach said that he had talked about it, but that he was going to put everything in her name. Not this... partnership."

"It's very odd," Terry said, shaking his head. "I agree with you that it seems to defy logic, why he would say one day that he was going to leave her everything and the next day, write a will that did the exact opposite."

"Yeah."

"We'll talk to his friends. See if he talked to anyone else about it. Find out who he was out drinking with. Sometimes... people just do weird things. You can't explain it. Maybe he did think it was a joke and thought that he would have a chance to undo it later. Maybe he had another will in another pocket that was meant to replace it. We'll know more after the medical examiner has a chance to examine the body and tell us what he finds."

They were stopped in the parking lot behind Auntie Clem's. It didn't take very long to get there and they had spent more time talking than they had driving.

"Well… hope the rest of your day is quieter," Terry said, leaning over to give her a kiss. "Though I don't imagine it will be, once word gets around that Mrs. Peach's husband died and that you were the last one to see him alive."

"Ugh," Erin groaned. "I hadn't even thought about that."

Erin explained to Vic and Bella where she had been and about Mr. Peach's sudden death during a lull. Luckily, word didn't appear to have gotten around yet, or there would have been no lull in which to discuss it. Erin gave them all of the details she could.

"Oh, poor Mr. Peach," Vic said. "Poor Mrs. Peach!"

"Yeah. I feel terrible for her. She's lived alone all of these years, and then she gets her husband back… only to lose him again right away. I can't understand why he went back to her in the first place."

"He wanted something from her," Bella suggested. "Or he was running away from someone and couldn't be at his own house, so he figured what better place to hide than with his estranged wife? No one would expect him to go back to her after so many years."

"I don't know about that." Erin shook her head. "Exactly who would be trying to harm him?"

"You don't know that no one was. Just because he didn't say so. Would you tell everyone if someone was after you? Especially if you'd been involved in something… shady?"

Erin looked at Vic. "No… probably not," she admitted.

"So, maybe someone was after him, and he went to Mrs. Peach's house to hide out."

"Maybe. I suppose it's possible."

CHAPTER 30

*M*rs. Foster came in toward the end of the day, which meant that she had all of the children with her, including Erin's favorite customer, young Peter Foster. A couple of years had passed since he had first come into her bakery, so he was older and more mature than he had been that first day when he had drilled her about her gluten-free products. He helped his mother to take care of the younger children in the brood the best he could and had been excited to finally welcome another boy into the family after three younger sisters.

Mrs. Foster often came during the school day so that she only had to have the youngest children with her. However, the older kids still had to come to get their kid's club cookies at some point. Peter was a master negotiator in getting his mother to buy additional baking that he "needed" for breakfast, lunch, after-school snacks, pizza dinners, and special occasions.

"Hi, how is everybody?" Erin asked as the kids swarmed up to the display case and got all kinds of sticky fingerprints on it as they picked out their cookies. But fingerprints wiped away, and Erin didn't get the same kick out of seeing her less-enthusiastic customers. It was always fun to see the children.

"We're going to go to the Statehood Day picnic," Peter offered, standing on tiptoes to make himself taller. "Are you going to have a booth there?"

"You bet. We'll have lots of fun treats there."

"And are you going to enter the baking contest?"

Erin smiled over at Vic, who was at the register. "We're getting it all planned out. I don't suppose that we'll win, but we're making something good!"

"At the Fall Fair, you won a cruise," Peter remembered. "You went to Alaska."

"That's right," Erin agreed. That had been an *interesting* vacation.

"Did you see puffins? And seals? And polar bears?"

"We saw lots of puffins and seals. No polar bears. And we saw whales too."

"Cool!" Peter drew the word out, breathing excitement into it.

"Pick what you want now," Mrs. Foster instructed, bouncing Alan in the baby sling. The baby was looking a little happier than he had been. He was getting bigger, his face fat and round, and Mrs. Foster thought that she finally had his allergies under control. "I need to make my order, and we need to get home for supper. Everyone will be crabby if they don't eat soon."

"But we're going to have cookies," Peter pointed out, "so *we* won't be crabby."

"But I still will. So tell Miss Erin what you want."

Peter told the little girls to go first. Traci shrieked tearful directions to the one cookie she wanted, until Erin finally put her hand on it, and then squealed with delight when it was handed to her. The other girls were less challenging, giving her their orders politely. After some more deliberation, Peter finally picked a chocolate cookie with white chocolate chips. Mrs. Foster gave her order in a tired voice. At least the children were occupied with their cookies and Alan was quiet, sucking on his fingers.

Erin saw Beaver come into the bakery. Instantly, she remembered that Beaver had been looking for information on Mr. Peach and that Erin and Terry were supposed to tell her if they found out anything about him. Beaver had probably heard by now that Mr. Peach was dead and knew that Erin had not bothered to contact her when he had reappeared. Erin had no idea whether Terry had informed her of the fact or whether she had found out through other channels.

She bit her lip and finished gathering Mrs. Foster's order together. When they said their goodbyes and left, Beaver turned the door sign over to Closed and turned the bolt on the door. Vic looked at Erin, brows raised. She would normally clear the cash register at that point, but Erin suspected that Beaver wanted to talk to her alone. Or at least with some semblance of privacy.

"Why don't you see if Bella needs any help in the kitchen? I'll close up here."

Vic nodded and retreated into the kitchen, leaving Erin and Beaver alone.

"Been a long day?" Beaver questioned.

Erin shrugged. Most of her days were long. "I'm sorry I didn't call you about Mr. Peach coming back. I wasn't thinking about it this morning. And he… wasn't in any shape for visitors anyway."

"And now it is too late."

"I didn't have any way of knowing he was going to die in his sleep."

"No. But unfortunately, now we've lost a witness in the prison break."

"Do you really think that he knew something about the prison break?"

Although it was hard to believe that his showing up at Mrs. Peach's house when there had been escaped prisoners in the area was entirely coincidental, Erin couldn't imagine Mr. Peach having had anything to do with the prison break. He was just a pastor, not a criminal. What reason would he have to be involved in it?

"He didn't just know something," Beaver said. "We have proof that he was involved."

People had repeatedly said that there was an inside man. Was Mr. Peach that man? Someone who had planned or assisted with the prison break?

But the same question returned. If he had been involved, then why would he have directed the escapees to Bald Eagle Falls? Especially since that was where his wife was? He had shown that he cared about her and had been concerned with her safety. He wouldn't have deliberately put her in the way of two violent criminals.

"You're sure?" she asked Beaver.

"An audit has been made of all of the key logs during the escape. I'm afraid that it can't be denied that Pastor Peach was complicit in the prison break."

"Maybe they stole his key card. Or maybe he was coerced. They... made threats to his wife to make him do what they wanted him to."

"Maybe. We can't ask him that now."

"I'm sorry."

"It's not your fault. It was too late by the time you brought him home. From what I gather, he wasn't that coherent at the time and he never woke up."

"Yeah."

"Aside from his wife, you are probably the person that had the most contact with him. I'd like to run through the conversations or interactions that you had with him to see if I can glean anything from them."

Erin sighed. She had already talked to Terry about it but, of course, Beaver would want to hear it straight from her rather than through someone else.

"Yes... do we have to do it now? Or can it wait until I've had a chance to get home and get settled?"

"Tonight, then? I don't want to put it off for too long."

"Yes. In a couple of hours."

Beaver nodded and chomped on her gum. "Appreciate that."

She turned back to the door and, in an instant, she was gone. Erin re-locked the door and finished clearing the till.

CHAPTER 31

*E*rin had time for a quick dinner with Terry before Beaver showed up at the house. The animals had been fed and were snoozing or bathing and Erin was just putting the last of the dishes into the dishwasher when Beaver knocked at the door. Terry let her in and they exchanged polite greetings. Terry didn't sound too excited to be sharing further information about the investigation with Beaver. Maybe he was feeling territorial and was irritated by the fact that Beaver hadn't given him what he felt was a fair exchange of information.

"If I could talk to Erin first," Beaver said, "then I need to have a more in-depth conversation with you."

Terry shrugged. "Fine."

Erin joined them in the living room. She and Terry sat down on the couch and Beaver took one of the chairs. She leaned back in her seat, chewing her gum. Erin was glad that she didn't tip the chair onto its back legs. She looked like she would if she thought she could get away with it.

"So, tell me about the first time you saw Gregory Peach," she told Erin.

Erin thought back. She told Beaver about first seeing Mr. Peach in Mrs. Peach's backyard, though she hadn't known who he was at the time. Even though she didn't think that was the information Beaver wanted. Beaver said to start with the first time she had seen him, so she did.

Beaver nodded encouragingly, listening intently to every word and chewing her gum slowly.

"Has anyone searched the yard and shed to see if he hid something out there?" she asked Terry.

"I took a quick look when he was missing to make sure that nothing had happened to him. But it wasn't a thorough search. I couldn't see anything out of place. But at the time, I was really only looking for a body."

Beaver nodded. "Might be a good idea."

"I'm not sure Mrs. Peach is going to give you permission to search the yard and shed. I had a hard enough time getting her to agree to show me his bag."

"If she doesn't agree, I can get a warrant."

"You think you have enough for a warrant?"

"When he's implicated in the prison break? You bet. I can get anything I want at this point. Only way it could get better is if he was a terrorist."

"He's not a terrorist," Erin said.

"This is based on your limited experience of seeing or talking to him what, three times?"

Erin set her jaw. "Yes."

Beaver's eyes danced. "Well, I happen to agree with you. I don't think he was a terrorist. I'm just saying that I can get into whatever place or records I want if we're dealing with a terrorist."

"He was a nice man."

"I think he was probably protecting his wife, so yes, he was here for an altruistic reason. If he wasn't also here to cover up his secrets."

"He must have been forced to use his key card as part of the escape," Erin reiterated what she had told Beaver at the bakery. "He wouldn't do that voluntarily. He was a pastor. I know they're not perfect, but he's someone who is supposed to help the prisoners with their spiritual lives. And he's been there for years without any suspicions being raised about him. Why would he help with a prison break after being there for thirty years?"

"We'll come back to that. In the meantime, maybe you could tell me about when you saw him next."

Erin described taking the sparkling grape juice over to the couple and what she could remember of her conversation with Mr. Peach. It hadn't been a long conversation; there really wasn't much to tell. And there was even less to tell about helping him home when he had reappeared, so drunk he could barely walk.

She did her best to describe his condition to Beaver, to recall what he'd had to say—mostly concerns about whether his wife was okay—and about him giving her the sealed envelope to give to his wife.

Beaver sat and chewed her gum thoughtfully, clearly trying to put all of the pieces together into something that made sense. A whole picture instead of just the fragments they had.

"He had to have known what was in the envelope and that it would make his wife unhappy," she said finally.

Erin nodded. She was having trouble making sense of that as well.

Beaver looked at Terry. "It's too early to have had a proper handwriting comparison done, but did you have any samples of Mr. Peach's writing to give you an idea of whether it was actually his writing?"

"The penitentiary scanned and emailed over a few pieces of correspondence that they had on file. Mr. Peach wrote recommendations and reference letters for Kevin Hatch or other inmates who had left the prison. Incident forms. That kind of thing. It looks the same to me. But I'm no expert."

"Huh. And you don't have any thoughts about this partnership that he left his estate to?"

"Not yet. We're looking into it. But partnerships are not required to register anywhere, making it impossible to do a record search. And we're assuming that it is an entity operating in Tennessee. Maybe they own one of the memorabilia stores in Nashville or something like that. But it's going to take a lot of legwork and phone calls to find out if that is the case."

Beaver looked at Erin. "And there was nothing else? No impressions? Things that didn't fit? Something that surprised you or made you uneasy?"

"Well…" Erin frowned, the muscles in her forehead tense and sore, "I don't know. It's hard to put my finger on anything."

"That sounds like a yes. There is something that didn't feel quite right."

Erin pressed her lips together, thinking about it. She wished that Beaver would spit out her gum or at least stop chewing it so vigorously. It was distracting.

"I guess… just… the whole thing."

CHAPTER 32

*B*eaver raised one eyebrow. Terry turned and looked at Erin, frowning.

"What do you mean, the whole thing? You didn't tell me that you had any doubts about anything."

"I know. It's just…" Erin shook her head, trying to put it into words. "It isn't any one thing that I can put my finger on. I just felt like something was off, that he wasn't really drunk."

"You think he was faking it? And if he was faking it, then what did he die of? That was just a coincidence?"

"Officer Piper," Beaver drawled his name, "let's just slow it down. I'd like to hear what Miss Erin has to say. Without her being backed into a corner or having to defend herself."

"Well, I didn't mean to…" Terry sputtered, his face turning red. "I just was asking. I'm surprised, Erin, that's all."

"I know."

Erin was glad for Beaver's intervention, because she didn't know the answers to Terry's questions. She wasn't even sure how to put any of her doubts or impressions into words.

"I don't think… he was faking anything. I'm just not sure that he was drunk. He was having trouble walking and wasn't very coherent… and he smelled like whiskey. But… it seemed a little *off*."

160

Erin thought about it. Both Terry and Beaver remained quiet, giving her time to think it through. She replayed the scene in her head several times. It had been such a brief incident, but there was so much information to process.

"I've lived with drunks. And when they were really impaired, they would stand with their feet wide and sway. And when they walked, they had their feet wide and went from side to side, and they stumbled sideways." Erin looked at Beaver and then at Terry to see what they thought of this. Both of them were nodding, recognizing the description. "Mr. Peach was lurching and stumbling… but his feet weren't wide and he wasn't moving side to side."

"What was he doing?" Beaver asked.

"He was… taking small steps. Mincing."

They all thought about that, but no one came up with any possible explanation. Beaver chewed her gum slowly and thoughtfully, like a cow chewing its cud.

Terry asked, "Anything else?"

"I don't know. When we were there at noon, after he had died… the room didn't smell like he was drunk."

Terry shook his head, chuckling. "I could smell the alcohol. You certainly should have been able to with your sensitive nose. Maybe you have a cold."

"I could smell alcohol on his clothes," Erin clarified. "But someone who's had a lot to drink, they sweat alcohol, and they breathe it out. So the room stinks. It's in the air, this foul, sweaty, drunk-breath smell."

"And it didn't smell like that." Terry thought about it. "I didn't notice that… but you could be right. I smelled that sharp alcohol smell, but not *body* smell. But maybe he died shortly after you brought him home. If he died in the early morning, then by noon, that smell could have dissipated."

Erin nodded. "Yeah. You're right. That's probably all it was."

"I'm not arguing your premise. I'm saying that you're right… but maybe there's an easy explanation."

"I know."

"The medical examiner will be able to tell us his stomach contents and blood alcohol level," Beaver said. "Then we'll know for sure whether he was drunk or whether it was something else." She shrugged. "Maybe another drug. Not alcohol, but something else."

"Maybe," Erin agreed.

"What else could you smell?" Terry asked. "Did you notice anything?"

"Not really... I mean... he smelled like a bathroom. Really bad. Drunks do. They have... accidents. But I could smell soap too, so maybe he'd tried to clean himself up. And... cat food."

"Cat food?" Beaver repeated.

"Something like that. It was faint, under everything else. I don't know what else to associate it with. Maybe... he went back to his house and fed his cats. Or a neighborhood stray. It was just faint, but I don't remember it being there when I talked to him the first time. The night that I took the sparkling grape juice over."

"Well... we'll keep that in mind," Terry said, though he didn't sound too sure he thought any of it was important. And it probably wasn't. Erin couldn't explain any of it.

"You said you were going to have Moose River do a welfare check at his residence out there," Beaver addressed Terry.

"Yeah, I did ask them to. Of course, he wasn't there."

"Did he have cats?"

"Uh... not that they said, but I didn't ask."

Beaver didn't say anything. Terry took the hint and pulled out his phone. Erin watched as he found Jack Ward's name and tapped on it. She snuggled into Terry, wishing that they were alone, relaxing, without having to talk about drunks or dead people or any danger that might remain from Davis, who had still not been found.

Terry put the phone on speaker and set it on his knee while it rang.

"Jack Ward," Jack answered brusquely, then apparently saw the caller ID, "Oh, Piper. What's up? Did you find your missing person?"

"We did, actually. He showed up at the wife's house."

"There you go. All's well that ends well."

"Well... he died. So, no."

"Died? What happened? Not while in custody...?" Jack asked with concern.

"No. At his wife's, sleeping on the couch. I should tell you that you're on speakerphone. Sorry. Erin and Rohilda Beaven are with me."

"Ladies," Jack acknowledged. "So.. what do you need from me? Sounds like this happened in your jurisdiction."

"Yes. It did. I just had one question for you. When you did the welfare check... did Mr. Peach have any pets?"

"Pets? No."

"You're sure?"

"It's part of our protocol. If someone is missing and has pets, we don't just leave them in the house to starve. We see that a family member or neighbor takes them or call a rescue group. So, no. No pets."

"Great, I appreciate that. That's all I wanted to know."

"That's it? Well, have a nice evening, y'all."

Terry ended the call. "He didn't have cats, so it must point to something else."

"I'm not even sure it *was* cat food," Erin said.

"I'm familiar with your nose... I'd say if you think it was cat food, then it must be. Or something darn close."

Erin shrugged, not sure what to say to this. He had more confidence in her than she did. She wasn't sure that it had been anything like cat food; that was just what had come to her mind. And what did that mean? That he had some kind of disease that made him smell bad, and that was what had killed him? That he had rotten teeth or she was catching a whiff of what he had eaten for supper? It didn't necessarily have anything to do with his death. And his death didn't necessarily have anything to do with the prison break and Bruel's death. It could just be a coincidence.

"Why don't you go in the kitchen and make us some tea and cookies?" Beaver suggested. "I need to talk to Officer Piper alone."

Erin was irritated by the suggestion. There was no reason to be upset; of course Beaver couldn't talk in front of a civilian about her investigation. But Beaver had said she needed to speak with Erin and then was summarily dismissing her.

But she got up without complaint and walked into the kitchen.

As she put on the kettle, she realized that while Beaver had asked her to leave the room, she was making no attempt to lower her voice so that she wouldn't be overheard.

"We got access to his financial records through the prison break investigation," Beaver told Terry.

"Is that relevant to his death?"

"We won't know until your investigation progresses further. I suspect that both of our cases will be intertwined."

"So, what did you find?"

"Prison pastors do not make a lot of money. That probably doesn't surprise you."

"No."

"But the amount that he had in his bank account was significant."

"He told his wife that he'd been saving for thirty years and would arrange to leave his nest egg to her."

"He lied on both counts. Looking at the historical bank records, he did not build it up gradually, one paycheck at a time. In fact, he spent more than he made from the penitentiary. He had significant cash deposits."

The kettle started to whistle, but Erin had no intention of interrupting the discussion. She worked slowly, ears pricked to hear what else Beaver had to say about her investigation.

"Cash deposits," Terry repeated.

"Yes."

"Did he have a second job? Something that paid under the table?"

"Something. But he spent the majority of his time at the prison. He wouldn't have had a lot of time to spend at another job. And the cash deposits were more than his regular paychecks. So the chances that it was a legitimate business are... low. Sure, he could have had a hobby making and selling high-end handcrafted furniture or some other venture, but I don't think that's what was happening."

"Where do you think it came from?"

"I don't know yet. We are investigating. But if he was complicit in the prison break, that would suggest that he was willing to work outside the law."

"Smuggling contraband into the penitentiary?"

"Possibly. It may take a while to figure out exactly what he was selling and to who. But we'll figure it out."

Erin couldn't hear Terry's murmured response.

"How's that tea coming along?" Beaver asked.

Erin grinned. Apparently, the ostensibly confidential portion was over and she could again be in the room. She grabbed the tea tray and cookies and took them out to the living room.

CHAPTER 33

*A*fter the Sunday morning ladies' tea, Erin had the rest of the day to do some planning, and she and Vic were going to take a run at making a gluten-free slab pie to make sure that the crust would hold up. And maybe catch up on some accounting if she had the time.

As she walked from the garage to the back door, her phone rang. Erin pulled it out and checked the display. It was Mrs. Peach. Erin answered the call.

"Hi, Mrs. Peach. How are you doing today?"

"I'm sorry to bother you, Erin, but I saw that you were back…"

"Yes, I'm taking some time off today."

"You wouldn't want to spend your time off running me around town…"

Erin thought about all of the tasks Mrs. Peach must have in the wake of her husband's death to get things in order, notify friends and family, and begin making funeral arrangements. Erin had seen enough deaths from the perspective of a care worker to know how overwhelming it could be for the next of kin.

Especially a widow like Mrs. Peach, who didn't have any children or other family to help her manage it all.

"Of course I would. Where do you need to go?"

"It's your day off. You must have a hundred things to get done."

"They'll get done or they'll wait. Do you need to go into the city?"

That would be where they'd have sent Mr. Peach's body. Erin didn't know if she'd have to go to a funeral home in the city to arrange for transportation.

"No, no. Just a few places around town. Maybe that wouldn't be so bad…"

"I'd be happy to help. Do you have a schedule? Certain places you have to be at certain times?"

"No, most of them just said 'come by any time.'"

"Okay. We should probably go earlier rather than later, when you still have energy and things won't be as busy. Do you want to make up a list and I'll pop over?"

"Thank you so much, Erin. That would be such a load off my mind."

"I'm happy to help. I'll be there in a few minutes."

After hanging up, Erin called Vic to let her know she wouldn't be available until the afternoon and ran through the top items in her planner to see if there was anything she could dash off. She could, perhaps, run a few errands of her own while she was taking Mrs. Peach around town. She turned to her list of shopping and errands to do and took note of the various accumulated tasks. Many stores would be closed on Sunday. But she could fit a few in and around Mrs. Peach's errands. She was probably going to some of the same places.

Erin put her planner back in her purse and walked to Mrs. Peach's front door. She knocked and opened the door. She heard Mrs. Peach's invitation to let herself in, so she did. No point in making Mrs. Peach get up to answer the door.

"Good morning, Mrs. Peach."

The older woman was sitting on the couch where her husband had died, writing out a list on a pad of paper on the coffee table.

"You don't know how much this means to me. It's such a relief to have someone to drive me around. Normally, I get around just fine on foot and the bus, but there is so much to do, and I can't spread it out like I normally would."

"I believe it." Erin went over to her and sat beside her on the couch to look at the list. She felt a little creepy sitting there where a man had died, but she knew that she would stop feeling anxious about it if she just acted normally. "Do you want to go to the lawyer's first? You don't have a set time to meet?"

She was surprised that the law office was open, but maybe they used Sunday as an overflow day.

"Yes, it would probably be best to go early. I'm sure they don't spend all day waiting around for old ladies."

"That sounds good. Maybe while you are meeting with the lawyers, I can—"

"Could you come in with me? I'm worried that everything they say is going to go over my head. I need someone who can tell me what steps to take… in normal English."

Erin grinned. "Well, I can't guarantee that I'll understand it any better. Didn't you say that Betty Thompson used to work for a law firm?"

"Oh yes, she did," Mrs. Peach agreed, her voice getting a bit higher. "Do you think she would come with us?"

"You could ask her if she's free. If there's a better time, we could schedule it for when it would work for her."

"I'll give her a call."

Mrs. Peach pulled an old-style landline phone with push buttons closer to her and carefully pressed them one by one to call Betty without looking up her number. Erin hardly knew any phone numbers by heart. Her phone did all the work for her.

"Betty? It's Gladys."

Erin only half-listened while Mrs. Peach made arrangements with Betty, looking at the rest of the errands on Mrs. Peach's list and comparing it mentally with her own. She looked back at Mrs. Peach when she placed the receiver into the cradle.

"Is she going to go with us?"

"Yes, she said she would be happy to." Mrs. Peach sounded almost cheerful. It was obviously a big relief for her to know that they would have someone with expertise with them. Someone who could tell her what to do in normal English. Erin smiled.

"Great. Now, or did you have to arrange a later time?"

"She wants to go now. Get it over with. When I have that out of the way, I will feel so much better. Right now, it feels like such a big burden."

Erin nodded. "Okay. Do you want me to pull the car around back or front? Which one is easier for you?"

"The front is best."

"Okay. I'll be right back."

In no time, they were all in the car and on their way to the lawyer's office. Erin felt a little embarrassed trying to make everyone comfortable in the bug. It wasn't really built with little old ladies in mind. But Betty Thompson and Mrs. Peach giggled and seemed to be enjoying themselves.

"You should see how many people we could squeeze into this little car when we had a church do when Clementine was still around," Betty chuckled. "Of course... we were all a little younger and more flexible then!"

Erin tried to picture all of the old ladies carpooling together, laughing like teenagers. "It sounds like a lot of fun."

"Oh, it was, dear. It was. One of the best times of my life."

It was good to know that Clementine had had such nice friends. Erin hadn't really thought about who her aunt had socialized with. She pictured her spending all of her nights at home, alone in the house, but there was no reason she couldn't have gone out with friends regularly. Movies, church events, painting the town red...

"It must be in this building," Erin said, peering at one of the storefronts that had office suites up above.

"Yes, this is the right one," Mrs. Peach confirmed.

"Perfect." Erin got out and helped each of the ladies out, making sure they were steady on their feet before letting go. Hopefully, there was an elevator to the second floor. She didn't want to be trying to get either one of the women up a full flight of stairs.

Luckily, there was.

The lawyer, a Mr. Benz, was a little surprised to be dealing with the three of them instead of just Mrs. Peach, but he was gracious and found a meeting room for them and offered everyone coffee or juice. Eventually, everyone was provided for and sitting down.

Benz already knew about the death of Mr. Peach, so he wasn't surprised when Mrs. Peach produced a copy of the will.

"Officer Piper gave me a copy. He still has the original," she explained as she passed him a photocopy of the handwritten will. "He said that it is a holographic will. And that they are legal in Tennessee."

"Well, if they meet certain requirements," Benz agreed, taking it from her and scanning it. "And... this does appear to be in order."

"So that replaces any other wills that he has written."

"Yes, it does," he agreed, giving Mrs. Peach a smile. He clearly thought that this was what Mrs. Peach wanted.

At Mrs. Peach's unsmiling return gaze, he dropped his eyes back down to the will, doing more than giving it a cursory skim this time. His eyes stopped when he reached the Willie Nelson part and he made a little noise of surprise.

"This will... does not include you as an heir," he observed. Brilliant. Even without legal expertise, Erin had figured that out.

"No." Mrs. Peach agreed. "And no one has any clue what the Willie Nelson Partnership is."

Betty gasped.

They all turned to look at her. Erin thought it was simply surprise at Mr. Peach not leaving his estate all to his wife. But Betty leaned forward, looking at the piece of paper.

"The Willie Nelson Partnership? But I know who that is!"

CHAPTER 34

*I*t was their turn to be shocked.

"You know who the Willie Nelson Partnership is?" Erin repeated, stunned. From what she had heard from Terry and Beaver, finding anything out about the participants in a partnership could be challenging since partnerships were not required to be filed with the corporate authorities like a company was.

Benz looked at Betty too, curious about the turn in events.

Betty looked at the will as if she weren't sure whether to believe what she was seeing. "Yes. Isn't that odd! The firm that I used to work for set up that partnership."

She looked at Benz, who raised an eyebrow.

"Of course… there is client confidentiality. I can't really say anything about it without the client's permission."

"Is the client still around?"

"Oh, yes."

"Who is it?" Mrs. Peach asked. "You can tell us that much, can't you? You don't have to tell us anything confidential about how it was set up or what it was supposed to do, but you can tell us *who* it is, can't you?"

Betty shook her head. "No… but I can tell you that it wasn't anything to do with Willie Nelson, the singer."

Erin laughed and shook her head. "We kind of figured that much out already. Why would Mr. Peach leave all of his money to someone like Willie Nelson, who is already so fabulously wealthy?"

Betty pursed her lips. Erin got the uncomfortable feeling that Betty had been expecting a different response and had been disappointed. Erin tried to pay better attention in order to pick up on any nuances that she might have missed.

"What do you know about partnerships?" Betty asked Mrs. Peach.

"Well… nothing, really. I don't have any legal training and we never had a business of our own."

"A partnership is set up when two people—or more—are working together on a venture," Betty explained. "Two people," she repeated.

Erin got it. "Willie and Nelson! Not Willie Nelson, but two different men named Willie and Nelson."

Betty nodded, looking satisfied. Then Erin's joy over having solved the riddle disappeared, her heart plunging downward.

"I only know of one Willie around here. Willie Andrews."

Betty didn't give anything away.

"I guess we could ask him," Mrs. Peach said. "He'll tell us whether this is his partnership or not."

"But why would Mr. Peach leave everything to Willie? And whoever Nelson is."

Again, something twinged in her brain and she thought about Nelson, someone Willie might have a business venture with. She remembered Nelson Dyson talking with Willie about firewalls and Nelson setting up his own organization within the Dyson organized crime family. Or maybe outside of it, she wasn't sure. Willie said that he helped Nelson with computers and electronic toys.

And apparently, he and Willie had set up a partnership together.

"Nelson Dyson?" she asked Betty breathlessly. "Is that the Nelson in the partnership?"

"I can't tell you anything about it. You'll have to talk to the partners yourself." But she gave a slight nod that told Erin she was on the right track.

"Willie Andrews and Nelson Dyson?" Mrs. Peach said. "I don't understand what that has to do with my husband or why he would leave money to them. If they set up this business venture, they must have plenty of money. The Dysons… they're not exactly scrounging for pennies."

"I don't know of any connection with your husband," Betty responded. "I don't know why he would leave his estate to them."

"It doesn't make any sense."

Benz spoke up. He nodded to the copy of the will. "At any rate, that appears to be a legal will. If you want to challenge it in court, you can try. But it won't be easy. The fact that he didn't at least leave you the house means that you can challenge it under the Right of Surviving Spouse clause." He frowned and rubbed the back of his neck. "When did you marry? Was it before 1977?"

Mrs. Peach nodded. "Yes." Her eyes were watery. "We've been—we had been—married for fifty years."

"Then you have dower rights too. That gives you one third of his estate."

"But I have to go to court?"

"You'll have to draft a court application, yes. But you don't have to stand up and testify in front of a jury or anything like that. It's just a statement of facts for the judge."

Mrs. Peach looked at Erin and then at Betty, her eyes worried.

"You should do that," Betty asserted with a firm nod. "You have rights under the law. He can't just give everything away to this partnership. It's just like stealing what's rightfully yours."

Erin nodded her agreement. "That's not fair. You're the one who stayed married to him all of those years. You deserve it. You don't want to lose your home."

"No… I always planned to stay there for as long as I could take care of myself. And when Gregory came back, I thought that it would be both of us together again. I don't understand why he had to drink. We were never drinkers."

Erin kept her mouth shut, not wanting to suggest that maybe it had been something else. Though she had her doubts about things not smelling right, she didn't have any proof that Mr. Peach *hadn't* died from alcohol poisoning.

"Have you heard anything back from the medical examiner yet?" Erin asked.

Though she supposed that if there was anything strange, the ME wouldn't report it to the next of kin, but to the police.

Mrs. Peach shook her head. "I've been trying to call them to find out when we can get Gregory's body back, but they have not been returning my calls. The lady who answers the phone keeps saying they'll let me know… but they don't. So what am I supposed to do?"

"I suppose these things can take time. Hopefully, it won't be much longer."

CHAPTER 35

$\mathcal{E}$rin was back from driving Mrs. Peach in enough time to bake with Vic. They reviewed Erin's pie crust recipe, even though both of them could probably make it in their sleep, and assembled the ingredients.

"About three times a single crust recipe for one slab?" Vic guessed.

"Maybe four. Better to make too much."

"Okay, four times. We do that all the time at Auntie Clem's. And you think it will be strong enough that the middle pieces will hold together?"

Erin looked at the cookie sheet that they planned to bake the slab pie on. "I hope so. We won't know until we give it a try."

Vic nodded. "Yep, you're right. When you're right, you're right."

They began preparing the pastry. Erin looked at Vic sideways as they worked.

"Do you remember Nelson Dyson?" she asked tentatively.

Vic blinked at her. "Remember him? The three of us bearding the lion to try to rescue Charley from the Dyson clan? Yes, I think I remember that."

"Well, except he wasn't the lion. The big boss, I mean. He kind of... does his own thing. Remember?"

"Sure I remember," Vic agreed. "What about him?"

"How well does Willie know him? It seemed like they knew each other fairly well."

"I don't know. I don't get involved in Willie's businesses. He likes to do his own thing, and I do mine. I suppose he probably thinks that I'm not very motivated since I only work at one job, and he's got all of these different things going on. But I like the bakery. And it's enough to pay my expenses."

Erin nodded. She didn't pay her employees large salaries, but she tried to be fair about it. And Vic had lived as Erin's tenant rent-free the whole time that she'd been working with Erin. So it was *like* having a higher-paying job.

"Why?" Vic asked. "What made you think about Nelson Dyson?"

"I just wondered how much Willie worked with him. It sounded like he was pretty involved in Nelson's computers and security."

"Yeah, I guess."

"But you don't know anything about it. How often they see each other or what the terms are, or even what they are working on."

Vic raised an eyebrow and looked at Erin. "What business is it of yours? Or even mine?"

"Well... I know. It isn't. I'm just worried... don't you worry about him still being involved with the Dysons? I mean... he said that he wasn't with them anymore, that he wasn't associated with them at all and didn't do jobs for them. But then there's this thing with Nelson, where clearly, he is involved somehow. With an organized crime figure."

"Nelson isn't the Godfather."

"I know that. And he said that he's setting up his own network separate from the Dysons... but that's kind of worrying too."

"Why would you be worried about it?"

"If he's splitting off into his own faction, then aren't his dad and the rest of the Dysons going to be mad? They're not going to want him infringing on their business, trying to take away their territory. They'll be enemies, just like the Dysons and the Jacksons, if he splits away from them."

"So? Let them fight with each other."

Erin studiously cut lard into the flour mixture. Vic waited for an answer, and when one wasn't forthcoming, pushed it further.

"Erin? What's going on? Why are you suddenly asking all of these questions? I thought you didn't want to know anything about the clans or what they were doing."

"I don't. It's just… Willie and Nelson. Don't you see? The Willie Nelson Partnership. It's a venture between Willie and Nelson Dyson."

Vic's jaw dropped. "What?" She shook her head. "Where did you get that idea? There's no way, Erin. No way. Willie is not in business with Nelson that way. He just helps him to buy and set up his computers and equipment. That's all."

"How do you know that? Because that's what Willie told you? What if he's not telling you the full truth?"

"The Willie Nelson Partnership. No." Vic shook her head. "It's a joke. Can you see either one of them picking a name like that? No."

"And Mr. Peach left all of his estate to the Willie Nelson Partnership. Do you know if he and Willie even knew each other?"

"No. I told him about Mr. Peach coming back to his wife after thirty years, and he thought it was an interesting story, but he didn't talk about Mr. Peach as if he knew him at all."

"Maybe Mr. Peach only knew Nelson."

"I don't think there's any connection," Vic said dismissively.

"There has to be a connection. He wouldn't put them in the will if he didn't know the name of their venture."

"You don't know that this Willie Nelson Partnership has anything to do with Willie. That's just speculation."

"But Betty was working as a legal assistant when it was set up. She knows."

"Did she tell you it was Willie and Nelson?"

"Well… no. She couldn't. Because of confidentiality."

Vic nodded triumphantly. "So you don't know. You're only guessing."

"Well, Willie will be able to say whether it is him or not."

"Even if it was," Vic argued, "that doesn't mean that Willie had anything to do with any of the stuff that has happened. The prison break or Bruel being killed or Mr. Peach dying. None of that has anything to do with Willie."

Erin nodded and decided that she had gone far enough with it. She didn't want to alienate Willie and Vic.

She just wanted to know what was going on. And so far, she didn't feel like she was getting any farther ahead.

CHAPTER 36

It was nice having Terry home every evening. Erin knew that she had better enjoy it while it lasted, because it wouldn't be too long until he told her that the danger had clearly passed and that Davis was long gone. There would be no need for him to avoid night shifts if he knew that Erin was safe.

So she did her best to make their evenings relaxed and comfortable and that they spent plenty of quality time with each other. Even the animals seemed to be more relaxed with him there on a regular schedule.

Erin's phone rang. She looked down at it, half-expecting it to be Vic, maybe with Willie's feedback on the slab pie. Erin and Terry had eaten some for dessert, and the pieces had held together well. Erin was pleased with the results. With the base recipe established, she could start experimenting with fancier variations and plan something really good for the Statehood Day picnic.

But the caller ID said it was Mrs. Peach. Erin suppressed a groan. She wanted to help her neighbor, but she also wanted to be left alone and have time to relax at the end of the day. Mrs. Peach had lived on her own for thirty years. She was a strong, independent woman and shouldn't have to rely on Erin for everything in the wake of her husband's death.

But she pushed the negative thoughts aside, put a smile on her face, and answered the phone with a warm, polite greeting.

"Good evening, Mrs. Peach. How are you managing?"

"Well, I'm fine, I'm fine." Her voice quavered a little. Erin didn't know whether it was because of fatigue and age or something else was bothering her. She wasn't sure she wanted to know what else might be wrong. She was happy to help, but it was still a burden, and she was already putting a lot of time and energy in at the bakery.

Erin got up from the couch and walked to the bedroom, where she could talk privately and not disturb Terry by talking over the show he was watching on the TV.

"That's good. How can I help you?"

"I finally got a call back from the medical examiner in the city."

"Oh." Erin nodded to herself. "So are they releasing Mr. Peach now?"

"Yes, they said they would. But… they said he did not die from the alcohol."

It felt as if something had clicked into place in Erin's brain. Finally, someone had confirmed the uneasiness she'd been feeling about the last time she had seen Mr. Peach alive. She knew it. She had known that he hadn't been drunk, or at least not that drunk. So what was it? Had he been faking it? Giving them all an easy explanation of why he had been MIA?

"Was there any alcohol in his system?"

Mrs. Peach didn't answer right away. The seconds ticked by, and she waited, wondering if Mrs. Peach had heard her or if she had been distracted by something else. Or if she was crying, the phone muffled to prevent Erin from hearing her.

"Mrs. Peach?"

"No. No, they said he didn't have any alcohol in his system. But I could smell it on him, Erin, and so could you. And you could see how drunk he was. The man could barely stand."

Then she suddenly started crying, long, wrenching sobs. Erin looked at the phone, wondering if she should just wait or if she should run over to Mrs. Peach's house and be there for her in person. It was hard to talk to someone on the phone when they were crying.

She would see Mrs. Peach and hear her better if she were there in person.

But then, Mrs. Peach might not want company, either. She hadn't come over to Erin's house or asked her to go over to hers. It might be easier to talk to someone at the end of the phone line and not have to look her in the face or to excuse herself for streaked mascara and being in a mess.

Erin waited until there was a slight slow-down and quieting of the sobs. "I'm sorry, Mrs. Peach. Can I do anything for you? Do you want me to come over there?"

"They said he was beaten," Mrs. Peach said. "He had bruising on his body and on the bottoms of his feet. I asked how you get bruises on the bottom of your feet, and they said that it's a method of torture. Somebody tortured my husband!"

Erin gasped in shock. She held her breath, trying to sound calm for Mrs. Peach. She needed someone who could support her, not someone who was going to break down.

"They're sure? It couldn't have been from something else?"

"They said they can only tell me the most basic information. It will be up to the police department to decide how much else they are going to tell me or release to the public." Mrs. Peach snuffled noisily. "They will investigate it, won't they, Erin? They won't just pretend that he was drunk?"

"Yes, of course they will." Erin thought about Mr. Peach's mincing steps, how he had stumbled and had such a hard time making it up the stairs to the door. Her heart hurt. At the time, she had judged him for being so drunk, for showing up like that and treating his wife so badly. And all along, he was in terrible pain. The victim of torture.

She thought of him repeatedly asking if Mrs. Peach was okay. Of course he had. He'd been afraid that whoever had tortured him would go after her too. That they would hurt her to get whatever it was that they wanted from him.

But who had done it?

Davis?

She couldn't see him in the role of a torturer. He hadn't killed face to face. He hadn't used his hands to torture and kill. He had put other people in the role of killer or had used a weapon that kept him separated from the victim so that he would not have to look at their faces. Was that the kind of man who got a kick out of hurting someone? Or could stand to torture someone until they screamed to get some piece of information from them?

Mrs. Peach was talking again. Erin tried to focus on the conversation.

"I don't want people spreading it around that he was drunk. That isn't fair to him. I told you we don't drink. I told you that."

"Yes, you did. And you were right," Erin agreed, trying to keep her voice as soothing and encouraging as she could. Mrs. Peach deserved to know that her husband hadn't wronged her. He hadn't been out carousing while she sat at home and waited for him to return. Instead, something had happened to him. Someone had stolen him away and had tortured him.

Had he escaped? Been released? Been dropped off by the torturers onto his own street? Erin wasn't sure how he had gotten there. She hadn't seen him until he had been in front of her house. He couldn't have walked very far. Not in the shape that he was.

Erin remembered trying to take Mr. Peach's shoes off to get him settled more comfortably and the way that he had sat up and yelled at her not to touch them. He must have been in agony when she had tried to take his shoes off. She felt sick for any extra pain she had caused him while blind to his actual condition.

"I'm so sorry that happened to him," she consoled Mrs. Peach. "No one deserves to go through that. Will you be okay? Do you want someone to sit with you?"

"No. I'm going to take a sleeping pill and go to bed. I can't think about it. I can't think of my poor Gregory being tortured by those goons."

"Do you have any idea who?"

"Well, it must have been the men from the penitentiary. It had to be something to do with the prison break. They... they must have had a grievance with him because of something that happened there."

"Maybe," Erin agreed, not pointing out that of the men who had escaped prison, one of them was already dead. He couldn't have had anything to do with Mr. Peach's torture.

Could it have been just one man? Davis?

She supposed that physically it was possible. Davis was much younger than Mr. Peach. But he was also slight, not a big man. Mr. Peach was heavier. Maybe taller too. Erin thought that Davis would have needed an accomplice. But maybe if he'd had a weapon, that would be enough to persuade Mr. Peach to do what he said. Then once he was restrained, Davis could do what he wanted.

Erin expressed a few more platitudes, hoping to tell Mrs. Peach what she needed to hear.

CHAPTER 37

*E*rin felt like she was coming out of a long, dark tunnel. Even though she had only been away from Terry for a few minutes, she felt like she had been gone for longer. He had probably barely noticed her absence, but she felt like the world had tilted on its axis. Like nothing would ever be the same again.

She kept seeing poor Mr. Peach, staggering home, wanting to reach his wife to know that she was safe. And not telling anyone how badly he was hurt.

Terry looked away from the TV to Erin. He immediately picked up the remote and pointed it at the TV, shutting off the show he had been enjoying.

"What is it, Erin? What happened?"

"That was Mrs. Peach."

"Is she okay? Does she need to be taken to the hospital?" He started to rise from his seat.

Erin shook her head. "No. Nothing like that. She's fine, just upset. She said she's going to take a sleeping pill and go to bed."

"I hope she's careful about how much she takes. She's not a young woman."

"I'm sure she'll be fine." Erin waved off his concerns. Mrs. Peach had been taking care of herself for years. She knew what she could do, how much a sleeping pill would affect her. "It's not that."

"What is it, then?" Terry patted the seat where Erin had been and fluffed up the pillow, making it more comfortable for her to rejoin him. Erin sank into the couch beside him. She lay her head against his shoulder and closed her eyes. Imagine how it would be, sitting next to this same man for twenty years. To be married to him for fifty. To lose him to something so terrible.

"Mrs. Peach talked to the medical examiner. I guess the police department must have a copy of his report, right?"

Terry nodded. "One would have been sent to the sheriff. He'll see it in the morning. What were the results?"

"According to what the medical examiner told to Mrs. Peach… he was beaten. Tortured."

Erin looked at him. Terry's eyes widened. He didn't ask her, "Are you kidding me?" but Erin was sure it was on his lips. They had all been so wrong about Mr. Peach.

"They're sure it was torture? Not just… a fall down the stairs? Some kind of accident? He wasn't a young man."

"They said that the bottoms of his feet were bruised."

Terry blinked, taking this in. He tried to come up with an alternate theory and shook his head. "That's incredible. I can't believe it. I do, of course, but… wow. I didn't see that one coming."

"No. Me neither. What a terrible thing."

"Mrs. Peach is okay?"

"Like I said… she's going to take a pill and go to bed. Not think about it." Erin shook her head. "She might be taking a sleeping pill every night for the rest of her life to forget it."

"We'll have to make sure she knows she can get counseling… Get in touch with victim services. That poor woman." Terry shook his head. He looked at Erin, touching her cheek. "And you too. If I had known…"

What could he have done? Gotten up earlier in the morning so that he was the one to walk Mr. Peach home? There wasn't anything he could have done to protect Erin. And she couldn't allow herself any self-pity. She hadn't suffered anything. Mr. Peach had suffered.

And Mrs. Peach had suffered from his loss. Erin had just been a bystander.

"Is there anything you can think of…? Anything that Mr. Peach might have done or said that would indicate who it was that hurt him?"

"No. He didn't tell me anything. He just kept asking if Mrs. Peach was okay. And he wanted me to give her the will. Why would he write Willie's stupid partnership into his will?"

Terry frowned at her. He scratched his stubbled jaw, brows drawn down. "Willie's stupid partnership?"

"That Willie Nelson…"

"Willie? Our Willie?" Terry demanded. "Andrews?"

"Well, we don't know for sure. Betty couldn't actually say what it was she knew about the partnership, but… well, she said it was a partnership. Two people. Not just one."

"Willie and Nelson." Terry blew out his breath. He swore. "How long have you been sitting on this?"

"Umm…" Erin tried to come up with a good answer. "Uh…"

"Why didn't you call me as soon as you found out? This is a vital piece of information."

"Because… I don't actually know anything. It's just speculation. Unless Betty confirms it to you, or Willie does, or you have a copy of the agreement…"

"Willie."

Erin could see rapid calculations going through his head. Adding up everything he knew about Willie and Nelson and seeing how they could be twisted around to implicate Willie in everything. As if Willie hadn't been the target of enough police investigations lately.

"Vic said it couldn't be Willie."

Terry shook his head. "She can't know that. She can't know where he is every minute of the day. She has no idea what he might or might not be involved in."

"She knows what kind of a person he is."

"I'm not sure she does. I'm not sure any of us can know that. People wear masks. They hide who they really are. Some criminals, even very violent ones, are the most cultured and polite people you could imagine. But under it all… they are animals."

Erin remembered Adele's husband referring to one of the men at the penitentiary as a "gentleman." Someone who wouldn't stab another person without provocation.

"Willie can't have had anything to do with any of this."

"Willie is an expert in security and computers."

"So what? That doesn't prove anything. A lot of people know about computers."

"Up until now, there hasn't been anything to connect him to the prison break. But there has to be a reason Mr. Peach left him all that money."

"What? He couldn't have known that he was going to die. Mrs. Peach said that he told her he was going to leave it all to her. Why would he change his mind all of a sudden and write a will that left it to Willie?"

"Maybe he did know he was going to die. Maybe he owed it to Willie. We know that he was getting periodic cash payments. Maybe some of that money was supposed to flow through to Willie and Nelson. Maybe they had set up a pipeline to get contraband into the penitentiary, so they were all supposed to get a share. Maybe he was behind and hadn't paid out what he was supposed to."

"No…"

Terry rubbed his forehead, still working through all of the possibilities.

"I guess I should make a few phone calls. Sheriff Wilmot is going to want to look at that report right away. And I should probably loop Beaver in if she hasn't already been brought up to speed."

Terry put his arm around Erin's shoulders and gave her a squeeze. "Sorry, I wanted to spend some more time with you tonight, but I think I'd better get this squared away first. And you're going to get to bed before long."

CHAPTER 38

Though Terry had done his best to put the sheriff and Beaver on to the new clues that night, things hadn't worked out. The sheriff had listened to the news and agreed to read the report in the morning. When they'd all had a good rest and were fresh. Nothing they did was going to help Mr. Peach; what was done was done. An all-nighter wasn't going to get them to a solution any faster.

And Beaver was unreachable. She wasn't answering her phone. Jeremy hadn't seen her and didn't know where she was. Terry left messages for her to call him back but was left frustrated, unable to advance the case any further until the next day.

But that's what police work was like. Slow and tedious much of the time. Having to wait to talk to witnesses or other law enforcement officers. Going over the facts of the case again and again, hoping that something would break.

Erin went to bed knowing she wouldn't be able to get to sleep right away and that, all wound up over the case, Terry was unlikely to get to bed until much later. She had resigned herself to the fact that their sleeping schedules would rarely match, but it was frustrating when she wanted him there to hold her and help her to calm down, and he was too intent on his work to do it.

As usual, she went to Auntie Clem's in the morning and let the work take her away from her troubled thoughts. There were cakes and cookies and loaves of bread to be made, and all manner of other gluten-free treats. Customers to be greeted and served, a steady stream of people through the bakery, some of whom had heard that Mr. Peach had died of drink and some of whom had not. No one seemed to know of the autopsy results. Erin tried to give vague answers to their questions and not say anything that Mrs. Peach wouldn't want to be spread around or that the police would not be releasing. It was a tug-of-war, with the ladies wanting to know the latest details and Erin holding back on what she knew.

Mid-morning, she got a call from Sheriff Wilmot. She looked at his name on the phone screen and guessed that he wasn't calling to order a box of muffins. While they were more than happy to stuff themselves with treats from Auntie Clem's Bakery, it was rare for anyone but Melissa to buy anything for the police department. Erin would take free food over to them from time to time, when it was convenient for her to see what was going on with the little police department and possibly get to overhear the latest news on an investigation.

It was strange not to have heard at all from Melissa. Maybe she really was sick. Erin had thought that she would miss a day of work and then would be back the next day on her schedule. But she hadn't been back to the police department and hadn't come into Auntie Clem's to get any treats and spread the latest news.

"Erin here."

"Miss Price," Wilmot's voice sounded somewhat hoarse, but warm and friendly. "I wonder whether you would be able to come over to the police department for a talk. Nothing you need to be concerned about, just going over your interactions with Mr. Peach again in light of the most recent revelations."

Having found out that he had been beaten rather than drunk meant that everything had to be put under a microscope again to examine the significance of each detail.

"Sure," Erin agreed. "I can come after the lunch rush. Would that work?"

"I'm sure that would be fine."

"Do you want me to bring anything with me? Some dessert?"

"Well… you know I wouldn't turn down anything that comes out of Auntie Clem's Bakery. If you happen to have something you can spare, we're always happy to receive it."

Erin laughed. "I'll see what I can pull together, then."

Despite knowing that she was not a suspect and was not in trouble, Erin was still anxious about going to the police department offices to talk things over with Sheriff Wilmot and whoever else might be involved in the investigation. She felt sad and heavy thinking about Mr. Peach and how she had let him down. If she had recognized at the time that he was hurt instead of drunk, would they have been able to do anything for him? If he had been rushed into the city and treated by a trauma team at the hospital, would they have been able to save him?

The sense of failure weighed heavily on her. Mrs. Peach had lost the opportunity for a few more years with her husband because of Erin's failure to recognize his condition. She had been a care worker. She should have known the difference between someone who was drunk and someone who had been tortured.

When Erin walked into the police department offices, Clara lowered her glasses and smiled. She was a tough woman and, while Erin had felt somewhat intimidated by her when they had first met, Erin's continued attempts to be friendly—or maybe her baking—had noticeably softened Clara's hard shell.

"Miss Price. I'm supposed to take you straight in."

Usually, Erin had to wait in the outer reception area until Terry or whoever she was there to see was ready for her. She had previously been caught wandering where she should not be, so the sheriff was pretty strict about it.

Clara stood up and led Erin toward one of the interview rooms. Erin held out her box of treats, expecting Clara to take it to the little kitchen nook where the coffee maker was. Clara shook her head. "Just take it in with you."

She took Erin to the largest interview room, where Terry, Beaver, Sheriff Wilmot, and Officer Rod Stayner were assembled around the table. It was not the formal sort of meeting where everybody was sitting up straight and were following an agenda. Instead, they were lounging around in their office chairs. There were remnants of lunch on the little counter at the end of the room, the smell of coffee that had been sitting out for too long, and loose papers covering the table. They had probably been there all morning discussing the case.

"And here's Miss Price with the goodies," Wilmot observed, standing up and touching his forehead as if he were saluting her. "Thank you for coming in, Erin."

Clara went to the back of the room to tidy up the food and wrappings. Erin handed the box to Wilmot, and he selected a large slice of banana bread. Carrying out the remnants of their meal, Clara paused to see what was in the box and snagged a brownie. She nodded at Erin. "Thank you!"

"Happy to make everyone's day a little sweeter," Erin offered. "Say… have you heard anything from Melissa? I was wondering if maybe I should take her something… a casserole or…?" Erin shrugged. "I'm just wondering how she is feeling?"

"I don't know." Clara adjusted her glasses. "She says she's sick, but she sounds fine. Usually, when there is something like this going on… well, *you* know. She likes drama. So she must really be sick."

Erin nodded. "Maybe some chicken noodle soup," she murmured. Though the only chicken noodle soup in her house was the kind that came in a red and white can.

Clara nodded and walked out of the room. She didn't shut the interview room door. Erin's box of goodies was passed around the table. Terry got up to kiss her on the cheek and offer her a treat from the box, but Erin shook her head. She had to be careful how much of her own baking she ate, or she would end up as big as a house.

"Have a seat," Terry offered, pulling a chair out for her and sitting down in the one next to it. Erin sat. She wasn't sure what to expect. She had expected a one-on-one meeting with Sheriff Wilmot, going over her previous statement and trying to remember any additional details. Or maybe Sheriff Wilmot and Terry together. She hadn't expected to see the others there or be part of some kind of interdepartmental meeting.

No one made any attempt to gather up the papers spread across the table. Glancing at them, Erin could see that they were evidence in the case. Statements, reports, handwriting samples. She shifted in her seat and looked around at them, raising her brows to ask what was happening next.

Everyone's eyes turned to Sheriff Wilmot, who munched happily on his banana bread for a moment, then put the rest of the slice down on a napkin.

"Thanks for joining us, Erin. I know that we usually do our best to keep you out of these things. Still, the fact is, you have been a witness to several events and conversations. We felt that it was best to read you in on some of the investigation and see if anything connects up with what you have discovered, even though you might not be aware of the significance of what you know yet. However, what you hear here is not public knowledge and you will need to file a Confidentiality and Non-Disclosure Agreement." He started pushing around some of the papers on the table, then found a stack of three stapled agreements clipped together in a bundle. He pushed them across the table to her. "If you want to give that a quick scan, we can proceed after you have signed it."

"Basically, it just says that anything you hear or see here is confidential and you won't repeat it to anyone," Terry explained.

Erin looked up from the papers to his face. "I *have* signed Non-Disclosure Agreements before."

"Oh. Sorry," he looked properly chastened. "I didn't mean to talk down to you."

Erin skimmed through the agreements and didn't see anything problematic. She scribbled her signature in triplicate and gave them back to Sheriff Wilmot, who witnessed her signatures.

CHAPTER 39

Sheriff Wilmot tapped the bottoms of the documents against the table to square them, and put them to the side.

"That's the formal stuff out of the way. Now… I know this is a pain and that you've already repeated yourself more than once, but if you could run through a few events one more time. The discovery of Christian Bruel's body. Your discussion with Mr. Peach at his home the night before he disappeared. And what you saw and heard when you helped him home the morning he passed. I also understand that you visited with Mr. Windsor at the penitentiary."

"Oh… yes."

Erin glanced at Terry, but he didn't have anything to say about this or look upset about it. He'd had enough time to get over being angry about her going to the prison without telling him ahead of time and running into not just Rudolph Windsor, but also Daniel Jackson.

"If you could include that as well. I'm not sure where it lands in the timeline, but if we could go roughly chronological, that would help." Wilmot sighed and picked up his slice of banana bread again. "So I guess that means starting with the discovery of the body, unless there is something that happened before that that you think might be connected. Anything you saw or heard."

Erin nodded. She watched Wilmot take another bite from the

slice of banana bread and looked at Stayner and Beaver. Beaver, of course, was lounging back, looking completely relaxed, chewing her gum and watching Erin. Stayner didn't look entirely comfortable with the proceedings. Erin didn't know whether that was because he was new to an investigation like this or because he didn't like a civilian being brought into the room. He sat more rigidly than anyone else in the room, except maybe for Erin herself. He had a pen in his hand and a notebook in front of him, poised to write down any bit of evidence he thought should be followed up on. Erin decided not to watch him while she was talking. It would be too distracting. She swiveled her chair slightly so that her view of the room was limited mainly to Terry, and began recounting her tale yet again.

Already, some of it was fading. She stumbled a few times over details, having to go over the same ground a few times before she was sure she'd gotten it right. But she worried about what she might have forgotten.

She couldn't remember much of the conversation with Rudolph Windsor at the prison. She had been there as moral support for Adele, and a lot of what had been said at the short interview had failed to stick. She remembered his charming smile, his teasing, and not much else. He had denied having anything to do with the prison break. He had said that Pastor Peach hadn't had anything to do with the escape but, apparently, he had been proven wrong on that score by the computer security logs.

"Which of the clans was it that Windsor worked with before he was arrested?" Stayner interrupted, hand hovering over his notepad.

Erin paused.

"Jacksons," Beaver advised.

"Is that why Windsor wasn't part of the escape plan? Plaint was with the Dysons. So is Willie Andrews. It sounds like it was split along clan lines."

Erin didn't jump in and defend Willie. They all knew that she was friendly with Willie and figured she would rush to his defense on any accusation. It was her job to stay focused on the story she was telling and not to let Stayner sidetrack her.

"Rudolph said it was because he just wants to serve his time and get out, because then he'll be free for good. He wouldn't have to keep looking over his shoulder. He said that it's the lifers who make escape plans."

Stayner's scowl said that he wasn't sure that Rudolph was telling the truth or that Erin should have believed it, but he didn't argue the point. She noted that he didn't write it down.

"Go on, Erin," Beaver encouraged.

She tried to pick up the thread of her narrative again. She dredged up what she could of what had happened during the penitentiary visit.

"And before we left, I asked him whether Mr. Peach had had anything to do with the prison break."

"Why did you do that?" Beaver asked.

"I thought that being on the inside, he would have a different perspective and he might have heard something."

"No, I mean, what was it that made you think that Mr. Peach might have had something to do with the prison break? At that point, you had talked to him only once. What made you connect him?"

"Just because he had suddenly shown up in Bald Eagle Falls. He'd been away for thirty years, and he came back the same week that there was a prison break where he worked. The escapees ended up practically in his backyard—in the backyard of his wife."

"You thought he had sent them there?"

"No… but they could have been there to meet him… maybe to get cash for expenses or something. Maybe he didn't want to direct them to meet him in Moose River because then they would have known where he lived? I don't know. I just thought it was too coincidental that he worked at the penitentiary."

"And Windsor told you that he didn't know of any connection."

"Right."

"Do you remember Mickey, Erin?"

Erin looked at her blankly for a minute before remembering Mikhail, a Russian gangster that she'd had the misfortune to meet a couple of times. A man who had eventually tried to kill her and who had been arrested and put in prison instead. At the same prison? She hadn't even thought about *him* being there.

"Oh. Mickey. Yes, I remember."

From what Erin could gather, Mickey had been some kind of informant for Beaver, at least part of the time.

"I've been talking with Mickey about it, and he had some interesting things to say about your Mr. Peach."

"He's not *my* Mr. Peach."

Beaver nodded. "Okay. Well, it sounds like he's been running a number of rackets at the penitentiary. He's made a significant amount of income outside of his salary as a prison pastor on these... ventures."

"Can you believe Mickey? I mean, he's an organized crime figure. Can you believe anything he says?"

"Can I take it for gospel? Of course not. But it is a starting point for investigation. I take what he gives me and see what can be verified through other sources. And I knew before I talked to him that Pastor Peach was making an income on the side. And that his card swipes coincided with the movements of the escapees. Whether Mickey had told me anything or not, I knew Peach was involved in some shady dealings inside the penitentiary."

Erin shook her head slowly. "He seemed like such a nice old man. He was polite, charming. I can't believe that he was a criminal."

"You can't tell by looking at a person. There are criminals from all walks of life. Some do it out of need or because of the families they were raised in. Others are addicted to the adrenaline rush. There are as many different reasons as there are criminals."

Erin was very disappointed to hear that Mr. Peach had not been the upstanding, law-abiding person she had thought that he was. Maybe she had been swayed by the fact that he was a pastor, thinking that meant that he had strong principles. When in reality, it had all been a mask.

Erin looked over the papers that were scattered on the table in front of her. "So what was he doing?" she asked, picking up a couple of them.

Terry had said that they had received some reference letters from the penitentiary to compare Mr. Peach's handwritten will to, and that's what the papers she had picked up appeared to be. One of them was commending a man who had served his time and was looking for a place to live. Mr. Peach had testified that he was a quiet, respectful man who had done his time and learned better ways during his stint in prison, and that he was sure that the man would be no problem as a tenant.

The other had a name that she recognized, but she had to stop and think about how she knew it. Kevin Hatch. It was a letter to some kind of industrial factory recommending Mr. Hatch for a job there. Mr. Peach related how Kevin Hatch had been wrongly convicted so that his record should not be held against him. He was a law-abiding citizen looking for a job to support himself and should be given every consideration.

"Oh... I remember this guy. Rudolph mentioned him. He was convicted based on evidence that had been fabricated by the police."

Terry took it from her and looked it over, then put it back down, unmoved.

"Don't you think that's sad?" Erin persisted. "He didn't do anything, and he ended up serving thirty—no, forty—years for it, until one of those innocence projects proved that it had all been a set-up."

"I remember hearing about the case around the time that his conviction was reversed. There was quite a bit of publicity about it. The cops who had been involved said that they knew that he had done it, but they hadn't been able to provide the level of proof that was required for the case." He shook his head. "I don't condone cops taking the law into their own hands, but I can sympathize with them knowing that he killed his girlfriend and not being able to prove it."

"That doesn't excuse it, though," Erin protested.

"I said that it didn't. But if they thought that he killed her, he probably did. They probably did the world a favor putting this guy behind bars instead of letting him go on killing other women until they finally caught him in a case that they could prove."

"What if he was innocent? He was in prison for forty years." Erin knew that prisons were not intended to be comfortable places to live, and she shuddered to think of what kind of conditions prisoners were kept in forty years earlier, before many prison reforms came in and lawmakers started thinking about rehabilitation instead of just punishment.

"I doubt he was innocent," Beaver said, "Officer Piper is right. If the cops were that convinced that he did it, they were probably right. They were wrong to go about it the way that they did, but they probably still had the right guy behind bars."

"So this referral…" Erin fingered it. "If you were an employer, you wouldn't even consider it?"

"Nope. I wouldn't want someone like that working at my plant. Too big of a risk. There are many programs that help reintroduce felons into mainstream society. Give them apprenticeships in car repair shops and industrial work where they are closely supervised. Best to let the parole officers and social workers get them into rehabilitation programs and ensure that he is properly reintegrated. Just dumping him into a place like this where no one is keeping an official eye on him? I wouldn't want him."

"But he couldn't get into a program like that if his conviction was overturned, could he?"

"Nope." Beaver was unsympathetic and unapologetic about it. But then, she thought, like Terry, that he probably was guilty anyway. He had just been lucky to get out.

Erin shook her head.

"To get back to your previous question, though," Beaver said, "a reference letter like that would not come cheap."

Erin looked at Beaver, then looked at the letter again. "What do you mean?"

"Apparently, Pastor Peach did not just give references to anyone who asked."

CHAPTER 40

"ou're telling me that he charged for this? For writing a letter for someone?" Erin was flabbergasted. It seemed like such a little thing. Wasn't that something that a pastor at a prison did to minister to his little flock? He helped them find their way in the outside world if they confessed and repented and all that?

She knew that there were cases where people were expected to pay the priest to be forgiven for something or pay the way for a relative who had died. Still, she didn't think *that* was particularly ethical either.

"Yes. He apparently expected payment for writing letters or helping the prisoners out in other ways. Someone on the outside would have to pay, because the only money that the prisoners have access to is the commissary funds, and that's apparently not enough to buy off a pastor."

"So Hatch must have had money to pay Mr. Peach for this letter?"

"*Letters*," Beaver corrected. "He wrote several references for Mr. Hatch. It seems that even when he has been able to get a job, he can't hold it down for more than a few weeks or months. So each time, he needs another letter setting out what a great guy he is. He's worked at an automotive shop," Beaver consulted a notepad, "pizza delivery, dishwasher in a restaurant, flipping burgers, and packer in a fish processing plant."

Not very glamorous jobs. Erin didn't think that the standards for pizza delivery or dishwashers were particularly onerous. Had he just made people around him feel uncomfortable? Or had he really not been able to perform those tasks to the satisfaction of his managers? Maybe he had PTSD or agoraphobia after being in prison for so long. He wasn't likely to be very sociable.

"So…" Beaver flapped a hand at the letters. "That was one of Peach's sidelines. From what Mickey said, it's possible that he was also blackmailing prisoners who had confessed to him as their spiritual advisor."

"Oh, no." Even an atheist like Erin knew about the sanctity of the confessional. Priests were even given the protection of the law. They didn't have to go to the authorities if they knew that someone had committed a crime. And their religious principles wouldn't allow them to. So a man could confess to the most heinous crime—like those that men in the penitentiary might have committed—and the priest and the law couldn't do anything about it.

But if Mr. Peach threatened to report a prisoner's confession to law enforcement or to someone they had wronged… it was unconscionable. If the prisoner or a loved one on the outside had access to money, they would probably pay any amount not to have his crime revealed.

"Could he really make money doing these things, though?" she asked. "Like you said, these prisoners only had their commissary money. What are the chances that they would have someone on the outside who was willing to pay anything substantial? They probably come mostly from poor backgrounds."

"There are ways to make money if you are desperate enough. Pastor Peach was apparently very… *motivating*." Beaver spoke the word as if it tasted bad.

Erin wished she could wash her hands of the whole affair. She had been wrong about Mr. Peach, thinking that he was a good person, and he hadn't been. Not at all. All of that money that he had promised to leave to his wife was dirty, tainted money. He had told her that it had been all of his savings over the years, but he had lied about that, just like everything else.

Which, of course, led to the next question.

"What did Mr. Peach say to you about the money that he was leaving to his wife and about the will?" Sheriff Wilmot asked.

"He didn't say anything to me about it. Mrs. Peach talked to me about that, told me that he had said he was going to leave it to her, but Mr. Peach didn't tell me that."

"What did he say to you when he gave you the envelope?"

"He wasn't really saying anything at that point. He would start to say something and then lose his train of thought. He just pushed it into my hands. Wanted to make sure that Mrs. Peach got it."

"Are you sure that's what he was doing?" Terry asked.

"What do you mean?"

"If he wasn't coherent, then maybe he wanted something else. Maybe he wanted you to get rid of it, rather than giving it to Mrs. Peach. Maybe he wanted you to shred it."

Erin thought back to the scene, Mr. Peach getting the envelope out of his pocket and giving it to her. He hadn't said to give it to Mrs. Peach, but her name was on it, so what else would Erin do with it? If Mr. Peach had intended for her to destroy it, he had waited too long to tell her. By that time, he couldn't say anything intelligible. Other than telling her not to touch his feet. Erin remembered again with horror how he had yelled at her and pushed her back when she had tried to remove his shoes. It must have been agonizing to him when she had touched his feet, but she hadn't had a clue.

Terry could see her expression change, even though she tried to keep her face blank. He put his hand on her back to comfort her. "It's not your fault, Erin. None of this is your fault. We're just trying to sort out the facts here."

"If I had just realized…"

"There was no way for you to know. Just focus on the one question. Are you sure that he was asking you to give it to Mrs. Peach? Or could he have been trying to ask you to do something else?"

"I don't know. You're right. It could have been something else. He could have been asking me to get rid of it. Mrs. Peach was out of the room, and he was very insistent that I take it. But why would he write it if he just wanted to destroy it again?"

"If it wasn't for the date on the top, he might have written it earlier," Stayner said. "It could have been the will that he meant to replace, to straighten things out so that Mrs. Peach would inherit everything."

"It's all backward," Erin agreed. "It doesn't make any sense."

"You were with Mrs. Peach when she took the will to her lawyer," Wilmot said. "She never gave any indication that she knew who was behind the Willie Nelson Partnership?"

"No. She didn't know."

"You're sure of that."

Erin threw her hands up in exasperation. "As sure as I am about anything else in this case. She didn't know. I'm *sure* she didn't know."

"So it was a surprise to her when Betty Thompson suggested that it was Willie Andrews and Nelson Dyson."

"Yes. We were both shocked."

"And you believe that's who was behind the partnership."

"I don't know. It makes sense, and it doesn't."

"How does it make sense?"

"Because I know that Willie did some computer stuff for Nelson Dyson. So it wasn't that much of a stretch that they might have done something together. Maybe set up some kind of tax shelter. I don't know how all of that stuff works, but I know that movie producers and oil companies set up partnerships or joint ventures for certain things."

Wilmot nodded. Everyone seemed to agree that it was a logical conclusion. "And it didn't make sense because…"

"Because there isn't any connection between Willie and Mr. Peach."

"Did you ask him?"

"No. I mentioned it to Vic, but she said no. He hadn't even known who Mr. Peach was."

"Hearsay. She told you something that he told her. You don't know for sure."

"How could I know for sure? You haven't found a connection, have you? Between Willie and Mr. Peach? Or the penitentiary?"

"Willie has connections with people incarcerated in the prison."

"Well, so do I. So does Adele. So does Beaver." Erin looked around the table. "Probably all of us have some kind of connection with someone in the prison."

"But Willie's connections are to clan members. A criminal organization that he was once a card-carrying member of," Terry pointed out.

"That doesn't mean that Willie is connected with everything that the clan does. It doesn't mean that he has anything to do with them anymore. You can't keep assuming that because he was once involved with them that he still is."

"But the partnership is proof that he is. That partnership wouldn't exist if he wasn't still involved with the Dysons."

"We don't know anything about what that partnership does. At least I don't. It could be... to provide computers and security for schools. It doesn't necessarily have anything to do with the clan. Nelson isn't the boss of the clan."

"He's not that far removed. His father is."

"But they don't get along. He doesn't have any interest in taking it over from his father."

Terry frowned at her. "That may or may not be true. Where did you hear it?"

Erin thought back. "Uh... I guess... when I met Nelson. Willie said that he wasn't really part of the clan workings, that he was interested in other things, and that's what Nelson said too. That he was building his own network and wasn't interested in the family business."

She remembered what Vic had said about this. That Nelson starting up his own faction would just cause more problems with the clans. Introducing another criminal organization into the mix would make things more volatile.

"So even if this isn't related to the larger Dyson clan, it could still be related to Nelson and whatever he thinks he's building outside of the clan," Beaver suggested.

Erin couldn't find any way around that. Somehow, the partnership between Willie and Nelson seemed to be connected with Mr. Peach. She could only assume that it was something to do with the penitentiary.

"I assume you guys have talked to Willie. What has he said about the partnership?"

"Willie declines to speak to us about it," Sheriff Wilmot said. "What would you expect?"

"We're doing what we can to get a subpoena for the partnership records," Beaver offered, "but it is a stretch. We can't prove any connection between the prison break and Willie and Nelson. So we can't connect it to the partnership. We're doing our best to tie it to the investigation into Peach's death, which is being classified as a homicide. He left his money to the partnership. But it's going to take a bit of convincing to get a judge to agree that it is relevant to his murder."

"And I don't suppose Nelson wants to talk to anyone about it."

"He laughed," Terry growled. "Said that it was none of our business and didn't have anything to do with our investigation, so we could stuff it."

Erin suppressed a laugh of her own at Nelson's response and Terry's outrage over it. Terry, with his hand still on her back, must have sensed her laughter. He shook his head, glaring at her.

"I'm sorry." Erin wiped her forehead and allowed a little laugh to escape. "I think I'm tired and overwhelmed by this all. I think… I've told you everything that I can. I don't know how any of it is helpful, but I tried."

Terry took his hand from Erin's back. Sheriff Wilmot straightened some of the papers in front of him. Stayner flipped his notebook closed.

"We may have additional questions or things to talk over with you," Beaver advised. "But we know how to get you."

"Yeah, of course. If there's any way I could help, I would. I don't exactly want to have to worry about whether Davis is stalking around the woods. I'd rather have him back in prison. And if he's the one who killed Mr. Peach…" Erin shook her head. "I thought he was a nice old man, and I guess that he wasn't, but that doesn't justify Davis killing him. If that's what happened."

"*Torturing* and killing him," Beaver amended.

As if Erin could forget that part. "He died from internal injuries…?" she asked tentatively.

Beaver nodded. "We're still waiting for all of the final tests, of course. But yes… the medical examiner says he died from internal bleeding, shock, the extent of his injuries…"

"I feel so bad that I missed it. He had some cuts on his face. I figured he'd just been in a spat with someone at the bar. I should have seen it."

"You couldn't have known."

CHAPTER 41

*B*eaver's last warning to Erin had been to remember the confidentiality and non-disclosure agreement that she had signed. As if she could forget. But she supposed Beaver had to be extra aware of these things and whether or not her informants were following the rules she had given them.

That gave Erin pause. Was *she* an informant now?

She thought not. An informant was someone who was mixed up in whatever crime was being investigated, and Erin didn't have anything to do with it personally. She was only a witness, not an informant.

It was later than she had expected it to be. She hesitated between going back to Auntie Clem's to help close or just going straight home. But she had driven Vic that morning, so she really should go back to pick her up. Vic could walk home or call Willie for a ride, but an escaped felon was on the loose and Erin didn't know what Willie was doing. He might be in one of his mines. Or in Moose River. With the police questions about whether he was involved with Mr. Peach and threatening to get a subpoena for his partnership records, she supposed that Willie was probably as far away as possible. He wouldn't want to be around if they decided they had more questions or wanted to serve that subpoena. If they couldn't find him, they couldn't bother him.

So, Erin decided that the polite thing was to go back to Auntie Clem's to help close up and drive Vic home.

"Ah, the prodigal returns," Vic observed when Erin walked through the kitchen to the front of the shop.

Erin smiled. "Back for a few minutes."

"I wasn't sure whether you would make it back or not."

"Neither was I. How has the afternoon been?"

"Just fine. No problems. A lot of questions about Mr. Peach, though, and I don't know how to handle them."

Erin shook her head slowly. "I don't either. The more I hear, the less I know what to think of him."

"I was wondering whether we could do something for Mrs. Peach. I mean, there will be all the usual. Helping out at the funeral and a reception afterward, casseroles, and she's right next door, so we're there to check up on her or see if she needs to run any errands, like you helped her with at the lawyer's office. But I wondered about *baking* something."

Erin raised her brows. "Like what?" Mrs. Peach was in the bakery regularly, buying bread or whatever else she needed. Erin couldn't see how baking more would help. Unless Vic meant giving food to Mrs. Peach without charge.

"I just thought… Mr. Peach… peaches… maybe dedicating a day next week to peach baking or making a Pastor Peach Pie or something like that. A little… acknowledgment of him."

Erin nodded slowly. "It would be nice to do something for Mrs. Peach," she agreed. She was careful to word it as something for Mrs. Peach, not something for Mr. Peach, since it turned out that he was a bad apple, to mix her metaphors. "I kind of like the peach day of baking. It's easy to do, and peaches are in season right now. There are some really nice ones this year. We could do some peach tarts, muffins, peach crumb bars. It would be a nice variety. We could make it the day of the funeral, once we know when that is going to be, and we could make enough to supply the reception with a tray or two as well."

Vic smiled and nodded, pleased that Erin had picked up on her suggestion and was running with it.

"We could even do a peach slab pie for the funeral," she suggested. "Test out your revised pastry recipe."

"Peach slab pie," Erin agreed. "You bet. We can have all of the slices arranged in pinwheels…" She started to think of any other details. "Maybe with a crumb topping. Lots of brown sugar…"

"Oh, you're making me hungry!"

"I'd better stop, then," Erin looked at the clock. "It will be a while before we can get supper. What are you doing tonight? Anything with Willie?"

"No, he's off tending to something. He didn't say much about what it was. A mine, I guess."

Or going to see Nelson Dyson to talk to him about the police closing in on their business? Erin pushed the thought aside and focused on what she did know. Willie was a good guy. He had helped Erin numerous times in the past and was very protective of her and Vic. He was dedicated to Vic and wouldn't do anything to hurt her. And as far as Erin was concerned, that meant staying out of shady dealings with the clan or Nelson Dyson too.

"Do you want to go over with me to see how Melissa is doing? She hasn't been at work for a few days, and I thought I could take over some chicken noodle soup."

At Vic's skeptical look, she added, "I was thinking of picking some up at the family restaurant."

"Ah. Yes, that sounds good. It would be nice to do something together and to see how Melissa is doing. It's been strange not having her around at all throughout all of this. Usually, she's the first to be in on the gossip and tell us what's going on with the police department. It's weird not having an *in*." She surveyed Erin. "I don't suppose you can tell me anything about what they had to say? They just wanted to hear what you had to say about finding Bruel's body and Mr. Peach when he was… sick?"

"I had to sign a non-disclosure agreement."

"You did?" Vic's eyebrows went up and she looked thoughtful.

"That's interesting. Then they didn't just want to hear your witness account again. They shared some of their investigation with you."

Erin shrugged, not sure she could answer that question.

"Hmm. Very interesting," Vic repeated.

Erin looked at the clock again. "I think we're close enough to start clearing the till. I'll see what needs to be prepped for tomorrow."

She left Vic at the front and went back into the kitchen to see if everything had been cleaned up and put away properly, and what batters they already had soaking in the fridge. They already had most of what they would need in the morning. She just had a couple more things she wanted to mix up while Vic was finishing in the front.

CHAPTER 42

*D*espite her skill with baking, Erin didn't often have the time or energy to spend on other cooking. So her meal preparation at home tended to be pretty dull, making use of prepared foods and leftovers from the bakery. She did not have a good recipe for chicken noodle soup, although as she thought about it, she imagined making long, flat gluten-free noodles to add to a rich chicken broth and her mouth watered. If she had the time and energy, she could make a good chicken noodle soup. But since she didn't have that kind of time and energy at the end of the day and didn't want to take Campbell's Chicken and Stars over to Melissa, the best choice was the family restaurant.

She called ahead to make sure that they had chicken noodle soup on the menu that day. They usually had some simmering on the stove, but it would be just Erin's luck if they had decided to forego it and instead had only borscht. She didn't think that would be quite as appropriate an offering for someone who was sick. Even though Melissa was probably more worried or embarrassed than sick.

As a result, there was a family-size order of chicken noodle soup awaiting her when she arrived at the restaurant, and she and Vic headed directly over to Melissa's house to deliver it.

Erin had never been to Melissa's house before. She had seen her at the police department, the bakery, and other events that Erin had gone to around Bald Eagle Falls, but never her house.

It was a nice little bungalow, early fifties construction, but well-kept-up. Erin liked the green with white trim. It looked friendly and welcoming. And the borders along the sidewalk and small gardens on either side of the front steps were a riot of color and texture that suggested Melissa had spent a lot of time maintaining them over the years.

It didn't take Melissa long to get to the door when Erin rang the doorbell. She opened the door and looked out at them, smiling but uncertain. The dark spirals of curls spilled around her face, making her skin look pale. Maybe she had been sick after all. Or maybe it was just a trick of the light.

"Hey, we were sorry to hear that you were sick," Erin told her. "So we brought you some chicken noodle soup." She displayed the bowl.

"Is that from the family restaurant?"

Erin couldn't very well deny it with the restaurant's logo stamped prominently on the bowl in bright red lettering. She covered the logo with her hand and pretended that she was trying to hide the fact from Melissa.

"Why no, I made it myself. Why would you ask?"

They all laughed. Melissa stepped back, motioning them in. "Why don't ya'll come in. I'm feeling pretty good. We could visit for a while." She eyed the bowl. "And I don't think I can eat that all by myself."

Which was exactly what Erin had hoped she would say.

"Are you sure? We could just leave it for you, if you're not feeling up to a visit. I wouldn't want to impose."

"Come in," Melissa insisted.

So Vic and Erin stepped into Melissa's house. Vic held up a paper bag. "I've got rolls from Auntie Clem's as well. We had a few extra left over at the end of the day."

"What a feast," Melissa declared, even though it was only soup and rolls. "This will be fantastic. Do I need to heat anything up...?"

"It's all warm from the oven," Erin told her.

"Let's just sit down, then. I'll get out some bowls."

They walked through to Melissa's kitchen and arranged themselves around the table. Melissa cleared some flyers and junk mail away. "I don't even know why I look at this stuff. I never actually shop the sales. I might as well just put it straight in the recycling. But I feel guilty when I do that."

Erin nodded. She usually reviewed the grocery flyers in order to plan her purchases for the week, both for herself and for Auntie Clem's, but the rest went directly into the recycling bin.

Melissa got out bowls and spoons for everyone, and a serving ladle. As Erin lifted the first spoonful of soup to her mouth, Melissa held up her hand to stop her. She looked at Vic, then back at Erin, turning a little bit pink.

"Do you mind if we say grace first?"

"Oh." Erin put her spoon back into her bowl. "Yeah, of course. Sorry."

She hadn't grown up in any families that prayed over every meal, but she knew that some people did. She put her hands in her lap and stared down at her bowl, waiting.

Melissa's prayer was, luckily, not too long. Erin waited until Melissa picked up her spoon to begin eating before picking up her own, ensuring that she wasn't missing some other ritual.

"So, how are you feeling?" Erin asked after they had each eaten some of the soup and rolls and commented on how nice the simple meal was.

Melissa looked at her. "I'm okay... but I feel... pretty anxious about going back. The way everything is right now, every time I think about it, I just feel sick. You know how you get all nauseated and crampy when you have to write an exam or something like that?"

Erin nodded. Yes, she knew that feeling very well. And she'd been feeling it a lot with this case. "That's rough," she agreed. "But maybe you'd feel better once you got there? Sometimes, when you jump into something, even when it is uncomfortable, it's the best thing. Avoiding it will just make you more and more anxious until you feel like you can't ever go back."

"Yeah. That's sort of what's been happening. I keep saying to myself, 'I'll go tomorrow and get back into it.' But then the next day, it's just so hard, and I keep thinking about what people are going to say and how they're going to be looking at me, and how I'm going to feel. And what if I throw up at work? Because I hate being sick anywhere else. It's just... so gross. And so I can't really go in. Not until this is all over."

"But when is it going to be all over?" Vic asked. She took another swallow of the soup and shook her head. "Even if they get Davis back in prison, the investigation is still going to be ongoing."

"And people aren't going to forget that I'm friends with him," Melissa sighed. "They're always going to look at me differently now."

"I don't think it's that big of a deal," Erin tried to comfort her. "I know at first Terry was a little shocked, but I think that was mostly because he didn't know that the two of you were friends. Davis grew up in Bald Eagle Falls, so there are plenty of people who know him and might have been friends with him on some level at some point in time."

"Not really." Melissa stared off at nothing, lost in her memories. "He never had very many friends. Trenton was the more popular of the two. Davis just... never really got along with anyone. And everyone was always comparing the two of them, including his own mother. She was always putting Trenton up on a pedestal and then running down Davis. Even before..."

Before he got into drugs? Before he ran off the rails? Before his father had been killed?

"Well then, shame on the rest of the town," she told Melissa. "If they wouldn't be friendly with him and treat him like a person and kept comparing him to his brother and acting like he didn't measure up, then that's on them. You aren't the person who should be embarrassed for being friends with him. They're the ones who should be ashamed for being stuck up and not treating him like a human being."

CHAPTER 43

*V*ic's eyes widened at these strong words. She lifted one eyebrow. But she shouldn't have been surprised. She knew that Erin had strong feelings about the way that people should be treated. Especially teenagers who were so vulnerable to the harsh words of others. Erin hated the culture that tried to shame children who were different or who were struggling. Those were the very children that the community should be supporting and encouraging and trying to help along the way.

Melissa dabbed at the corner of her eye. "Do you really think that?" she asked Erin.

"Yes. I do. Don't you think so? Isn't that what your Christian religions teach? Love each other. Your neighbors, your enemies, all that? They don't say it's okay to shame and alienate people who are different or who are struggling."

Melissa nodded. "You're right. And that's supposed to be one of the most important commandments. Love God and love one another."

"Then, like I say, the people who didn't show him any friendliness are the ones who should be ashamed of themselves."

"Maybe they are," Vic suggested. "Maybe that's why they act like they do. If they can put everyone else down, pointing out their sins, that raises them up in their own eyes. Proves that they are more important."

Erin nodded. "Yeah. Something like that."

"Hmm." Melissa sipped some more of her soup. "Maybe if I focus on that, it will be easier when I think everyone is looking at me and judging me."

"Good. Because you're a good person. A lot better person than I could be," Erin said. "You're very loving toward everyone. Not just a few people that you decide are worthy of it."

"You're loving too!" Melissa insisted, her voice louder and firmer than it had been. "You're always trying to help people out. People you don't even know. Even when everyone tells you not to bother. And you take action. You don't just say that we should feed the hungry. You *feed the hungry*."

Erin chuckled at that. "Well, I guess I take a more literal interpretation than some."

"You're a better Christian than most of the Christians." Melissa rolled her eyes and looked away. "I hope you don't think that's an insult, because I don't mean it that way. I really do think that you're a better person than the ones who go around judging everybody else."

Erin looked for a way to get the focus off of her. She had not gone to visit with Melissa to be praised. "It's just my nature as a baker. What do they call it? My love language." She actually disliked the term, but that didn't mean she couldn't use it to her advantage.

"For sure," Melissa agreed. "For my mom, it was food too. Any time she wanted to show someone how proud she was of them, or if someone was sick and needed to be taken care of, or anything else, she would cook for them. Some big, showy dinner or their favorite, richest dessert. That was my mom. No point in trying to stop her, because she couldn't. That was just the way she was, right until the end."

Erin didn't know very much about Melissa's family. "Your mom has passed?"

"Well... no, not really." At Erin's expression, Melissa laughed. "I mean... she's still here with us, but she has dementia, so the part of her that was really my mom, that is gone now. I wish I could sit down and talk to her like I used to, or she could whip me up a roast beef or fried chicken dinner with gravy and mashed potatoes. But *that* mother is gone."

Erin felt bad for her. "That must be really hard."

"I guess. But it can't be as bad as her being dead, right? Your mom died when you were a little girl, and that's completely different from me fussing about how she can't remember my name or make me dinner anymore. You had to grow up without her."

Erin shrugged. It was true. But she didn't know that it was any better than watching a parent fade with dementia. She'd only had her mother for a short time, but at least she hadn't had to watch her slowly failing. She hadn't been aware that her mother had survived the car crash by several months. She'd been told that both of her parents had been killed instantly, so that was what she had assumed to be the truth.

"Tell me what it was like growing up here," Erin suggested. "What did I miss out on? What were all of the things that you guys did as kids and teens?"

"Oh…" Melissa thought about it. "You're younger than I am, and I suppose your generation would have had totally different experiences than mine. But then, some things are universal. Or long-standing traditions. We did a lot of things together as school kids. It was just a small school, so they did a lot of things to foster unity and make sure that we knew each other well. The kids the same age or in the grades below and above us."

"Like what?"

"I don't know. Sports. Book clubs or homework clubs. Science fairs. Family movie night. Whatever they could think of to get us together. Holiday parties. There was always something going on."

"Like the Statehood Day picnic?"

"Yeah. That was one of them. I don't know for sure, but it seemed so much bigger when I was a kid. I don't know if that's because it really was, or just because I was smaller and it felt bigger. There had to be more farm animals and more entries in the baking contests than there are now, I'm sure of it."

"Are you going to enter anything?"

"Me?" Melissa laughed. "I'm not exactly the best baker in the world. No, I'm not going to enter anything into the baking contests. There are some for flowers or quilts… maybe I'll enter one of them."

"What about Davis? Did he go out for sports and all of these other things too?"

"No. He was never very good at sports. Not like people would give him a chance, though. How was he supposed to be as good as the boys whose fathers were always out playing with them and training them? Davis's dad… He was never at home. And when he was… I don't think he ever got along with his wife and kids. From what I gathered, it was a war zone over there all the time when he was home. When he wasn't, then maybe they got to relax a little, but learn sports? Or get help entering the science fair or doing something else worthwhile? No. I knew what Angela Plaint was like, and trust me, she wasn't one of those moms who thought that her kids could do no wrong and who bought everything they could ever want."

"I feel sorry for the guy. Did he have anywhere to escape to?" Erin remembered Bertie Braceling's description of how Davis had called Bertie while hiding in the closet after his father had been killed. Not a kid who could feel safe in his own home.

"When they went on family vacations, they had a place in the woods. Where Davis's great-great-grandmother had lived, I think. Rustic."

"In real estate agent talk, that means no indoor plumbing," Vic informed Erin.

Melissa laughed. "I think that would be accurate. Maybe a well pump over the kitchen sink, but no indoor toilet or gas stove out there. It was camping, just in a rickety old house instead of a tent. A little bit bigger and more civilized… but not by much."

"And they went there for the summer every year?"

"No. For a week or two. Not all summer. I think they probably would have killed each other if it had been all summer." Melissa stopped, thinking about what she had said and getting red. "I mean… well, you know what I mean. I didn't mean it literally."

Some of the family vacations Erin had endured had been pretty tense. Putting a dysfunctional family into a hotel room or tent and adding in extra concerns over finances and spending wasn't really the way to increase family unity, which was always what they had said it was about. Spending time together as a family to make them stronger and closer together.

Yeah. If they didn't kill each other, like Melissa had said.

"Where was this cabin?"

"I don't think I ever knew exactly where it was. I was never there. They wouldn't have been allowed to take friends out there."

"And he never took you there when you were older and he could sneak out? You know, a private place where you could... visit."

Melissa's curls bounced as she shook her head insistently. "No! We never went out there to make out. You should be ashamed of yourself for even saying such a thing, Erin Price." But she was laughing, not accusatory, so Erin knew that she didn't actually mean it seriously.

"Okay, sorry. I was a teenager once too..."

"We weren't like that. Just talked to each other sometimes. We weren't ever actually dating. Boyfriend and girlfriend."

"Right. Okay."

Melissa shook her head. "I was a good girl, Erin. I never would have considered such a thing. Especially not with a boy like Davis. He was... already in a lot of trouble by the time we were in high school. With drugs and everything, I mean."

Erin suspected it was probably true. If Melissa had been able to keep her adult friendship from the people of Bald Eagle Falls, then it was probably because they had never been aware of her friendship with him as a teenager. If they had been causing all kinds of gossip when she was young, then a renewed friendship as adults would have garnered a *lot* of attention.

Eventually, what was left of the soup was cold, and Melissa put it in the fridge for lunch the next day. She politely thanked Vic and Erin for coming to see her and spending some time visiting to boost her spirits. Erin dug a brownie out of her purse from where she had stowed it for safekeeping and presented it to Melissa.

"I thought you might like a little something for dessert. If you were feeling better."

Melissa leaned forward impulsively to give Erin a hug and a quick kiss that blew past her cheek. "Thank you for everything, Erin. That's so sweet!"

"That's the way you like them," Erin said, smiling, putting a different meaning on Melissa's words.

Melissa giggled. "Well, yes, I do. I never was one for all of the bittersweet stuff. Give me sweet chocolate any day."

"Let us know if you need anything else," Vic told her and, in a few minutes, they were out the door and sitting in Erin's car.

"I'm glad you suggested that," Vic said. "I think she really needed a friend tonight."

"And she got two of them," Erin said, touching Vic on the arm. It hadn't just been her. Vic had definitely held up her end of the conversation as well, and eating the delicious soup together had made them all feel close and intimate. "You're a good friend too."

"Yes, but *I* didn't have a brownie in my purse."

Erin laughed.

She started the car and they traveled the few blocks home.

CHAPTER 44

The next day, Erin walked into the kitchen at Auntie Clem's as Vic placed a pink note at her workstation. Erin raised her brows questioningly.

"Adele called," Vic explained. "She asked if we would bring a bit of extra day-old home with us today that she could pick up later."

"Sure, of course," Erin agreed. Usually, Adele came to the bakery to pick up the day-old bread but, of course, she didn't need to, living in the woods behind Erin's and Vic's homes. There was no problem with having them take food home for her to pick up from there, which was more convenient.

Erin frowned, thinking about it.

"What?" Vic asked

"Nothing. It's just… not her usual day. She's kind of fallen into a rhythm, and she wouldn't normally need any extra yet. And usually, she comes here."

"She didn't say, but I guess something came up." Vic shrugged. "Maybe the family that she collects for has company this week. Or a teenager who is suddenly eating more."

Erin nodded. "Yeah. Or she has picked up someone else that needs the help."

"How is it that Adele ends up making contact with people who need help? She's so reclusive. I can't see her just running into anyone around town and offering help. And even if she does, how does she talk them into it, when neither of us has ever had any success in getting people to accept help?"

"I don't know. I guess she just has that way about her. People know that they can trust her. Maybe because they know that she can keep quiet and isn't going to go blabbing their secrets to anyone else."

Vic chuckled and nodded.

"And as far as the people that she meets—I think it might be through her rambles in the woods. She knows she can't let people camp on my property, because it's her job to make sure they don't. But once past my property line, she might have contact with people who are squatting on one of the adjoining properties. Out past the west town limits, I don't know who owns those properties. They're pretty wild; I don't think they've been kept up by anyone."

"We used to play out that way when we came to see Aunt Angela. We'd hop on our bikes and go play war or hunting or 'surviving in the wild.' It was always a lot of fun. I liked that it was so wild, but it was close enough to town that we wouldn't get in trouble if someone was looking for us."

"It would be a good place to squat if no one is enforcing any kind of security out there. Out of the way and independent, but close enough to town to access the amenities when necessary."

Vic nodded. "It's a short list," she said, pointing to the pink phone message. "She only needs a few things."

"As long as it isn't for Adele herself. I always worry about whether I'm paying her enough. I don't want her to be suffering because I'm not paying her a living wage."

"She really doesn't have many expenses," Vic pointed out. "You give her a place to live. She doesn't have a car. It's just food and minimal living expenses. And it's not like she lives a lavish lifestyle."

Erin shrugged. She'd run the numbers several times herself and believed that Adele was making enough as Erin's groundskeeper to survive on, outside of whatever she made with the wildcrafted items that she sold through the General Store and herbs and remedies that she sold as a "wise woman of the forest." She believed that Adele was making enough to be comfortable.

But it always worried her that she didn't know where the day-old goods for the homeless were going. Maybe she shouldn't have had a "no questions asked" policy. But it was too late to remove it now.

Erin called Adele before they left Auntie Clem's Bakery to tell her that she would bring the baking out to the cottage. Adele didn't need to come to the house to fetch it. Adele made noises of protest, but Erin shrugged them off. "I'm bringing it out to you," she insisted.

She counted off the reasons in her mind. It would be good exercise for her and the opportunity to reconnect with nature. Something she had made a goal of but still didn't do as often as she should. It would give her a chance to look surreptitiously around Adele's cottage to make sure that she appeared to have everything she needed, just to settle her worry that Adele might need the food donation for herself. She could see the new cat again and make sure that it was healing well and didn't need further medical attention. And, of course, it would give her the chance to talk to her groundskeeper and make sure that she didn't have any concerns.

Any one of those reasons would have been reason enough to take the meandering path through the woods to Adele's cottage.

It would require a little courage on her part, going by where she had found Bruel's body, but if she didn't face up to her fears, she would be letting them control her.

That didn't mean that she had to go alone. "Do you mind going with me over to Adele's to deliver the food?" she asked Vic.

Vic shrugged. "Sure, no problem. I should take Nilla out for a walk. He always likes it if we go into the woods. So much more interesting than the dog run in the backyard or the street."

"You'll have to leave him outside. Adele won't want him in the cottage if she still has the cat there."

She hoped that the cat was still there so she could see him again.

It hadn't had very long to recuperate. Though some animals did seem to heal much faster than she would have expected.

"I can leave him outside for a few minutes," Vic agreed. "I'll bring his leash so I can tie him up. He's getting a lot better about not running away, but I wouldn't trust him in the woods with all of the squirrels and other things to chase."

"Yeah, I don't think Adele would be too impressed if we let him chase all of her wildlife."

So as soon as they were home, Vic went into her apartment to get Nilla. Erin left her purse in the house for safekeeping and, with the bag of baked goods, they were ready to go to the cottage.

Erin was glad they had Nilla along. He was a good distraction. She was so busy watching and laughing at him that she didn't have time to think about finding Christian Bruel's body or the fact that his killer hadn't yet been brought to justice. The police really needed to find Davis and get him back in prison. Then Erin could feel safe again.

Erin heard a warning caw as they approached the cottage and looked around for Skye. She didn't see him on any of the nearby branches, but did see a magpie. Had she mistaken a magpie call for that of a crow? They weren't that much alike.

"Hi, there, pretty bird," she said to the magpie as they approached. His shining black feathers caught the sun, shining like oil with iridescent rainbows. "Are you the same magpie as I saw before? Where's Skye?"

She still couldn't see him when she got up to the door. Maybe he was out patrolling the woods or running some errand for Adele. Erin smiled at the thought of the crow following Adele's instructions. He did seem like a very smart bird sometimes, but she doubted he was smart enough to follow instructions.

Erin waited while Vic tied Nilla up. The leash still gave him plenty of room to roam around and smell things in the yard. When Erin looked back at the door, Adele was standing there waiting for them.

Erin walked to the door and offered the bag of baking to Adele. "That should be everything you asked for."

"Thank you. That will be of great help. Would you and Miss Victoria like to come in for a cup of tea?"

Erin looked at Vic as if to ask her, even though she already knew the answer. "Sure, we could come in for a minute. Thank you."

Adele motioned them in. Erin entered the cottage.

CHAPTER 45

*N*othing had changed since the last time she had been there. Nothing to indicate that Adele was in need or that anything was wrong. Erin was sure that the baked goods must be for someone else.

It hadn't been a lot of food, probably just enough for one person. Maybe two.

The black cat was not sleeping in his box by the stove, but had been lying on the bed. When he saw Erin and Vic enter, he jumped down off of the bed to investigate. Erin crouched down and reached her fingers toward him in invitation. He watched her warily for a few minutes, sniffing the air and waiting for her to do something threatening. Eventually, he walked toward her and sniffed her outstretched fingers.

"Hi, there!" Erin said to him softly. "He's looking a lot better than he was." His fur was smooth and clean, no longer rough with dirt or showing the wounds he had received from the birds. And he even seemed a little less thin, more rounded out, even though it had only been a few days.

"Yes, he's healing quickly," Adele agreed. "He's been much more energetic the last day or two. He'll probably be ready to leave here soon."

Though Erin would have preferred Adele to keep him indoors, she knew it wasn't an argument she could win, so she didn't comment.

"Did you give him a name?"

Adele gave her a sideways look as she put the kettle on the stove. "Why would I give him a name?"

"You gave Skye a name."

Adele blinked and gave her a slow smile. "Bernt."

"Bernt?" Vic repeated. "That's so cute! What a great name."

Adele gave a little shrug. "It seemed appropriate."

"Hi, Bernt," Erin moved her fingers slowly to scratch the black cat's ears, and he tolerated her touch. In a few minutes, he was rubbing against her fingers, enjoying the attention.

"He likes you," Adele commented. "Maybe you should take him home with you."

"No, I think I'd better not become the neighborhood cat lady. With a cat and a rabbit and a dog around already, that's probably enough."

Nilla gave a yip from outside.

"And another dog," Erin said, grinning at Vic.

Vic smiled back. "I suppose it has kind of become pet central. But Bernt really is darling."

"Maybe he'll stay around here, now that he knows you," Erin said to Adele. "It would be nice if he at least had somewhere to go when he was hungry or cold."

"Of course," Adele agreed. "The animals seem to know where to go."

"Does that include the humans? They seem to know that you'll feed them too."

Adele looked at the bag of baking that she had set down on the wooden table. "Yes," she agreed, eyebrows raised as she nodded. "I suppose the human animals know where to go too."

"Do the humans need anything else? It's not winter, so I don't suppose they need any extra blankets or clothing…"

Adele didn't answer immediately. Then she shook her head. "No, I don't think so."

She set a cup in front of each chair at the table and poured the boiling water into them. "Any special blend you would like?"

Vic picked out an Orange Pekoe tea bag and gave a polite nod. "This is good."

She would only take commercially prepared tea at Adele's. Erin couldn't believe that she was still superstitious about anything that the witch made. She said that she wasn't, that she knew Adele would never try to poison her or put a spell on her, but her actions said something different. Erin chuckled to herself.

"Do you have anything interesting?" she asked Adele.

Adele opened a small cupboard, just deep enough for single rows of small jars, each one filled with different herbs or blends. She glanced over her stores.

"How about this one?" she suggested and put a jar of finely-ground leaves on the table.

Erin sniffed the jar. The spicy smell was evocative of Christmas and gingerbread men. She closed her eyes. "Ginger, cinnamon, and cloves…" Those were obvious. But there was something else. "White tea leaves. And… rose…" She was going to say rose hips, but it didn't have the fruity smell of rose hips. "Rose petals?" she suggested. "Rosebuds?"

"Rosebuds," Adele agreed. "You are very good."

Erin carefully measured the blend into her cup and gave it a stir. "It smells lovely. I love ginger tea."

Vic didn't say anything to warn Erin against not being poisoned or magicked by Adele, but her eyes were on Erin's tea as she let it steep.

"So… everything has been quiet in the woods?" Erin asked. "At least, since Bruel's body was found?"

Adele gave a nod. "No more bodies," she confirmed.

"Well… that's good. Any trespassers? Anything I need to be worried about?"

"No. Some kids, but there are always going to be kids. It's not hard to get them on their way. They want privacy, so if they think someone might be watching them, they'll leave pretty quickly."

"To say nothing of the business end of a shotgun," Vic said.

"That does have its own convincing power," Adele agreed. "But I try to use it judiciously. People get too accustomed to a gun, and it stops having the same effect. You don't want to have to fire it to convince them that you're really serious."

Erin shuddered at the thought of Adele firing her gun at someone in the woods. She didn't mind Adele being armed for her own protection. Who knew who she might run into in the woods when she was out and about at night? Especially when there were escaped prisoners in the area. But she did not want Adele to ever actually have to shoot at anyone. The hope was that having the gun with her, she would never actually have to use it.

"You haven't seen any sign of Davis?" Erin asked. Just to be absolutely sure. Sometimes Adele chose not to tell her things.

"He hasn't been in your woods," Adele confirmed, shaking her head. "You can rest easy."

"Hopefully, he's gone somewhere far away," Vic said, stooping down to pet Bernt as he wound around her legs.

Erin nodded. She kept watching Adele, who didn't meet her eyes, but focused on stirring her tea.

"You haven't seen Davis at all?" Erin asked.

Adele looked up at her. For a moment, the three of them just looked at each other, calculating.

Erin had not missed that Adele was trying to answer her question without being dishonest, but without giving Erin the information she was asking for.

"He hasn't been in my woods. But maybe you have seen him somewhere else?" Erin looked at the baked goods. "Maybe he's hiding out and in need of some new provisions?"

"Perhaps."

"Adele!"

"You don't judge," Adele said. "The food goes to who needs it, no questions asked. And you weren't upset about Ryder's murderer getting away free."

"No, but that's different. There's a big difference between that and what Davis has done. Don't forget that he tried to kill me and to burn down my house."

"But he didn't succeed."

"He did succeed in killing Bertie Braceling, and that's not exactly easy for me to forget."

"Which is why I thought it better if you didn't know anything."

"We can't give aid to an escaped convict."

"You aren't."

"If I'm giving him food, I am. If you're helping him to hide from the police, then you are. We really can't, Adele. We need to obey the law."

"You don't know anything about it. He isn't here." Adele raised her hands to indicate the cottage, looking around her significantly. "You have no idea where he is. You gave the food to me."

"So you're the only one on the hook? I don't want you to have to go to prison either, Adele. Please. Just tell me where he is, and we'll get him back in prison. That's the only way to make sure that everyone is safe from prosecution."

Adele sipped her tea, reminding Erin that she hadn't yet had a taste of hers. The light, spicy-tasting tea was very nice.

"Maybe being safe from prosecution is not the most important thing," Adele said.

CHAPTER 46

hat are you worried about, then?" Erin asked.

"That justice is done. That no one is hurt or killed because of something they didn't do. That everyone, especially the people I care about, is safe and doesn't get hurt."

"Okay... well, that seems doable. That doesn't stop us from turning Davis over to the authorities."

Even though Erin knew that Adele would prefer to have nothing to do with law enforcement, it didn't seem like they had much choice. They couldn't harbor a fugitive. Especially one that had just killed his fellow escapee and maybe Mr. Peach too. He had a proven track record against Erin.

"He's not... the person you think he is."

Erin shook her head. "You can't believe his 'poor me' act. I know he's had a tough life and that a lot of things have gone wrong for him. But he is violent and he has killed more than once. I feel bad for what he's been through, but he's not innocent."

"He didn't have anything to do with Gregory Peach's death. And I don't think he had anything to do with Bruel's death either. The police are going to assume that he did. They'll come in guns blazing, and if they do manage to take him without killing him, they're going to throw him in with the worst offenders on the assumption that he escaped prison to kill two people. And that's not true."

Erin looked at Vic to see what she was thinking. Vic didn't seem to be any more convinced by Adele's plea than Erin. Erin knew Davis. She had seen him kill violently and with no apparent remorse.

"How do you know he didn't have anything to do with Gregory Peach?" Vic asked.

"Because… he was alone. He's been alone this whole time. He didn't kidnap Peach and hold him hostage and torture him. I know where he was, and he didn't do that."

"If he was alone, then you don't have any proof that he was there the whole time," Vic pointed out. "He could have left and come back while you weren't there."

"He wasn't coming and going. I would have known."

Erin couldn't help looking around Adele's cottage once more for a closet, shoes under the bed, or some other hiding place Davis could be. But he wasn't there. She thought about where he could have been that was within eyesight of the cottage but couldn't think of anywhere. There was no way that Adele could have been keeping track of Davis all the time. Not that closely.

Erin sighed. "And Bruel? You don't know that Davis didn't kill him. You said you didn't think he had anything to do with that death, but you don't know."

Adele shook her head. "No. I can't tell you I'm one hundred percent sure. But… I'm pretty sure."

"How could you be? And if Davis didn't kill Bruel, then who did? He didn't kill himself."

"Peach, maybe. But I don't believe it was Davis."

"Because that's what he told you?"

"Because… he was afraid."

"He was afraid of getting caught," Vic said flatly.

"No. He was afraid of someone coming after him. Killing him like they had Bruel."

"Who?" Vic rolled her eyes. "Has he at least come up with a plausible reason that someone killed Bruel? Who it was and what their motive was?"

"No. He didn't know who did it. That was why he was afraid."

"You should have told the police as soon as you saw him. You knew that he had escaped from the penitentiary and that he might have been the one who killed Bruel even if he said he didn't. You should have called the police."

Adele stared at Vic, expressionless. "If you'd had the experiences that I have had with the police, you would understand. I don't have any reason to trust the authorities."

"You know Officer Piper. You could call him. You know he wouldn't go off the handle."

"The police would do what they were required to do. Arrest him and put him back in prison. Where he would be vulnerable to retaliation."

"Retaliation from who?"

Adele sipped her tea. She looked at Erin when she replied. "Retaliation from whoever helped them escape prison."

CHAPTER 47

Whoever helped them? That was Mr. Peach. He was the one who helped them to escape prison, and now he's dead, so Davis doesn't have to worry anymore. If that's what he was concerned about, then he can go back to prison without fear."

"He said it wasn't Mr. Peach. That Peach could never have organized the whole thing. He'd just been a tool for someone else."

Erin and Vic looked at each other. They looked at Adele. None of them had any better theory of what had happened. Erin had to believe that Davis was the perpetrator of both murders. It was the only logical explanation. And it meant that they needed to find Davis and get him back in prison.

"Where is he?" Erin asked.

Adele's shoulders lifted in a shrug. "You'll have to find him. You won't get it out of me."

"Because you don't think that he had anything to do with either death."

"That's right."

"You think that he's scared and there is still someone out there who killed Bruel and Peach."

"Yes." Adele's eyes were steady.

"Why?"

Adele's eyes went down and she frowned. "You wouldn't like it if I said that I just know."

"You have to have some reason."

"I have… a sense about some things. And I can sense that Davis is telling the truth. That he's scared and doesn't know who is behind the killings. That if he is exposed… he will be the next victim."

And Adele had said what she wanted was to see that justice was done and for nobody else to die.

She wasn't going to give up Davis's location. Even if Erin called the police, she would have nothing else to tell them. They would still have to find Davis on their own. It wouldn't get them anywhere and Erin's relationship with Adele would be ruined. Adele would never trust her with any sensitive information.

"Okay… if you won't say, you won't say," Erin said finally. She had one last sip from her cup and put it down on the table. "We should be getting on our way."

Vic opened her mouth, startled and starting to protest, then shook her head and pressed her lips together and said nothing. Adele studied them both. She seemed relieved, yet still anxious at the same time.

"It's been nice to have you," she said carefully. "Thank you for bringing the bread."

Erin nodded. "We're always happy to help people out. I hope you'll keep giving us the opportunities."

Adele nodded.

Erin looked around for Bernt. The little cat was once more curled up in the box by the stove. She and Vic could let themselves out without worrying about whether the cat was going to bolt. They went back outside, untied Nilla, and headed for home.

"Tell me that we aren't just going to go home and pretend that nothing happened," Vic said peevishly.

"We're not."

"Adele knows where Davis is. I can't believe it. We need to let the police know and get him back in prison."

Erin looked at Vic, a slight smile on her face.

"What?" Vic demanded.

"It wasn't that long ago that you were talking about how you'd grown up being taught never to involve the police ever. That you should go to the clan, and they would help you."

"Well, that's true. But I can tell you—and so can Jeremy if you don't believe me—that I don't always do what I was taught to growing up. I didn't back then, either."

Erin knew very well how widely Vic had strayed from the path that her parents had tried to cut for her. "No, really?" she asked in a mock-horrified tone.

"What are we going to do?" Vic asked.

"We're going to call somebody. But we're going to have to be really careful how we go about this."

Vic would, of course, expect Erin to call Terry. But if so, she was wrong. Nor did she call the sheriff or the penitentiary authorities. She called Beaver.

She didn't tell Beaver exactly what she wanted on the phone, just said that she needed her and could she come over right away?

Even over the phone, Erin could hear Beaver chewing her gum. She grimaced and tried to remain focused on the conversation rather than the annoying sound.

"Is this about the case?" Beaver asked.

"Yes."

Chomp, chomp, chomp.

"Then I'll be right there."

Bald Eagle Falls was a small town and Beaver had obviously not had reason to go back to the city since she was at Erin's door about ten minutes later.

She looked around as she entered, confirming to herself that Erin and Vic were alone. She sat on one of the chairs, wide-legged, looking casual and sloppy when Erin knew very well she was anything but. She was professional and attentive, every sense on alert, and the mannerisms were just an act.

"Ladies. What do you have?"

"I think… we're close to figuring out where Davis is," Erin said slowly.

"You don't believe that he's gone? Someone smart would have gotten himself as far away from here as possible, knowing that the police were on his trail."

"No. He's still here. He's close by."

"Oh?" Beaver looked amused, raising an eyebrow in query.

"I have… an informant."

"Oh, you do, do you? Informants need a lot of handling. And you can't believe everything they have to tell you. It all has to be cross-checked and confirmed."

"I know. Or… that makes sense, anyway."

"Your informant knows that he is still in the area?"

"Yes."

Vic looked at Erin as if she were crazy. "But we don't know where to look. We have no idea where to find him."

"When we were talking to Melissa, she said that Davis and his family used to go on family vacations in the summer," Erin reminded her.

"Yeah. But she didn't say where."

"Melissa?" Beaver repeated. "Is she your informant?"

"No… we just took some soup to her, to help her feel better."

"If she was really sick, that would be commendable."

"Whether she's sick or not, she still needed it," Erin told Beaver firmly.

Beaver cocked her head, considering. Then she nodded. "Okay. Maybe she did." She waved a hand. "Sorry. Go on. I interrupted."

Erin looked at Vic. "She talked about family vacations."

Vic nodded, remembering. "Right. He didn't like them. Camping."

Erin shook her head. "Not camping."

Vic thought about it for a minute. "Right. Not camping. In a cabin in the woods." She stopped abruptly and looked at Erin. "And A—our informant said that he wasn't in *your* woods."

"Yeah. Which makes me think that maybe he *is* in the woods. Just somewhere a little more remote than mine," Erin motioned toward the back of the house where the woods bordered on her property.

Vic nodded. "Yeah… yes, I think you could be right about that. So what do we do? How are we going to find out where this cabin is? There must be some kind of record, I guess, if they had some land-holdings from his great-grandmother or whatever she was. How do we go about searching for title deeds? And we can't assume that it would be in the Plaint name. It could be something different. Some-thing really common in Bald Eagle Falls."

"I think you already know where it is."

"What?" Vic crinkled her nose. "What are you talking about? I don't know anything about it."

"You said you used to go play in the woods to the west of mine. When you were in town visiting Angela Plaint."

"Yes…" Vic thought about this, frowning.

Beaver leaned forward slightly, her eyes glittering.

"Why did you go there?" Erin asked.

"I don't know. Because it was close, but it was wild. It was more fun to play there."

"But why *there*? Why not in my woods? Or in something at the other end of town, closer to the Plaint home?"

"Because…" Vic trailed off. "You think it was because Aunt Angela's family owned that land?"

Erin shrugged. "Who showed it to you? How did you know to go there?"

"I don't know. My brothers knew about it, so they would take me there. But I don't know who told them. *Maybe* Trevor and Davis?"

"Was there a cabin on the property?"

"I don't know." Vic rubbed her temples and closed her eyes, trying to visualize it. "Our parents would kick us out to go play outside. So we played outside. Yeah…" She shook her head, unable to remember for sure. "I think there might have been a cabin. But it was really old."

"Pump in the kitchen sink?" Erin prompted.

"Yeah… That sounds familiar. We might have hung out there

sometimes to use it as a fort or play 'survival.' Do you really think that's where Davis is?"

"It's close enough to—*here*—that our informant was aware of it and aware of him staying there. She said she would know if he'd been coming and going, so it must be a spot she can keep an eye on regularly. That means that it's within a short walk. She doesn't need a car to get there."

Beaver had probably figured out by now who Erin's informant was, but she wasn't going to out Adele in so many words. All that she had given away was that it was someone who lived close by.

"Why did you call me instead of Terry?" Beaver asked.

Erin squirmed, uncomfortable with the question. "Vic and I can't go rushing in there like some heroine on a TV movie. But I think that… we might be able to talk Davis into giving himself up. I know Vic has her gun," Erin glanced sideways at Vic, "but I don't know if Davis is armed. He might be dangerous if we corner him in his hiding place."

"So you need someone to back you up. Some protection in case things go off the rails. Why me instead of Officer Piper?"

"Davis knows Terry. If Terry goes in there, Davis is going to come out guns blazing. I've seen him under pressure. He won't be thinking things through logically. If he's desperate, there's no telling who he might kill."

"But he doesn't know me."

"He doesn't, does he? He's not another informant? You haven't met him before at the prison or in an undercover investigation?"

"No. He wasn't active in the Dyson clan or any other criminal organization. He was only ever acting for himself. Not someone I would have had contact with."

"We can pretend that you're just one of us. A friend or someone else who works at the bakery. Then he won't feel cornered, but you're there in case something goes wrong."

Beaver nodded. "Sounds like a plan."

Erin waited for her to protest that they couldn't go in by themselves, that it was a stupid idea. Beaver didn't. One reason Erin called her was that she figured Beaver was impulsive enough to go rogue.

Beaver had demonstrated previously that she was willing to bend or break the rules to achieve a goal. That was the kind of attitude she needed if they were going to bring Davis in without a shoot-out.

Vic was looking Beaver over. Beaver's chewing slowed and then stopped.

"What?"

"You look army. Or at least like a hunter. If you're going to look like a baker or just 'one of the girls,' you need a makeover."

Beaver looked at Erin. "What have you got me into now?"

CHAPTER 48

*G*iving Beaver a makeover probably involved more negotiation than they would have to go through with Davis. Beaver was comfortable in her own skin and didn't care what other people thought of her. Her image and the personas that she presumably adopted while working undercover with one of the organized crime families were not "girly." She wasn't Annie Oakley, a sharpshooter in a dress with long, curly hair. She was one of the guys, who just happened to be female.

She and Vic were close enough in size for Beaver to be able to wear some of Vic's clothes, though her well-muscled shoulders and biceps presented a challenge. Each article of clothing she tried on required a lengthy negotiation and discussion of how she would carry her various weapons with her in a way that would allow her to access them quickly and smoothly if the situation required.

Erin had forgotten how much equipment Beaver actually carried. She didn't just have a small gun in a bra holster like Vic. There was her main gun, quite a bit larger than Vic's and a smaller throw-down on her ankle. A knife in a sheath on her arm. And the hunting jacket she invariably wore had numerous pockets filled with other equipment that Erin probably didn't even want to know about.

Vic couldn't talk Beaver out of the hunting jacket. But she

managed to get Beaver into a pink t-shirt in place of the army green halter top, and flared blue jeans that allowed her easy access to her ankle holster in place of the camouflage cargo pants. Vic banned the camouflage cap as well and turned Beaver's long blond ponytail into a messy bun.

The hunting jacket looked a little out of place, but Vic had done what she had set out to do, and Beaver no longer looked like she was in the army; just eccentric.

Erin added an artistic smudge of flour to Beaver's face. Just enough to suggest that the bakery employee had wiped her face with the back of her wrist and not realized that she had gotten flour on it.

She and Vic surveyed their work.

"I think that will do it," Vic said, nodding. "He's not immediately going to think that you're packing, anyway."

"Sometimes, it's best if people think you are," Beaver countered.

"I don't think you want to trigger Davis," Erin said. "I don't want you to, anyway. He's volatile."

Beaver gave a nod. "I'll defer to your opinion on the matter."

"Well, then…" Erin looked at Vic. "You remember the way?"

"Not exactly, but I'm sure I can find it."

They had a choice between Beaver's old station wagon and Erin's equally old yellow bug, and Beaver insisted on her car.

"Just give me a minute to get it warmed up and we'll be on our way," she advised, sauntering out the door.

Erin looked at Vic, shaking her head. "If it has to be warmed up in this weather, we might be in trouble."

"Maybe she just needs a minute to herself to get into character. That pink shirt might have thrown her off her game."

Erin chuckled. "I don't think pink is her favorite color."

"She looked as uncomfortable as a rooster in a pond," Vic agreed, giggling loudly. "That poor woman."

"Well, it's only for a little while tonight, then she can get back into her soldier clothes." Erin looked at the green clothing neatly piled on the coffee table. "I'm not sure how she works undercover when she looks so much like she's military."

"There are a lot of baddies who like to dress in camo too. Hunters, militia groups, and wannabes. People who could never pass the army psych exams or background checks but like to look like bad boys. It makes them feel more powerful or part of a bigger movement. So she could still have good cover. But it doesn't fit if we're going in there as non-threatening bakers who just want to help him out or get him to turn himself in." Vic pursed her lips, looking at Erin. "What exactly are you going to tell him?"

Erin's stomach tightened and her guts gave a sluggish gurgle.

"I don't know, exactly. If Adele is right, and he's not the killer and there's someone else out there that he's afraid of, then prison is the safest choice for him. Hiding out in the woods… someone else is going to find him sooner or later. Not everyone knows about his family having a cabin there. Still, sooner or later, someone is going to figure it out. He can't hide forever."

Erin tried not to think too deeply about what she was about to do. She focused on Davis's face, on the way that Bertie Braceling and Melissa had talked about him. A vulnerable teen when his father had been killed. Someone who didn't have a lot of inner strength and resolve, who had been traumatized and succumbed to addiction. Davis was still stuck in that mindset, lashing out wildly, not knowing whom he could trust, trying to protect himself from any further hurt. That was who he was on the inside. That was the part of him she needed to appeal to.

"Think we've given her long enough?" Vic asked.

Erin looked at the station wagon, which appeared to be chugging away just fine, though the blue exhaust coming out the tailpipe probably wouldn't pass any emissions testing. "Looks fine to me. Let's go before I start having second thoughts about this."

They armed the burglar alarm and locked up. Vic got into the front seat beside Beaver, where they both had room for their longer legs and Vic had a good view through the windshield, and Erin squeezed into the bench seat in the back.

Beaver pulled out and they started off traveling west. The daylight was fading and Erin hoped that Vic would see their surroundings well enough to lead them to the cabin in the woods. She knew it was a gamble relying on her vague memories of where she had played war games with her brothers several years ago. How long had they kept going to those woods? Until Vic was ten? Into her teens? Her older brothers probably wouldn't have remained interested in playing survival with her as older teens.

Vic started off strong, directing Beaver to the woods following the same route she would have taken on her bike. But as they got farther into the woods and daylight faded, it became harder. She had to remember the landmarks and try to pick them out in the darkness by the light of the headlights.

"There. There it is," Vic jabbed her finger against the window emphatically.

Peering through the trees, Erin could barely see the dark shape of the cabin. It would have been easy to miss it. Beaver crept closer on the gravel road that had been overgrown by weeds and bushy under-growth. It was evident that no one had driven down it for a long time. She turned her headlights off so that they wouldn't alert him to their presence. Better to catch him inside the cabin than to be trying to chase him through the trees on foot in the dark. Erin was not particularly adept at running or navigating through the wilderness in the dark. Even walking, Vic always accused her of crashing through the bush like a buffalo because of how loud she was.

Beaver stopped. "I don't want to get any closer than this. I don't want to tip him off or end up cutting off my exit route."

Vic nodded and popped her door open. "Let's go, then."

Erin noticed that the cabin light in the station wagon did not light when the doors were opened. She was a little more reluctant to get out of the car, but it was her plan. Vic was waiting for her to take the lead. Beaver too was holding back, ready, Erin assumed, to see how everything played out before taking any action. Erin hoped that she wouldn't end up having to drive back sitting in the backseat with Davis, handcuffed or not. She hadn't thought that part through.

She followed Vic. Vic paused as they got closer to the house to speak to the two of them in a low voice. "There's a front door and a back, so he could run for it. But it's all just one room, like your summer cottage," she aimed the comment at Erin, "so we'll know that there isn't anyone hiding in another room, or closet, or downstairs."

"Good." Beaver nodded at the description. "Do you two want to go in the front while I cover the back?"

"No, not if you're supposed to just be one of our friends," Erin said. "We're not supposed to look like we have any police training or are there to capture him. Just to talk."

Beaver chewed her gum and didn't say anything. It was too dark to tell if she were rolling her eyes or regretting her agreement to go along with them.

Erin walked up the large rocks that formed a paved path to the front door. No hiding or creeping up on the house if they were just a trio of bakers coming for a visit. They needed to look unprofessional and unafraid.

Erin could see a light in the window, which was helpful. It gave her a more concrete reason to be there.

Erin knocked on the door.

CHAPTER 49

*E*rin imagined Davis's reaction at hearing someone at the door. Heart leaping to his throat and pounding wildly. Reaching for a book or lamp or anything that could be used as a weapon if he didn't actually have a weapon. Looking around in panic, wondering if this were to be his final stand.

"Hello?" Erin called cheerily. "Anyone home? I saw your light."

She hoped this would calm him. A concrete reason someone would be there. Not because someone had figured out who he was and where he was hiding out, but because she had seen his light and was curious about it.

It was still a couple more minutes before there was any response from within. Erin knocked again, with a few more friendly hellos and yoo-hoos. She looked at Vic. Hopefully, the man's training in Southern hospitality would take over and he would feel compelled to welcome whoever had come to his door, despite the circumstances.

There was a scraping sound on the other side of the door.

"Who's there? You're trespassing on private property."

"See, I told you there was someone here," Erin said loudly to Vic. "I told you I had seen lights out here. Welcome to the neighborhood, hon. Do you need anything?"

The door opened a crack. "I don't need anything. I just want some privacy."

"It's so good to have someone new here. It always worries me, these properties not being used. Abandoned houses are just a magnet for crime." Erin kept her voice falsely high and bright, but was afraid that Davis would see right through the facade.

He opened the door farther, his eye pressed to the crack, peeking out at them. Erin didn't think he recognized her at first, but then he took a step back and started to shut the door. Vic shoved the toe of her shoe in the door to prevent him from closing it.

"Invite us in," she told him.

Davis shook his head, scowling. "Go away. I don't know what you're doing here!"

"Go away? And tell the police where you are?"

His eyes widened in alarm. "No." He hesitated, trying to figure out what to do, but caught between a rock and a hard place. Of course he didn't want to invite them in and to have to talk with them, but he didn't want them going right back to the police, and he couldn't stop them if he just shut the door and let them drive away. After a few moments of indecision, he opened the door wider to permit them entrance. He shook his head as he watched the three women enter, angry and alarmed. Keeping one hand in his jacket pocket, he shut the door firmly, then went to the windows to tug the tatters of curtains together, trying to block the light from spilling outside.

Erin took a quick glance around the interior of the cabin. It was hardly livable. Melissa had compared it to camping, only in a building instead of a tent, and it was certainly rustic. There was a bed with a wooden frame, maybe handmade. The ancient mattress, probably a canvas slipcover filled with straw, was blotched with mold or mildew. There was a rough table with a couple of chairs. A sink with a hand pump, as Vic had remembered.

Erin could see stars through some of the holes in the roof, and the whole structure creaked as a wind blew through the interior.

Davis himself wasn't in much better shape. He had changed out of his prison uniform, but Erin wasn't sure where he or Adele had gotten the clothes he was wearing. Maybe they had been left at the cabin after the last family vacation. Old Levi's and a button-up shirt. They hung off of him like a scarecrow. He was even thinner than Erin remembered him, with a sharp, weasel-like face.

"What are you doing here?" he demanded. "You know who I am! You want to get yourselves killed?"

Davis faced them, one hand still in his jacket pocket, where Erin assumed he held a gun pointed at them. Little did he know that two out of three of them were also armed.

But Erin didn't want things to escalate. She wanted to calm him down, to get him to see that giving himself up was the only practical way to ensure his safety from both the police and whoever else was out there, if there was someone else mixed up in the whole thing.

"We know who you are," Erin said, trying to make her voice sound soothing, as if she were talking to a hurt animal or scared child. "And we're here to help. We know that you didn't hurt anyone."

He looked from one of them to the other, eyes jerking back and forth. He looked back at Erin when she said he hadn't hurt anyone, and his brows drew down.

"Why would you say that? You don't know what happened."

"You didn't kill Bruel," Erin asserted. "And you certainly weren't the one who tortured Mr. Peach. How could you be?"

"How could you know that?"

"You've been here the whole time. How could you have had anything to do with Mr. Peach's death?"

"I have been here!" Davis agreed, his voice slightly outraged. "Torture? Why would I torture someone who—" He cut himself off.

"Someone who helped you escape?" Beaver finished.

He looked at Beaver, eyes moving over her uncertainly. Erin held her breath, waiting to see if he would recognize the cop in her, despite her makeover. Beaver looked completely relaxed. She sounded calm and curious rather than challenging. She chewed her gum and grinned at him.

"How would you know that?"

Beaver chewed and popped her gum. "It's all over town. If you were actually in town instead of isolated out here, you would have heard by now. Everyone knows that it was Mr. Peach who got you out. His security card that was used to open the doors."

"They know that?"

"All of that stuff is logged by the computers." Beaver shrugged. "If Peach was smart enough to set up the escape, it's weird that he wouldn't know it would all be logged."

Davis was frozen, looking at her. He tore his eyes away for a moment to check the window, the doors, Erin and Vic, and then went back to Beaver again.

He was nodding. "Yeah. If he was so smart, why didn't he know that?"

"Maybe he never intended to go back to the penitentiary. Maybe he was just going to take his money and disappear. They said he had a small fortune in his bank account. Could have gone to one of those countries without an extradition treaty and retired on it."

Davis flushed. "He was dirty. Pretending to be a priest. Taking people's money all those years. At least now he's dead!"

"How well did you know him? Did he take your money?" Vic asked.

Davis sneered at her. "Why would I talk to *you*?"

The way that he said it made it clear that he wasn't just objecting to telling anyone his side of the story. He meant it personally. He knew, Erin supposed, about Vic being transgender and had his own prejudices against *people like that.*

"It doesn't really matter whether you tell us or not," she offered. "There's only one way you're going to be safe."

"What do you mean?" His expression was guarded, which Erin supposed meant that he'd already guessed where she was going with her comment.

"I mean… if there's someone else out there… someone smarter than Peach who masterminded this whole thing… then he killed Bruel, and he killed Peach, and there's still one other person who knows enough to put him behind bars. He just needs to take care of that one person and he will be safe."

"I don't know anything about it. Peach was the only one I dealt with."

"Oh." Erin let her voice go down. "Well, that's too bad."

His eyes flashed. He thought things through, looking at the situation from different angles. "Come in here," he ordered, motioning them to walk farther into the room, away from the door. He indicated the furniture. Erin and Vic sat down in the straight-backed kitchen chairs and Beaver remained on her feet.

"I couldn't just sit around," Davis burst out as if they had been pressuring him to explain himself. "I wasn't going to wait until I was eighty or older to get out of prison. That's fine for dopes like Windsor, who only had a few years to serve, but you think they were ever going to let me out of there? There are guys in there who've been on the inside for forty, fifty years before they die. I'm not going to sit around for fifty years waiting to die!"

"Some of them do get out. Like that guy the innocence project got released."

"Hatch?" Davis laughed. "Forty years on the inside! Because some cop set him up. And when he gets out, there's no way he can make it on the outside. The whole world has passed him by in there. It isn't the same place as it was forty years ago. He thinks that he's going to get out and get to be a paralegal at that law firm?" Davis shook his head. "They were never going to hire him. It didn't matter how good he got at filing briefs from prison. They were never gonna give a felon a job."

Erin thought of Hatch's long list of dead-end jobs. Pizza delivery guy. Who wanted to be a pizza delivery guy at seventy or eighty years old? And probably doing it on a bike because he wouldn't have had a driver's license when he got out. He wouldn't have a car of his own. Letting Hatch out after the reversal of his conviction without getting him into one of the transitional jobs that Beaver had talked about was cruel. A sentence to live out the rest of his life in poverty.

"He thought he could get a job at a law firm?"

Davis's eyes went to the front door, to the windows, and back again. His hand hadn't strayed from his pocket. He didn't relax his stance.

"The law firm the innocence project worked with. I guess they said that they were impressed with the motions he had written or something like that. He took it to mean that they could use someone like him on staff. That they thought he would be an asset." Davis shook his head in disgust. "Who would want a felon writing their legal documents? In prison, sure, it isn't like you can get anyone else to help. Once you're convicted, your lawyer doesn't care what happens to you. Not worth their time to help you. So you learn how to do it yourself or get a jailhouse lawyer to help."

"But that doesn't cut it on the outside," Beaver said.

"No one wants you on the outside. I know what it's like when you're on the skids and looking for someone to give you a hand up. It doesn't happen. Everybody's more than happy to kick you while you're down. Add a few decades of prison time to that… you might as well be invisible. You can't get the deadest of dead-end jobs."

Pizza delivery, dishwasher in a restaurant, flipping burgers at a fast-food restaurant, and packer in a fish processing plant.

The deadest of dead ends.

"Wait…" Erin said, holding up a hand as her brain stuttered and tried to fasten on to something. Something she hadn't realized before.

CHAPTER 50

*V*ic and Beaver looked at Erin curiously. Erin held on to the thought and let it grow in her mind. Davis's eyes got wider as he stared at her, trying to figure out what she was thinking.

"A fish processing plant," Erin said. "Hatch was working in a fish processing plant."

Beaver nodded.

Davis laughed, a cruel laugh at the expense of someone else who was worse off than he was. "Can you imagine how disgusting that would be? I remember when my dad ran the bakery, how good he smelled when he came home. Baking bread. Vanilla. During December, he smelled like gingerbread cookies."

Erin was nodding.

"Can you imagine what you would smell like at the end of a day working in a fish processing plant?" Davis asked. He made a gagging sound. "Can you imagine how you would have to scrub and scrub, but that smell would never go away?"

Erin looked at Beaver and saw that understanding was dawning on her features too.

"Mr. Peach. I thought he smelled like cat food. But it was fish. And soap. Like someone had tried to scrub the smell away but couldn't."

Davis looked at her, not comprehending. "Why would Peach smell like fish?"

"He didn't. I mean, he did, but it was because of Hatch. He'd been with Hatch. And the smell clung to him."

"Hatch." Davis's jaw dropped and he looked at her with sudden understanding. "When had Peach been with Hatch?"

"Before he died."

"You're saying that Hatch is the one who…" Davis's jaw worked, and he couldn't seem to get the rest of the words out.

"Hatch was the one who tortured him," Erin said softly. "And that means…"

"That he was the one behind the prison break," Beaver filled in. "He is the one who killed Bruel. Someone with deep knowledge about the penitentiary and how the systems worked over there. Someone on the outside who was in a position to mastermind an escape."

"He and Bruel were cellmates, weren't they?" Erin asked Davis. "Wasn't he Bruel's cellmate before Rudolph Windsor?"

Davis nodded, eyes wide.

"Cellmates learn things about each other," Beaver said. "The longer they are together, the more they learn about each other's lives. What they did to get there. What they got away with. The kinds of things that a guilty man might also tell his priest to get absolution."

"Bruel and Mr. Peach both knew things about Hatch that he didn't want to get out." Erin shook her head. "But I thought Hatch was innocent. They proved that he'd been set up."

"No, not exactly," Beaver said slowly. "The innocence project proved that evidence had been planted and manipulated to convict him."

"Isn't that the same thing?"

"No. He wasn't necessarily an innocent man who had been framed. He could just as easily be a guilty man there was not evidence enough to convict."

"Until the cops planted something."

"Right. The cops involved said that they knew he had done it;

they just hadn't been able to get the evidence that he had. So they manufactured evidence to get him put behind bars. A guilty man convicted for the wrong reasons."

"But he didn't even know me," Davis said, taking a step toward them. "Maybe he had reason to kill Bruel and Peach because they knew what he had done. But he doesn't have any reason to kill me." Davis straightened, looking like a weight had just been lifted from his shoulders. And maybe it had. If Hatch didn't have a reason to kill him, then he could stop hiding in the cabin in fear for his life. He could move on without being afraid that someone was after him. Hatch was probably long gone, running after he had killed Mr. Peach.

"You were supposed to be the patsy," Beaver surmised. "The one who would be blamed for killing Bruel. Stabbed with a shank? Who else would the police suspect but the other escaped prisoner?"

"But I didn't get caught. He probably thought that I'd get shot by the cops. He didn't know that I had someplace to go." Davis looked around exultantly at the dim, dirty cabin, ready to collapse like a house of cards at any moment. "Bruel said that we were supposed to meet with Peach to get the money we would need to start over and instructions about where we were supposed to go and who would help us. He said it had all been planned out. But I was on my own ground. My hometown. So I left Bruel there. Told him to go ahead, find Peach. It would be easier for him to make a clean getaway if he had all of the money and was on his own."

Bruel probably hadn't needed much convincing. But following through on Peach's instructions had gotten him killed. Hatch been waiting for him in the woods. For once, Davis had lucked out. Hatch had made it look like Davis had killed Bruel and Peach had been the one who had planned the escape. And made it look as though Willie or Nelson had tortured Peach into writing a new will naming their partnership as his beneficiary.

The pieces all fit into place. All along, there had been someone orchestrating it, but they hadn't seen his guiding hand, hadn't connected him to the escape or the murders.

Davis snickered to himself. He looked around the cabin. Erin could see him making plans to leave. Davis moved toward the dirty clothes and duffel bag on the bed, giving no further thought to the women. He had escaped prison; what did he have to worry about from three bakers?

CHAPTER 51

"H old it right there, Plaint!"

Davis whirled around to look at Beaver, who had drawn her gun and was holding it trained on him.

"You're under arrest for Escape under the Tennessee Code. Let's see those hands."

Beaver was standing several feet away from Erin and Vic. Erin wanted to jump in and warn Beaver about the weapon Davis was clearly holding. But of course, Beaver would have figured that out herself. She was the professional. She knew what she was doing.

Davis stared at her, scowling. "You're a cop?" His eyes went over her. "You don't look like any cop I've seen." He looked back at his possessions, judging whether he could go ahead and make his escape or whether Beaver really posed a threat to him.

"Hands!" Beaver shouted in a hard voice. "Let me see them now!"

She moved toward him, gun still raised and pointing directly at him. Sweat started to bead up on Davis's temple.

"I'm getting out of here," he said. "Put the toy gun away and get out of here before you get hurt."

"This is no toy and it isn't filled with blanks, either. I've shot plenty of men in my time, so don't think I won't. Get your hands up and turn around. Back to me."

He didn't. But he also didn't dive for the bed or make a dash for one of the doors. Beaver's body language was confident and powerful. She didn't look like a baker anymore.

"Hands, I said," Beaver growled, so close to him now that she jabbed the gun into his midsection. She grabbed the hand that he'd been keeping in his pocket the whole time they had been there and yanked it out.

Erin winced and shied back, expecting Davis's gun to go off. But his hand came out empty. Beaver manhandled him, wrenching his arms around to cuff them behind his back and then feeling his pockets for weapons. She patted them flat.

"You don't have a gun?" she demanded. "What kind of escaped convict doesn't at least have a gun?"

Davis was red-faced. "How am I supposed to get one without being spotted?" he demanded. "Do you see one around here? I'm known in Bald Eagle Falls. I show up anywhere around here looking to buy a gun, and someone is going to report me!"

Erin was breathing heavily. She felt like she had been running and could now finally stop. Beaver glanced at her, eyes amused.

"It's a rush, isn't it?"

Erin shook her head. She was no adrenaline junkie. She didn't enjoy the heart-pounding moments of danger like Beaver obviously did.

"Sheesh. Did you know that he didn't have a gun?"

"Suspected it. Couldn't be sure; he could have been holding a small caliber weapon. Or a knife." Beaver shook her head. "Not even another shiv?" she demanded from Davis.

"I'm not the one who killed Bruel. I never had a weapon."

"Are you telling me that you both escaped the penitentiary without any way to defend yourself? What exactly did you think was going to happen?"

"I thought... Peach said he was going to help us, but that we couldn't be carrying any weapons. He said that he had people to help. He was going to set us up for our new lives. He felt bad about the way we'd been treated and wanted to help."

"Just out of the goodness of his heart."

"Well… he was a priest, wasn't he?"

"You thought a priest would break the law to help you escape because he felt sorry for you? You already knew he was crooked."

Davis looked down at the floor. He no longer looked dangerous. He looked broken once more. The victim. The traumatized teen. The drug-addicted, disinherited man.

"I'd heard rumors," he admitted. "That he would help people for a price. But I thought that maybe he did stuff for free, too, when he felt sorry for someone. When he wanted to correct an injustice."

"Not Peach," Beaver said with a snort. "And it wasn't an injustice that you were in prison. You were convicted. You were not set up."

Davis opened his mouth to argue or complain, but his eyes went to Erin and he just shook his head unhappily. He couldn't very well say that he hadn't killed Bertie Braceling when Erin had seen it with her own eyes. He had tried to kill her too, more than once.

"All clear," Beaver said.

Erin and Vic looked at each other and looked at her, frowning. *What?*

They both jumped when the front door opened. Several black-clad figures in tactical gear stomped in. One of them caught Davis by the arm and pulled him away from Beaver. Davis, small and slight as he was, looked like a child next to the large men, bulked up even more in their gear.

"No weapons?" the man who held on to him asked.

"Give him a thorough search before you put him in the car. I did a quick pat down. Don't think you're going to find anything, but best to be sure."

He nodded, and the two of them escorted the escapee out. Davis didn't whine and protest, but seemed resigned to the fact that he was in custody and would be taken back to the prison. Beaver looked around. She poked through the bag and the clothes on the bed, but didn't pull out anything incriminating. No drugs or weapons. No pen, and no paper like Mr. Peach's will had been written on. Beaver glanced around the cabin for anything else of importance, but she didn't identify anything. It was pretty bare.

"This place doesn't look like it would stand up to a strong wind," she observed, shaking her head. "Amazing that it is still standing."

"Looks pretty much like it did a few years ago when we came here to play," Vic contributed. "I never realized how rickety it is! My parents would have had forty fits if they had known I was playing somewhere like this."

Erin looked toward the door, confused. "How did... how did your guys know you were here?" she asked Beaver.

They had to be Beaver's agency, of course. They were not law enforcement officers that Erin recognized. And Beaver had spoken directly to them, giving them the "all clear."

"I called them in while I was 'warming up' the car," Beaver chuckled. "Car's got GPS tracking. So does my phone. And I'm always wired for sound."

They both just stared at her.

Beaver chewed her gum. "You didn't think that I would walk into an unknown situation without backup, did you?"

Erin had to admit that she hadn't really thought about it. Beaver always seemed to be able to take care of herself in every situation. Erin had rarely seen her with any kind of backup. But she supposed that didn't mean that Beaver didn't have people close at hand when she needed them. They were supposed to be invisible until they were needed.

"Shall we...?" Beaver motioned to the door. Vic and Erin preceded her out. The yard was no longer empty, but filled with light from a few cars and floodlights, with various black-suited figures standing around, their big guns hanging at rest on straps as they talked to each other. Erin looked around, her eyes wide. They had been ready for anything.

"You ladies can wait in the car," Beaver told them, pointing to where she had parked it a distance away from the house. "I just need to have a quick chat with the boys."

Erin and Vic looked at each other, then headed over to the car.

"This is all... a little crazy," Erin said. "I thought we were just going to go in there and talk him into turning himself in. I wasn't expecting... this."

Vic nodded in agreement. "I guess maybe that was a little naive. Although… I do think you were right. The tactical team could just have kicked down the door, but they probably would have killed Davis. You would never have figured out the part about Hatch being behind the whole thing."

CHAPTER 52

There wasn't much discussion as they drove back to town. Erin's head was whirling, and she was half expecting Beaver to start in on her with a lecture about everything they had done wrong in assuming that they could walk into the cabin and talk Davis into giving himself up. But Beaver seemed cheerful and relaxed and didn't criticize them.

Erin supposed they had at least done one thing right in calling Beaver to involve her in their plan. Without her, they might have lost Davis. He hadn't pulled a gun on them, but he might have fled the scene, probably stealing their car and leaving them stranded. At least they were within walking distance of the house. A long walk, but not impossible.

Would Vic have been able to pull her gun and convince Davis to do what she said as Beaver had? She didn't have the same authority or experience. It could have turned into one of those situations that the police warned about, when a gun owner's weapon was turned against her.

Beaver missed the turn to Erin's house. Erin sat up straight, making a noise of protest.

Vic too was looking at Beaver, surprised by the mistake. Beaver was smiling. Obviously, she had something else in mind. Maybe she was hungry and thought they would all like to go out for a burger, though Erin felt somewhat nauseated.

But Beaver didn't turn down Main Street or take them to any other eateries close by. She turned into an area that was part residential, part commercial, with small apartments over shops and houses that had been renovated into small business offices all mixed together.

Erin wasn't sure where they were going. She remembered that her lawyer, the one who had helped her with the paperwork required to take possession of the house and store and to get all of the required permits for the bakery, worked out of one of those small storefronts. Since then, she hadn't had any other occasion to be there. Beaver turned down another street. There were a couple of police cars parked, their lights flashing. The red and blue lights were almost painfully bright.

"What's going on?" Vic asked, leaning forward in her seat and peering out the window.

"Looks like the police are up to something," Beaver observed.

Erin couldn't understand what they were doing there. Beaver parked beside the police cars. They watched as the door to one of the upstairs apartments opened and Stayner and Terry escorted a man out between them.

He was unremarkable. An older man, his cheeks somewhat shrunken and hair wispy, shorter than either Terry or Stayner. He wasn't fighting, though it looked like he was arguing with them. K9 followed Terry, his tail waving back and forth, watching the old man carefully. The law enforcement officers put the man into the back seat of one of the cars. He sat there, leaning his head back, obscured by the shadows inside the car.

Terry approached the station wagon. He nodded to Beaver, but it was Erin's window he leaned closer to. She fumbled with the switches on the armrest and managed to get the window rolled down.

"Well, Sherlock," Terry said, "another criminal put behind bars?"

She was surprised that he already knew what she had been up to. "Davis? Yes, he's on his way back to the penitentiary."

Terry turned slightly to look at the prisoner in his backseat. "And our innocent Mr. Hatch too."

"Is that Hatch?" Erin strained to see him better. "He was still here in Bald Eagle Falls? I thought he would be... somewhere far away."

"Didn't seem to think he would be caught. Didn't think we had anything on him."

"And you did?" Erin shook her head. "What do you have on him?" All that she had to tie everything together was that Mr. Peach had smelled like fish and soap, and Hatch worked in a fish processing plant. A plant that surely employed others in the area who also went home smelling like fish and tried to scrub the smell away.

Terry smiled. "He *might* have started talking when we said that Mr. Peach had given him up before he died and that we had Davis Plaint in custody."

"Oh!" It was somewhat devious on the police department's part but, of course, they were allowed to say things like that.

Vic tried to get a better view of the man in the back of the squad car. "He didn't seem like he was fighting you."

Terry nodded. "He's been conditioned to deal with the CO's and other officials for forty years. I doubt if he has much fight left in him. And from the way he folded... I think he has come to realize that he isn't equipped to deal with the outside world. It's probably a relief to be put back behind bars. He thought he could handle it but, as it turns out... it's a lot harder than he thought."

Erin would not have wanted to do the type of jobs that Hatch had been trying to do. She'd had her own problems with money and jobs that only paid a pittance. And she'd been a young woman without a criminal record. Hatch's opportunities would just get more and more limited the older he got and the more he cycled through low-paying jobs. With no family or friends, living in a world full of technology that he'd never used before, it must have been overwhelming.

Compare that to prison, where he knew people, knew how things operated, received three meals a day, and *didn't* have to work in a fish factory...

"How did Hatch pay Mr. Peach?" she asked. "Especially since Mr. Peach must have known that he wouldn't be able to go back to his old job once they figured out his security pass had been used."

Terry shrugged and looked at Beaver. "You looked at Peach's finances for your end of the investigation. Did he get a cash injection from Hatch?"

Beaver shook her head. "If he did, it wasn't anything significant. Not a retirement allowance by any stretch. Hatch probably turned the tables on Peach. Threatened to tell the authorities about *his* illegal activities."

"Dueling blackmailers? That seems like a dangerous prospect."

"Who had more to lose?"

"Hatch," Erin interjected. "If Peach turned Hatch in for something he said in a confession, then Hatch would be in prison for the rest of his life."

Beaver looked at Hatch in the police car. "Which wasn't much of a threat after having served forty years. First, they would have to retry him, if they could. Peach would have to break the seal of the confessional and would undoubtedly lose his job. There would be nothing to stop Hatch from telling what he knew about the pastor's illegal activities at the penitentiary, and Peach would end up behind bars himself."

Terry nodded slowly. "Peach would have lost his job no matter which of them talked first. So I guess he knew he was on his way out."

Erin shook her head. "Why didn't he just run? Why help with the prison break at all? It would have made more sense to just quit his job at the penitentiary and drop out of sight. Who would look for him? Even if someone filed a missing person report, there wouldn't have been a big investigation. It wouldn't have been so hard to disappear."

Beaver looked into the back seat at Erin. "I can only think of one reason."

"What?"

"Mrs. Peach. The pastor knew that Hatch *was* a killer. So if Hatch found out about Mrs. Peach and threatened her…"

Erin thought about her next-door neighbor, living by herself without even a burglar alarm. Even if her house had been secure, she walked around town with her walker regularly and would be an easy target for a criminal like Hatch.

So Mr. Peach had gone home one last time, to keep her safe.

CHAPTER 53

*T*he next afternoon, Erin paused at the edge of the woods, feeling reluctant to go on. Vic stopped and looked at her.

"It's okay. There's nothing to be worried about."

"I know," Erin agreed. "Nothing is going to happen." She wanted to believe it. She said it out loud to convince her brain that it was true. Her heart was already pounding hard, when she hadn't even set a foot into the woods. She hadn't thought that it would be so hard. She had, after all, been to Adele's cabin since finding Bruel's body in the woods, and nothing bad had happened to her on either of those occasions. So her body shouldn't be reacting so strongly with danger signals.

She wiped sweat from her forehead. Kevin Hatch had been arrested. He was back in jail, awaiting trial for Bruel's and Mr. Peach's murders. He was not walking in her woods, and neither were any other killers. It was the same serene, peaceful place that it had been before the prison break. And Adele was still keeping an eye on things, making sure that no one else trespassed on her property.

Even though Nilla was pulling eagerly on the leash, Vic took a couple of steps back and put her arm around Erin's shoulders.

"We'll go together, come on."

Her gentle encouragement was enough to get Erin to take that first step into the woods and then the next. She relaxed when she was a few paces into the woods, her muscles loosening and the anxiety cramping her stomach easing. She took deep breaths like she had learned in her tai chi practice, and her heart gradually slowed back to a normal speed. It was a beautiful spring day and the woods were lovely, the shade of the trees providing relief from the Tennessee sun and a light breeze blowing over her skin.

They walked together in silence for a few minutes, then Vic spoke up, diving into a discussion of their Statehood Day contest entry without any introduction.

"I think a berry slab pie would be best," she suggested. "Apples and peaches taste great, but berries are bright and colorful. We want it to be attractive to the eye as well as tasting good."

"Berries are good," Erin agreed. "And cherries."

"I thought strawberries would be really nice. They are at their peak right now, and red is a good color for something related to statehood."

"Red, white, and blue," Erin murmured, thinking about it. "We could do strawberries and blueberries. And when we serve it, a dollop of whipped cream for the white."

"That would be great. We can make the slab pie like a flag."

Erin nodded vigorously. Statehood day was all about patriotism. People would love a pie in the shape of a flag. A nice departure from a cake in the shape of a flag. "Yes. That would be perfect."

"We'll lay it all out when we get back to the house."

Erin saw movement in the trees up ahead and heard the caw of a crow. For a moment she froze, heart leaping to her throat. But she could make out enough of the tall, slim figure to realize that it was Adele. And maybe the caw had been Skye accompanying her, as he sometimes did. Give the bird a few peanuts and he would follow her anywhere.

"Adele!"

Adele turned toward them and they walked up to each other. "Good afternoon," she greeted politely. "Enjoying the beautiful weather?"

"Yes," Erin agreed. "It really is lovely. We agreed that we need to get outside more… so we're making an effort."

She wondered if that disappointed Adele, knowing that they would be walking around in her woods more often. Even though the woods belonged to Erin, Adele used them the most and she must feel like they were her territory.

There was a movement in the bushes behind Adele. She turned to look.

"Bernt."

The black cat poked its head out from beneath a bush.

"Come." Adele made kissy noises to call him, and he slithered out and trotted behind her like a dog.

Nilla, who had been investigating the trunk of a nearby tree, saw Bernt and ran over, barking. Vic pulled on his leash and tried to quiet him.

Erin expected Bernt to streak off into the trees, or maybe straight up one of them. But instead, he advanced, sniffing the breeze and looking interested in, but not at all afraid of Nilla.

"Crazy cat," Vic laughed. "Doesn't know when to be scared."

"Why should he be afraid?" Adele asked. "You have the dog on a leash and aren't going to let him do anything. Maybe Bernt is smart enough to know that."

Vic shook her head. "Maybe so. How is he doing? He looks really good!"

Adele nodded, looking down at the little cat. "He is almost fully recovered. Though he does still cower when a bird flies overhead."

"Poor guy," Erin said. "How did you get him trained so quickly?"

"I didn't do anything." Adele shrugged. "I guess he just trusts me."

Erin fought back her immediate reaction. The cat trusted Adele. But could Erin? Adele had kept details from her more than once. Important information

Adele kept too many secrets, not just about her private life, but about things that went on in the woods. Things that Adele shouldn't keep from her, since Erin was her employer and the woods did belong to her.

When Erin looked into Adele's dark eyes, she didn't see trust there. Despite everything that Erin had done for Adele and the time they had spent together, Erin sensed she still thought of Erin as a potential adversary. And Erin hadn't exactly earned any points by using what she had learned from Adele to have Davis apprehended.

They nodded politely to each other and went their different directions.

CHAPTER 54

*E*rin was awake when Terry got back from work. She was dozing just a little bit on the couch, her eyes tired from reading Clementine's genealogy book on the Plaints and studying her planner. She was doing her best to immerse herself in other things. With Davis and Hatch both back in custody, it was all over. She could relax.

Except her body and her brain didn't accept that. She still jumped at every sound, keeping an eye on the back window in case anything should happen in the woods or the backyard, and worrying over the details of the case over and over again, like a playlist on repeat. Except, of course, that it was something she wanted to turn off, not something she enjoyed.

Terry opened the door quietly, then saw after he stepped in the door that she was still up. He punched his code into the burglar alarm and smiled at Erin. A tired smile, but one that said he was happy to be home, not forced.

"Hey," he said softly. "Are you really awake?" He motioned K9 that he was off duty, and walked over to the couch and leaned down to kiss her. He touched her cheek that was warm from resting it against the couch when she had dozed off. Erin imagined it was creased and bumpy from the pattern of the fabric.

Erin tried to stretch the kinks out of her neck, but she knew that she really had to get up to stretch properly. And that meant moving the cat from her lap and the rabbit from her feet.

"Maybe you could give the animals a T-R-E-A-T," she suggested to Terry. Then she wouldn't have to feel guilty about upsetting them when they were so comfy and cozy.

"Ah, now you're the one being held hostage by them." She had teased him for exactly the same thing.

"Yes… I admit it. I don't like to push them off either. Now could you call them into the kitchen?"

Terry obliged by asking K9 if he wanted a cookie. Orange Blossom's eyes were immediately open and his ears pricked forward. As soon as Terry was over the line dividing the living room carpet from the kitchen tile, Blossom was off of Erin's lap and galloping into the kitchen. Marshmallow wasn't quite as eager to give up his warm spot. Erin wiggled her toes and prompted him a couple of times to go to the kitchen for a treat, and eventually the sleepy bunny hopped into the kitchen where he could be rewarded with some fresh vegetables.

"So how was your evening?" Terry asked, as Erin got out some kitty treats for Blossom and he went to the fridge.

"Uh—quiet. Just came home and tried to unwind."

Terry found a carrot and put it down for Marshmallow. "You were one step ahead of the police department again."

Erin shrugged. "I wasn't investigating," she told him firmly. "I told you everything I knew when we met at the police department. I just… happened to hear something, and the pieces started to fall into place."

"People like to talk to you."

"I guess."

"That's not a bad thing. But it does make things a little difficult when they would rather talk to you than to the police."

"Some people aren't comfortable talking to the police. They are worried about what is going to happen when they do."

Terry got himself a cookie out of the freezer and nibbled the edge without microwaving it first. "Is that how you feel?"

Erin shifted uncomfortably. "I guess." She rubbed her forehead.

"It's one thing when I tell you something in casual conversation. Even then, sometimes I feel like… things are out of my control. But having to report something officially… Well, I hate the whole process. Having to repeat myself over and over again and answer questions. People don't just trust that I'm telling the truth and know what I'm talking about. They have to examine every little thing that I say and decide whether it's the truth or not and whether it is important. That's… not fun."

"I guess not," Terry admitted. "Although we do have people around town who love to report everything. They love the attention they get when they have something to tell us. They like to feel important, needed."

"I really don't get that. I don't want the attention. And I don't want something that I say to be twisted around to accuse one of my friends."

Terry opened his mouth, then closed it. He nodded once. "That's fair. That's uncomfortable to you. But don't think it's any less uncomfortable having to question people you are close to. People who would be your friends, if you weren't a cop."

Erin hadn't looked at it from that perspective before. Of course Terry must have felt bad about having to question Erin, Vic, Willie, or any of their other close acquaintances. People teased her about how handsome Terry was and how good he looked in uniform. She invited people to dinner or went out with them to one of the restaurants in town, but other than Vic, most of them still maintained a certain distance. She had to assume that it was because of her relationship with Terry and they didn't want to spend a lot of time around a law enforcement officer. That barrier must leave him feeling pretty isolated and unable to connect.

She reached over and hugged him tightly. She didn't have the words to express what she was feeling, so her actions would have to convey it for her. "I'm sorry about that."

He kissed her, leaving cookie crumbs on her lips. "As long as I can always come home."

"Of course." Erin hugged him again and laid her head on his chest, listening to his heart thumping.

Terry was in the shower and Erin was tidying up before going to bed for real. As she shut off the kitchen light, she saw Willie getting out of his truck. He looked sharply toward the kitchen when the light went off, but he wouldn't be able to see her there with the inside lights off and the outdoor security lights on.

He stood there for a minute, and she wondered if he were trying to decide whether to come over to the house to talk to her, or thinking over the conversation he would have with Vic when he went up to the loft, or something else.

Maybe something about his partnership with Nelson Dyson. Word hadn't gotten around town yet as to the terms of Mr. Peach's holographic will, but she imagined they would before long. When a will was probated, it became part of the public record. Willie wouldn't be able to hide that the money had been left to him instead of Mrs. Peach. The town was suspicious enough about him because of his previous involvement as a soldier in the Dyson clan. The revelation of the fact that he was in partnership with Nelson Dyson wouldn't endear him to the hearts of the townspeople.

She wanted to know what the partnership was all about, but she wouldn't ask him. She wanted to stay friends with him, and maybe that meant having to overlook some things about him. He had never demanded that she explain her past or her business ventures to him, so why should she need to know about his?

Willie's face turned away from the window to the loft apartment, and he climbed the stairs up to the door.

CHAPTER 55

*E*rin took extra care to make sure that everything was nicely arranged in the display case. She wanted everything to be perfect. The bakery was filled with fragrant baking and spices. She looked at Vic.

"All set?"

Vic nodded. "All set. Let's open the door."

Erin went around to the front of the store. She flipped the sign to Open and unlocked the bolt. She pushed the door open and smiled at the waiting customers.

"Good morning! How are y'all today?"

Everyone else stood to the side as Mrs. Peach used her walker to enter the store first. She looked at the display case and smiled at Erin, her eyes tearing up.

"Happy Mrs. Peach Day," Erin told her.

Mrs. Peach dabbed at her eyes. "You girls are so sweet. Mrs. Peach Day." She shook her head. "I always did love peaches. And I used to say that I got the biggest peach of them all."

Erin smiled sympathetically. "I'm so sorry that you lost him."

She nodded. "At my age, it shouldn't be a surprise. I could have gotten a call any day to say that he had died from natural causes. It wasn't like the man took the best care of himself. But to have it happen like it did... I never expected that."

"No," Erin agreed. Who would expect her aging husband to be tortured to death? "It was terrible."

"I try to focus on being grateful I got to see him before he died. Having been apart for so many years... I hadn't ever expected to see him again."

"I guess not."

It was only thanks to Kevin Hatch's threats that Mr. Peach had gone home to her.

Mrs. Peach wiped her eyes again, then looked at the baked goods. "Peach slab pie and peach muffins. Those look really good."

Erin nodded and used the tongs to carefully pack Mrs. Peach's choices. She handed the box across the counter. Mrs. Peach fiddled with her purse.

"How much is that?"

"It's free on Mrs. Peach Day." Erin looked past her to the rest of the customers. "For her. Not for the rest of you."

Betty Thompson and the others laughed.

"Oh, I can pay!" Mrs. Peach insisted. "I don't have to worry about money anymore."

Erin frowned, surprised by this assertion. Mrs. Peach had always been very careful of her money, counting every penny. With Mr. Peach leaving everything he owned to the Willie Nelson Partnership, getting anything out of the estate would mean a fight in court to prove her dower rights.

Mrs. Peach read all of this in her face and shook her head. "No. The medical examiner said that he was tortured."

Erin nodded. "I know."

"That makes the will invalid. It was written under duress."

Erin blinked. "Oh! Really?"

Mrs. Peach nodded happily. "And the police didn't find any other will when they searched his apartment. He didn't have a safe deposit box, and I don't have a copy of any previous will he wrote. So he's intestate."

"And that means it all goes to you," Erin said, remembering the laws she had learned when they were trying to figure out who inherited The Bake Shoppe after Angela's and Trenton's deaths.

"Yes. That Beaven woman said he had quite a bit in his accounts. I won't have to worry about money for the rest of the time I have on this earth."

"I hope you're still with us for a long time."

Mrs. Peach shrugged. "I'm not in the ground yet." She pulled a bill from her purse and put it into the tip jar. "You girls have a nice day."

"Happy Mrs. Peach Day," Vic told her.

"Thank you. It was very kind of you to think of me."

Mrs. Peach said her goodbyes to the other customers, as regal as a queen, and made her way home. Betty Thompson was next in line.

"Well, I'm so glad we got all of that cleared up," she declared. "It would be a crying shame if Gladys didn't get Gregory's money after all of these years. I would never have stayed married to the man, but she was loyal to him to the end."

"Yes, she was," Erin agreed, thinking of how happy Mrs. Peach had been to have him home again, despite his abandonment of her and his very long absence. There were not many women who would have been happy to take him back. Especially when there were no children and grandchildren in the picture to keep them together. "It was so strange that Mr. Peach left everything to—or that Hatch made him leave everything to—the Willie Nelson Partnership. How did he even know about it? Did he just pull it out of thin air and get lucky that there actually was one? Or did someone tell him about it?"

Betty cleared her throat. "Maybe he knew one of the Dysons at the penitentiary and they mentioned it. The only other thing that I can think of is… that he saw the name on a file or piece of correspondence when he was at the law office."

"When he was at your law office?" Vic asked. "What was he there for?"

"Well, I couldn't say anything for sure, since I'm not employed there anymore. I'm retired," she reminded them, lest they think that she had been fired. "But it was a big deal when he was released from prison. I'm sure there were claims to be considered, paperwork to go through, making sure that everything with regard to the overturn of the conviction had been properly filed with the court, so he wouldn't end up back in prison over a technicality."

"And Davis said something about Hatch thinking he might be able to work for them," Erin remembered. "I don't know if he ever interviewed there, but it is a possibility."

Betty nodded. "I can't see them ever hiring someone like that, but they might go through the motions, just to show that they weren't discriminating against him. Jailhouse lawyers are great at filing spurious claims, so it would be best to cover themselves."

"There wasn't ever any connection between Hatch and the partnership?" Vic asked Betty.

"No… nothing that I know of."

Erin shook her head. "Do you think it's really possible that Hatch's only reason for torturing Mr. Peach into changing his will was to implicate someone else in the prison break and Bruel's death?"

Vic rolled her eyes. "Even after arresting Hatch, the police are *still* looking at Willie, thinking he must tie in somehow. So if that was Hatch's goal, he certainly succeeded."

Erin wished there was something she could say to Terry that would make him believe that Willie was no longer involved in the Dyson clan or any illegal activities. But she didn't have anything to go on other than her feelings.

Betty sighed and looked at the baking. "The peach slab pie looks lovely. And maybe… one of those small peach cobblers."

Erin agreed and got them packaged up for her.

"Are you entering something into the Statehood Day contest?" Betty asked.

"Oh, yes. We've got it all planned out," Erin agreed, thinking of the diagram in her office that she and Vic had drawn of the patriotic berry pie.

But she hoped that they would not win a cruise this time. She wasn't sure she ever wanted to get on a cruise ship again.

Did you enjoy this book? Reviews and recommendations are vital to making a book successful.

Please leave a review at your favorite book store or review site and share it with your friends.

Don't miss the following bonus material:
Sign up for mailing list to get a free ebook
Read a sneak preview chapter
Other books by P.D. Workman
Learn more about the author

Sign up for my mailing list at pdworkman.com and get Gluten-Free Murder for free!

PREVIEW OF WHAT THE CAT KNEW

Did you know that the Reg Rawlins, Psychic Investigator series is a spin-off of Auntie Clem's Bakery?

Check out the adventures of Erin's foster sister, Reg Rawlins in this fun paranormal series. Witches, fairies, cats, and more!

CHAPTER 1

*R*eg Rawlins climbed out of the car and stretched, her muscles cramped after being in the car all day. According to the dashboard readout, it was a few degrees warmer than it had been in Tennessee. Added to that, it was humid and the air felt muggy. She could smell the ocean. She'd heard that all points in Florida were within sixty miles of the ocean as the crow flies. She was looking forward to spending some time swimming and looking for seashells. She'd always wanted to live near a real beach. A warm, sandy beach.

"Witch!" accused a homeless man sitting on the sidewalk with a cardboard sign. He had long, scraggly hair and a beard, streaked with gray, and he was missing several teeth. His clothes were ragged, and even though he was a few feet away, Reg could smell his unwashed body.

She gave him a scowl, but didn't turn away. His reaction interested her. She was dressed for the part she intended to play—head-scarf, heavy jewelry and hoop earrings, a long, flowing peasant dress—so it was not unexpected that he would notice her and comment on her getup. But he had gone with *witch* rather than a fortune-teller or medium, which she thought was an odd choice. She wasn't wearing a pointed hat or black robe.

"What makes you think I'm a witch?" she demanded.

"All redheads are witches!" he informed her.

"Ah." Reg's red hair was all done in cornrow braids, which hung free around her face rather than being wound up under her headscarf. She liked the effect. And she liked the way the braids felt when she turned her head and they all swished back and forth. She ignored the homeless man and looked up and down the boardwalk.

She liked the atmosphere of Florida. Laid back and relaxed, not like in Tennessee where she had visited Erin. There had certainly been some uptight ladies there. She didn't regret leaving, though she was sad things hadn't worked out with Erin. Erin had been a lot more fun when they were kids. She'd grown up too much and become a stuffy old woman instead of the lost child she'd been when they had lived with the Harrises and then again when they had both aged out of foster care and had run a few cons together. Now she was grown up and mature and responsible, no longer interested in Reg's ideas.

"You don't know what you're missing, Erin," Reg murmured, looking around at the blue sky and the green vegetation, the tang of salt hanging in the air. Swimming in Florida was going to be nothing like a dip in the ocean in Maine. Miles of sandy beaches, warm water, and not a care in the world.

She gathered up her braids with both hands and pulled them back behind her shoulders, letting them fall again.

"There somewhere good to eat around here?" she asked the bum.

People looked at her oddly as they passed, and Reg didn't know if it was because of her outfit or the fact that she was talking to a non-person.

"Only if you like seafood!" the man cackled.

Luckily, Reg did.

"You should go to The Crystal Bowl," he told her. "That's where the witches gather."

Reg pursed her lips, considering him. "The Crystal Ball?"

"The Crystal *Bowl*. Get it?"

"Where is The Crystal Bowl?"

He gestured down the boardwalk. "Yonder about two blocks. Big sign. Can't miss it."

Reg had been told that Florida, and Black Sands in particular, was *the place* for psychics and mediums but she hadn't expected there to actually be enough of a community to warrant a restaurant of their own. She was glad she'd picked Florida over Massachusetts; she'd had enough of New England to last her a lifetime.

The Crystal Bowl had satisfyingly dramatic decor and furnishings. Blacks, reds, and golds combined into a rich tapestry of mysticism, lit by flickering candles which were actually tiny electric lights. East met West in a sort of a cross between an opium den and a carnival fortune-teller set. They worked together in harmony rather than clashing.

The patrons of the restaurant, however, were disappointingly normal. Shorts with t-shirts or light blouses, sunglasses propped on foreheads, everybody looking at their phones or calling across the room to greet each other. No sense of mystical decorum.

The sign said 'please wait to be seated,' but Reg walked across to the bar counter and selected a stool.

The bartender was spare, his skin too pale for a Floridian. He obviously spent too much time in the restaurant out of the sun. Either that or he was a vampire.

"Afternoon," he greeted, adjusting the spacing between the various bottles on the counter and turning their labels out.

"Hi."

"Don't think I've seen you here before."

"No, just flew in on my broomstick."

He eyed her. "Wrong costume."

Reg grinned. "Good. The old bum down the street said that I was a witch, and I was afraid I'd gotten it wrong."

"It's the red hair."

"So I hear. Mediums can't have red hair?"

"Mediums can have whatever they want. So what will it be?" He gestured to the neat rows of bottles behind the bar and the chalkboard on the wall behind them.

Reg looked over the options. Should she establish herself as someone with exacting and eclectic tastes? A connoisseur? Someone who was obviously unique and memorable?

But she wanted the bar to be somewhere she could let her hair down, not where she had to always be playing a part.

"Just a draft," she sighed. "Whatever is on tap."

He nodded and grabbed a beer stein. He filled it and placed it neatly on a coaster in front of her, pushing a bowl of pretzels closer to her. Something nice and salty to encourage thirst.

"So, Miss Medium, your name is…?"

"Reg Rawlins." She figured she was okay using the name, even though that was what she had used in Bald Eagle Falls. She didn't think any charges would follow her all the way to Florida. It wasn't like she was going to be filing taxes under the name.

He gave a nod. "Bill Johnson."

Reg took a pull on her beer. It had been a long drive and she was glad to be able to relax and recharge her batteries. Thinking of figurative batteries, she decided she'd better check her actual battery. Reg pulled out her phone and checked the charge. Not too bad. It would last her a couple more hours, and maybe by that time, she would have settled somewhere. She launched her browser and tapped in a search for lodgings. There were plenty of hits for short-term rentals. Lots of vacationers. Finding somewhere permanent might take a bit longer, but at least she'd have a place to hang her hat. Or her headscarf. And plug in her phone.

"You need a place to stay?" Bill asked, obviously recognizing the website.

"Looks like there are lots of options."

"Sarah Bishop is looking for a tenant. She's easy to get along with. You two would probably hit it off."

"Oh?"

Bill looked around the room. "She's not here yet. She often shows up for supper. If she doesn't, I can give her a call and let her know you're interested."

Reg raised an eyebrow. "You don't know me from Adam. What makes you think I would hit it off with Sarah Bishop or that you can recommend me to her?"

"Let's just say… I'm good at reading people. And I would know you from Adam, given that Adam was of the male persuasion."

Reg considered pointing out that there were plenty of men who could pass as women or had transitioned from one to the other, but decided that antagonizing him wouldn't be the wisest thing for her to do. So she took a sip of her beer and didn't challenge him.

"Okay. Well, I'd appreciate that. Being able to move in somewhere long-term right away would be a real plus. Thanks."

"No problem." He moved away to help another patron.

Reg continued to browse through the lodging listings to get a sense of what costs to expect for rent and what her options were if she didn't like Sarah Bishop's place. It could be a dump. Sarah Bishop could be Bill's sister or ex and he just wanted her off of his back. He had been pretty quick to offer his help and judge Reg worthy as a tenant for his friend.

Someone took the stool next to Reg's, and she looked up to see who it was. A strikingly handsome man. Thirty-something, short hair slicked back from his face to show off a widow's peak, a stubbly beard that at first glance made it look like he had forgotten to shave for a couple of days, but on a more careful examination was painstakingly trimmed. His eyes were dark but glowed almost red in the dim lighting of the restaurant, reflecting the red furnishings and wall coverings. Add a cape, and he'd be perfect to cast as a vampire.

He gave her an enigmatic look. Almost smiling, but not quite. A smirk. She thought he was going to greet her as Bill had, recognizing her as a stranger and asking who she was. But he merely inclined his head slightly and waited for his drink, which Bill brought over without being asked. Obviously his 'usual.'

"Reg Rawlins, Uriel Hawthorne," Bill said, making a gesture from one to the other by way of introduction.

Great choice of name. Reg was impressed. Still, Uriel said nothing, just threw back his shot and watched her.

"Nice to meet you," Reg said, thrusting her hand out to shake his, forcing him to acknowledge her presence.

He left her hanging for a moment, not moving to take her hand, and then finally responded, taking her hand in his in a soft, caressing gesture that made her immediately want to pull back. But she set her teeth and gave him a warm smile. She gave him one more squeeze before letting go and pulling back again.

"A pleasure to meet you," Uriel returned. "Are you thinking of joining our little community?"

"Well, we'll see how it goes," Reg said with a shrug. "I'm new in town and I've never been part of… this kind of community before. I've always just been on my own."

"There is something to be said for that."

Reg raised her eyebrows in query.

"Setting your own rules, doing your own thing," Uriel said. "No one with preconceptions as to how things should be done."

"Right." Reg nodded. Rules, in her opinion, were made to be broken. She wasn't about to buy into a social construct that tried to control her activities.

"Ah, here's Sarah," Bill said, hovering near Reg.

It took her a moment to remember who Sarah was and why she should care. Sarah was the landlord looking for a tenant.

Reg turned, following Bill's gaze. She was looking for a woman of around her age, since Bill had said that he thought she and Sarah would hit it off. But she didn't see anyone who fit her preconception.

Bill gave a little wave, and a woman nodded to him and corrected her course to join him at the bar.

She was an older woman, at least in her sixties, with a round face, bottle blond hair that curved around her face, and wire frame glasses. She looked like a friendly grandmother, lips pink with freshly-applied lipstick, a flowered shirt, pink slacks, and flat white sandals. She smiled at Bill.

"Good evening, Bill. How are you today?"

He nodded and didn't bother to answer the greeting. "Sarah, meet Reg Rawlins. She has just arrived in town and is looking for accommodations."

"Oh!" Sarah's face lit up. "Well, my dear, isn't that wonderful! I just happen to have a cottage that I am trying to rent out! Would you join me for dinner?" She motioned to the tables in the dining area. "I'm afraid I can't manage bar stools these days."

"Sure," Reg agreed, sliding down from hers and taking her drink with her. "That would be nice."

She didn't bother saying goodbye to Uriel, irritated with his distant, disinterested manner. Sarah led her to a table which was probably her regular, as there didn't seem to be any problem with her seating herself instead of waiting to be seated. She smiled and chatted with some of the other patrons as she made her way to her seat.

"Sit down, sit down," she encouraged Reg, as if Reg had somehow been holding her back. "Reg? Is that short for something? Where did you come from?"

"Regina. I've lived all over."

"Well, that's a pretty name. Did you pick it, or was it already yours?"

Reg laughed at the question. "I was saddled with Regina, but I picked Reg."

"Very nice. I like it. And what do you do?" She made a little gesture to indicate Reg's costume. "You read palms? Tarot?"

"A little of everything. Mostly, I talk to the dead."

"Oh." Sarah nodded wisely. "That's a good gig. Have you been doing it for long?"

Reg studied the woman, not sure how honest to be. She wasn't sure whether she should be open about being a medium or a con. Both paths seemed equally treacherous.

"I've always had… certain tendencies… gifts, if you like…" she said obliquely. "I'm just testing the waters now… seeing whether this is something I should pursue…"

Sarah nodded. A waitress came over and handed them menus, introducing herself and showing off a couple of rather long canine teeth when she smiled. Sarah took no note, and barely gave the menu a glance. She'd obviously been there enough times to know what she wanted.

"What's good?" Reg asked, glancing over the offerings.

"The seafood is fresh. Other than that... burger and fries... I wouldn't try anything too adventurous."

"Good to know."

After placing her order, Reg leaned back in her seat, looking Sarah over.

"How about you? Did you retire to Florida, or have you always lived here?"

"I've lived lots of places, dear. Florida is good for my old bones. As for retiring... maybe someday, but not yet."

"What is it you do?"

Sarah raised her brows, as if surprised that Reg didn't know. Was she supposed to have guessed? Did Sarah think that Bill had told her?

"Well, I'm a witch," Sarah said, as if it should have been obvious.

"Oh." Reg sat like a lump, with no idea what to say or how to respond. Sarah had turned the tables on her. Reg was used to provoking a reaction from other people. She liked to dress up and to say extravagant things to see how people reacted to her different personas. This time she was in the hot seat. "Oh. I guess I should have guessed." Reg threw her hands up in what was both a shrug and indicating their surroundings. "After all, we are in the Magic Cauldron."

Sarah blinked. "The Crystal Bowl."

"Whatever. This is a witch hangout, right? So of course that's what you are."

"I thought you knew. You didn't just wander in here of your own accord, did you?"

"There was an old bum down the boardwalk... he called me a witch, and he pointed me this way. So, yes... I knew... It's all just a bit much." Reg looked around the restaurant. "I mean, *everyone* here can't be a witch."

"Of course not," Sarah agreed. "We have people of all different spiritual and paranormal persuasions. Witches, warlocks, wizards, mediums," she gave Reg a nod, "fortune-tellers, healers... people who are gifted and people who are seekers."

"Okay, then." Reg looked around at the patrons and shook her head, having a hard time believing that they were all running the same con. "And there isn't too much competition for the same… customers?"

"Some people think Black Sands has gotten too commercial, and some people complain it has gotten too crowded. But for the most part… people are willing to live and let live. We are peaceful people."

"Uh-huh."

Sarah launched into a lyrical description of the town and its more interesting citizens. Reg tried not to sit with her mouth open as she listened. The waitress eventually came over with their meals. Reg hadn't realized how hungry she was getting, but when the platter was placed in front of her, she suddenly realized she was famished.

"This looks lovely," she told the waitress, not expecting to be getting a beautifully plated fish at the offbeat witches' diner. She dug in immediately, taking several delicious bites before looking at Sarah to ask her if she was enjoying her food.

Sarah's eyes were closed and her hands hovered over her plate as if she were warming them in the steam rising from the food. Reg turned to look at the waitress, but she was already gone. Reg looked uncomfortably at Sarah, wondering if she should follow suit.

Sarah's eyes opened, catching Reg staring at her.

"Uh…" Reg fumbled. "Amen?"

Sarah nodded slightly. Then she started to eat.

"It really is good," Reg said. "Really nice."

"I wouldn't eat here all the time if it wasn't," Sarah agreed. She patted her stomach. "I wouldn't have to worry so much about my waistline if I was cooking for myself!"

She was plump, but in a grandmotherly sort of way. Reg couldn't imagine her skinny; it just wouldn't have fit. Adele, Erin's witch friend back in Tennessee was tall and slender, and that worked for her, but it just wouldn't work for Sarah.

"So why don't you tell me about this cottage of yours?" she asked. "Bill seemed to think that we'd be able to come to terms."

"He's very empathic," Sarah said. "He reads people."

"Ah. Of course." It made sense for a bartender. Reg had known her share of good and bad barkeeps.

"It's just a little two-bedroom," Sarah said, answering Reg's question. "But it's just you…?"

"Yes. No dependents."

"So you could use one room as your bedroom and the other as an office, and still have space for entertaining in the living room."

"Right," Reg agreed. She hadn't thought about seeing clients in her home. She wasn't sure she wanted anyone to know where she lived. If they didn't like what she had to say, they wouldn't know where she lived to confront her. She had thought she would go to them, do readings in their own spaces. She could read a client a lot better if surrounded by their own things. People gave a lot away by the way they lived.

"It's separate from the main house, so we wouldn't be on top of each other. We can each keep our own hours. That can be a problem with night people and day people mixing. The kitchen is small, really just a prep area. You could come use the big kitchen if you needed to do any major baking or entertaining. I really don't use it that much."

"I don't expect I would either. I don't do a lot of my own cooking."

"You see? You'd be perfect. You wouldn't be complaining to me that there's no oven. It really does have everything you really need."

"Well, maybe we could go see it after dinner, and talk business."

"You're going to like it just fine. I can tell."

As Reg wasn't that picky, Sarah was probably right. If Reg didn't like it after a month or two, she'd have a good idea by that point of where to look for somewhere better. It wasn't a long-term commitment.

Which was good, because Reg Rawlins didn't like long commitments.

CHAPTER 2

*C*old, clammy fingers traced across Reg's face, awakening her in the wee hours of the morning.

She sat bolt upright, her heart racing. She looked quickly around her, trying to remember where she was and who was there with her. A chaotic childhood had conditioned her to be instantly awake and ready to fight. Strike fast to protect herself and escape to somewhere safe. But there was no one else in the room. Maybe the roof leaked and a drop of cold water had traced its way across her cheek.

She touched it, but it was dry, with only the memory of those icy fingers lingering behind.

Reg listened for a long time, hearing the lap of the waves in the distance. It was a restful, peaceful noise, and gradually the slamming of her heart slowed to its normal rate, though it was still pounding too hard to get back to sleep.

"There's no one here," Reg said aloud, very quietly. "You're perfectly safe, Reg. No one is going to hurt you."

It was comforting to hear those words.

When she was a kid, therapists had told her social worker and foster parents she had PTSD, and that was the reason for much of her unwanted behavior. It was nonsense, of course. Reg had never been in a war or terrorist attack. She'd never been kidnapped. Sure, she'd grown up rough, but a lot of kids had. And Reg was good at adapting. You couldn't call a few nightmares PTSD just because it was the fashion.

She listened to the waves for a long time. It was growing light as she drifted off to sleep again, still not sure what had awakened her in the night.

~

When she got up in the morning, it was with the clear plan to get a cat. She needed a cat. It would be a good prop. Witches had cats or other familiars. People instinctively felt that people who owned pets were kinder and more trustworthy than those who didn't. And it would give her a little company, without having to resort to having another person around the house. Reg liked company, but she liked having her own space.

A cat was the perfect idea.

Reg giggled to herself at the pun. A purrfect idea.

She checked addresses on her phone, thinking about what else she would need to buy in order to settle into her new living space. The fact that it came furnished was a bonus. She packed and traveled light and was used to operating on a shoestring. A fully-furnished cottage was a level of luxury she wasn't used to.

She picked up groceries and the basics she would need to care for a cat before going to the pound, patting herself on the back for thinking ahead and realizing that she wouldn't be able to do the other shopping once she had the cat in the car. She'd have to go straight home, and she wouldn't want to just abandon the poor critter there to go run errands.

At the animal shelter, self-styled as a pet sanctuary, before she was even allowed to look at the animals, Reg had to fill in a bunch of paperwork indicating her willingness to take care of a pet for the rest of its natural life and to follow all of the rules that the shelter set forth, such as not declawing a cat.

The place was noisy and smelly. Every effort had been made to make it a nice place, comfortable and humane for the animals, but it still stank. Reg thought about Erin. She probably would have run out of there puking, she was so sensitive to bad smells. Reg wasn't sure how she even managed to keep pets of her own, what with having to change litter and clean up after any accidents. They hadn't been allowed pets when they had lived with the Harrises, but Reg had seen enough examples of Erin reacting to human smells and accidents that she had no doubt she'd have difficulty cleaning up after animals.

There were old cats and tiny kittens and everything in between. Orange cats and tabbies and calicos. Short hair and long. Unlike the dogs, most of the cats didn't interact with the people walking by their cages, but simply slept, curled up in the corners of the cages. Occasionally, one of them would open its eyes or lift its head for a moment, but mostly they just continued to sleep.

She had thought she would be tempted by the playful younger kitties, but she thought of them keeping her up all night and wasn't sure that was what she wanted.

Maybe getting a cat had just been an impulse. Buying a pet was one of those things you were never supposed to do on impulse.

There were good reasons for getting a cat, but there were reasons not to as well. It might be noisy and wake her up nights. Have hairballs. Scatter litter and shed all over the house. It might jump up on the counter and get into things. Get out of the house and run out into the street.

It was probably a bad idea.

Reg looked into the next cage. The black and white cat raised his head, then climbed out of the nest of blankets in the corner, stretched, and walked up to the front of the enclosure.

"Hey, cat," Reg murmured.

He sat up tall and gazed at her, serious and still. Reg poked her finger through the bars at him, hearing a voice in the back of her head warning her never to poke her finger into an animal's cage. Even a hamster would bite you if you stuck your fingers through the bars. But just like she had ignored the foster mothers who had warned her not to do dangerous things, Reg ignored the voice in her head.

The cat's nose twitched as he caught her scent. For a minute, he just sat there. Then he leaned forward and took a step closer, touching his nose to her finger, and then rubbing his cheek against it. She felt his teeth brush over her finger as he rubbed. She scratched under his chin.

"Hey, you like that? Does that feel good?"

He rubbed against her and started purring a deep, satisfied rumble.

One of the shelter workers walked up.

"Wow, you connected with the tux!"

Reg looked at her. The girl was a teenager, maybe sixteen or seventeen, blond, with round cheeks. "The tux?"

"See, he's black with a white chest. Like he's wearing a black tuxedo and white shirt. So we call him a tuxedo cat."

"Oh, that's cool."

"And he has two different colors of eyes, too. I love that."

Reg looked at him and realized he had one green eye and one blue. "I guess that means he's special."

"I think he is." The girl poked her finger through the bars to try to scratch the tuxedo cat as well, but he only rubbed against Reg's finger. "He's been pretty depressed since he was brought in. His owner died and he hasn't really clicked with anyone. We've tried to play with him and to get him interested in things, but he's been so sad, pretty much all he'll do is sleep. He barely even eats."

In direct contradiction to her words, the cat stopped rubbing against Reg's finger and went over to his food bowl. He sniffed at the food, then began to eat, crunching the kibble.

Reg laughed.

"Well, he wouldn't!" the girl protested. "It must be you. Maybe you remind him of his owner."

Reg watched the cat. "What do you know about her?"

"Her? He's a he. A boy."

"No, I mean his owner. What do you know about her?"

"Oh. Well, he's also a he. A man. Don't really know much about him, just that Tux must have really been attached to him."

If she were going to get a cat, then it was obviously going to have to be that one. None of the other cats had shown Reg any interest at all, and she hadn't been particularly attracted to them. She clicked her tongue, thinking about it, and the noise made the cat turn his head to look at her again. He left his food bowl and again walked to the front of the cage, purring.

"I guess... this is the one," Reg said.

At least he was a short-hair, so he wouldn't get too much fur scattered around the cottage. And he seemed very quiet and sedate, not like a kitten that was going to jump on her face in the middle of the night and keep her awake.

"Oh, good!" the girl exclaimed. "I'll go get Marion, and she can help you with the adoption."

"Okay. Sure."

Reg waited there, scratching and quietly communing with her cat until the older supervisor approached to talk to her about the process.

If Reg had been expecting to just walk in and get a cat and walk out ten minutes later, she was sadly mistaken. Even the intake had taken longer than ten minutes. Apparently she needed counseling, needed to be walked through how to care for a cat, all of the things that could go wrong, budgeting for food and vets, what to do for behavioral issues, and on and on.

Reg had a headache by the time they were done and was ready to just pack it in and go home without a cat. But that would make the hours that she had been there wasted time, and she wasn't going to waste her first full day in Florida. Half of her groceries were already sitting spoiling in the car, and she wasn't going to walk out of there empty-handed.

Marion finally decided that Reg was ready to go and took the tuxedo cat out of his cage and settled him into a cardboard box, transferring the furry blanket he had been sleeping on into the box as well.

"That will help him transition, having something that already smells like home with him. Now you be sure to call if you have any questions about his care. Normally I would recommend that a first-time pet owner start out with a smaller animal, like a hamster, but... that tux needs a home badly, and he seems to like you."

Reg watched Marion close the box securely, and then took it from her. She didn't want to stand there discussing it any further. She wanted her cat home.

What the Cat Knew, Book #1 of the Reg Rawlins, Psychic Investigator series by P.D. Workman can be downloaded at pdworkman.com

ABOUT THE AUTHOR

Award-winning and USA Today bestselling author P.D. (Pamela) Workman writes riveting mystery/suspense and young adult books dealing with mental illness, addiction, abuse, and other real-life issues. For as long as she can remember, the blank page has held an incredible allure and from a very young age she was trying to write her own books.

Workman wrote her first complete novel at the age of twelve and continued to write as a hobby for many years. She started publishing in 2013. She has won several literary awards from Library Services for Youth in Custody for her young adult fiction. She currently has over 80 published titles and can be found at pdworkman.com.

Born and raised in Alberta, Workman has been married for over 25 years and has one son.

Please visit P.D. Workman at pdworkman.com to see what else she is working on, to join her mailing list, and to link to her social networks.

If you enjoyed this book, please take the time to recommend it to other purchasers with a review or star rating and share it with your friends!

facebook.com/pdworkmanauthor

twitter.com/pdworkmanauthor

instagram.com/pdworkmanauthor

amazon.com/author/pdworkman

bookbub.com/authors/p-d-workman

goodreads.com/pdworkman

linkedin.com/in/pdworkman

pinterest.com/pdworkmanauthor

youtube.com/pdworkman

Find P.D. Workman's books at

PDWORKMAN.COM

Scan the QR code below

www.ingramcontent.com/pod-product-compliance
Lightning Source LLC
Chambersburg PA
CBHW021217260626
47172CB00002B/477